Dating Mr. Darcy

Love Manor Romantic Comedy
Book 1

Kate O'Keeffe

Wild Lime Books

ISBN: 979-8667690634

Edited by Grapevine Editing
Cover design by Sue Traynor
Copyright © 2020 Kate O'Keeffe

Wild Lime
Books

About this book

Is it a truth universally acknowledged, that a girl must compete on reality TV to win a modern-day Mr. Darcy's heart?

Clothing designer Emma Brady is having serious doubts about how far she'll go to promote her new activewear line. Sure, being on a reality show would be great for business, but is putting up with Mr. Darcy-wannabe Sebastian Hunting-ton-Ross really worth it?

Sebastian is straight out of an Austen novel. But it's hard to focus on his chiseled jaw, broad shoulders and wickedly sexy accent when all Emma can see is his pride, arrogance, and smug demeanor.

But Sebastian has a secret reason for being on the show, and when Emma figures out what it is, her heart warms to him without her permission.

Will Emma hold fast and keep the aristocratic Sebastian at arm's length? Or will she put her reservations aside when the lines between reality and "reality show" start to blur?

MEDAL WINNER AT THE 2021 READERS' FAVORITE BOOK AWARDS

Also by Kate O'Keeffe

It's Complicated Series:

Never Fall for Your Back-Up Guy

Never Fall for Your Enemy

Never Fall for Your Fake Fiancé

Never Fall for Your One that Got Away

Love Manor Romantic Comedy Series:

Dating Mr. Darcy

Marrying Mr. Darcy

Falling for Another Darcy

Falling for Mr. Bingley (spin-off novella)

Cozy Cottage Café Series:

One Last First Date

Two Last First Dates

Three Last First Dates

Four Last First Dates

High Tea Series:

No More Bad Dates

No More Terrible Dates

No More Horrible Dates

Wellywood Romantic Comedy Series:

Chapter One

I s it a truth universally acknowledged, that a girl must compete on reality TV to win a modern-day Mr. Darcy's heart?

Of course not. That would be totally, off-the-charts insane, right?

And yet, here I am, moments away from becoming a contestant on the reality TV show, *Dating Mr. Darcy*.

I know, I know. You're judging me. Heck, *I'm* judging me.

But let me set the record straight. I'm not here for the guy. No way. I mean, who in their right mind would willingly date someone on national TV? Someone who's posing as Mr. Darcy, one of the most romantic fictional heroes of all time? The guy's got to be a total idiot, or at least have an ego the size of my home state of Texas. And even though my current dating life can be summed up with the word "laughable," there's no way I'm *that* desperate.

Yet, despite my lack of enthusiasm, here I am, sitting in a faux-leather swivel chair, my back to one of those Hollywood-lit mirrors as an overzealous, tweezer-wielding makeup artist plucks yet another hair from my poor, tortured eyebrows. Eyebrows that apparently I misguidedly thought up until about an hour ago were perfectly fine.

As another hair is pulled from its happy home, I scrunch my eyes shut. Ah, how I miss those carefree eyebrow times. Really, I didn't know how good I had it.

"You see, it's high def, honey. The cameras will pick up every little imperfection and totally magnify it," my torturer Linda says helpfully as she stands back to examine her handiwork. To my horror, she leans back in and begins to pluck some more.

I work hard at not breathing in her stale garlic breath while she continues to torment me. If she would let me turn around to see my reflection, I bet the skin around my brows would be so swollen, I'd look like Andre the Giant's kid sister right about now.

"The last thing you want to be known as is 'Monobrow Girl' or some other such name," Linda continues.

"People would do that?"

"You better believe it, girl. One contestant on the show a couple of years back had blackheads all over her nose. Bad ones, like someone had gotten a pen and jabbed it at her face, you know?"

I nod, pleased for the reprieve in the tweezer-induced torment.

She pulls out a large brush and starts applying face powder. "She got known as 'Dalmatian Chick,' which was kinda funny, but also kinda sad. People would hum the tune to *101 Dalmatians* when she passed by, and there were memes all over social media."

I knit my considerably lighter brows together. "That couldn't have been fun for her."

"I know, right? What I want to know is why she

couldn't have gotten her skin fixed before coming on the show? I mean, *duh*."

I blink at her reflection. *That* was the problem?

"She did get a great deal promoting skin products after the show, though, so it all worked out in the end," Linda adds.

"Right."

As though public humiliation can all be fixed by financial gain. I feel sorry for the girl, blackheads and all.

"My point is, honey, people can be mean. Remember that."

I nod at her. "And don't have unruly eyebrows."

She winks at me. "You caught on quick."

"Yes, ma'am."

She pulls off the barber's cape she tied around my neck and stands back from my chair. "There. Much better." She spins me around so I'm facing the mirror. "What do you think, honey?"

I sit up straighter in my seat as I take in my full reflection in the bulb-lined mirror. It's hard not to be impressed, even if I know it's not the real me. My eyes look larger and greener than they've ever looked in my life, my skin is glowing, and my lips are full and glossy. Despite the pain, my brows look perfect, and my brunette hair falls in soft waves around my bare shoulders.

Don't get me wrong, I'm a girly enough girl. I like to dress up to go out, I wear makeup, and I get my hair done with a guy called Stefaaan with three a's at a swanky Houston salon for a small fortune every eight weeks.

But I've never in my twenty-seven years looked like this.

"I love that red sequined dress on you. It totally complements your shape."

"Thanks," I murmur, still taking it all in.

"He'll love you. I bet you've got a real good shot at winning his heart."

I flick my eyes to hers. The Mr. Darcy imposter. Right. I'd temporarily forgotten about him. I paste on a smile and say what's expected of me. "I so hope you're right, Linda."

She leans in conspiratorially. "You know, I've seen him. He is *hot*. Tall and muscular and handsome. And that British accent of his?" She fans herself. "So sexy."

"Oh, great," I reply, not caring one bit. The guy could be Quasimodo as far as I was concerned. It made no difference to me.

"I heard he's super rich, too, from this aristocratic English family." She leans even closer to me and I take an accidental lungful of garlic breath. "I'm not meant to tell you this, but he owns some fancy house in England, like *Downton Abbey*. They call it his 'manor,' and I heard he's got servants, too."

An egotistical *rich* idiot.

Better and better.

"I tell you, if it wasn't for my Eugene, I'd be making a play for him for sure."

My phone beeps on the counter in front of me, saving me from having to comment on Eugene and the Mr. Darcy imposter. "I should check this."

"Sure, go ahead."

It's a message from Penny. My best friend since we met at college—all wide-eyed and out of her depth—and more recently, my business partner.

Call me! Last minute idea!! xoxo

I smile to myself. Penny has got to be the most enthusiastic person I know. Sometimes, I don't know how her husband Trey copes. But—and there's a big but— it was Penny's idea for me to apply for the show. Sure, we agreed that doing it could give our new, struggling activewear business, Timothy, a much-needed boost. But equally, if it wasn't for her, I would be home right now, curled up on my couch, watching Netflix with Frank, my tabby cat.

And I know practically every contestant on reality dating shows like this say they were put up for the show against their will by their friend/ mom/ podiatrist/ a pimply teenager who packs their groceries. But I *am* that girl.

Linda nods at my phone. "They'll be taking that off you pretty soon, honey."

I make a face. "It's going to be a nightmare."

As I begin to tap out my reply, I look up, startled, as loud approaching footsteps come to a sudden stop. In the mirror, I'm met with an extremely officious looking woman. She's probably in her forties, she's dressed in a navy suit, a clipboard in hand, and with a stern look on her face.

"Linda. You're needed in room fourteen," she says.

"No problem." Linda places her hand on my shoulder. "Good luck, honey," she says to me. "I hope you win."

"Thanks. And thanks for making me look like this."

"It's all you," she says with a smile before she slips away.

Sure. All me and a fancy dress I could never afford and expert styling. But I'll take it.

With Linda gone, the severe, frankly scary looking woman throws a critical eye over me before she consults her clipboard. "Emma Brady. Correct?" she says in a curt British accent that makes me want to slump down in my chair and hide.

"That's me," I reply brightly. I carefully slide my soon-to-be contraband phone under my sequin-clad butt.

"Well, it's an Austen name, even if it is the wrong book."

I shoot her an uncertain look. And this matters how, exactly?

"I'm Margaret Watson. I'll be coordinating the contestant's activities over the coming weeks. Anything you need, you come to me. Of course, I probably won't get it for you." She laughs at her own joke.

"It's nice to meet you, Ma'am."

"Mrs. Watson. That's what you'll be calling me from now on."

"Mrs. Watson. Got it."

"You'll be leaving to meet our Mr. Darcy in approximately ten minutes. We need you to hand him this." She fishes in a capacious bag she has slung over her shoulder and produces a piece of material. She hands it to me and I look at it in puzzlement.

"What is it?"

"It's an embroidered handkerchief."

"We're out of Kleenex, huh?"

Mrs. Watson's face doesn't crack. "It's meant to show your interest in him. Although traditionally a man would give his handkerchief to a woman in Regency England, in this instance we're reversing that moray. Look at it as a handkerchief you embroidered yourself, a personal, enchanting gift for a gentleman to treasure."

I look down at it in my hand. That sure is a lot for one small scrap of material to achieve. I scrunch up my face. "Do I have to?"

"On the red carpet when meeting Mr. Darcy, every girl has a bit. This is yours, Emma."

My bit's a lame handkerchief? Terrific.

I smile up at her. "Sure. No problem."

"Good. My assistant will come and get you when we're ready for you to go. When you exit the car onto the red carpet at the ranch, please remember to smile. You need to be open and friendly towards him. He's Mr.

Darcy, and it's your job to impress him as well as you can."

Well, if that doesn't make me feel like the little woman who should know her place, I don't know what will.

I nod, knitting my brows together to show how serious I am about this. "Smile. Friendly. Impress. Got it."

She writes something on her clipboard, and I'm dying to know what it is. Obedient? Impertinent? No way is Mr. Darcy going to go for this one?

Not that I care.

I'm not here for the guy.

"And Miss Emma?" she says, eyeing me once more. "That mobile you tried so dexterously to slip under your posterior when I walked in needs to be handed in before you get into the car. Need I remind you, no devices of any kind are allowed."

I shoot her a weak smile. Totally busted.

She turns on her heel and clomps out of the small room, leaving me alone with my now very warm phone. I abandon my message and instead dial Penny's number.

She answers almost immediately, and I can just imagine her sitting in our office (okay, her garage, if you've got to be nitpicky), waiting to hear from me. "Em. How are you? Are you nervous? What are you wearing? Are you ready for this?"

"So many questions, Penn."

"Sorry. I'm nervous for you."

Nerves hitting me for the first time. "I don't have long. I've got to get in the car to go meet him soon. What was your new idea?"

"Well, you know how we agreed that you're going to wear Timothy items out on dates with him and lounging around the mansion with the other contestants? Well, I thought to amp it up, you could wear some of our shorts and a top under your evening wear at the parties."

"Why?"

"That way you can whip your dress off and show our label!"

"You want me to take my dress off at the parties? Penny, this is *Dating Mr. Darcy*, not some sexy Vegas revue."

"Look, if you were wearing your underwear, I'd totally agree, but the whole point of you being on this show is to get publicity for our label. Everyone will be talking about you, and, most importantly, they'll be talking about Timothy."

We named Timothy for our dads, who are both called, you guessed it, Timothy. Penny's the creative mastermind and I'm trying to use my business degree from the community college where we met to make her vision a reality. We're two plucky gals, working hard to change our fortunes.

Wrong side of the tracks? We grew up so far from them, we couldn't even hear the trains.

Going on this show has got to work, for both of us. End of story.

"I'll think about it, Penn."

I've got zero intention of pulling my dress off to show our label. It's one thing to be a contestant on this tragic show, it's quite another to come across as a stripper on national TV. "I've got my Timothy leggings and top in my clutch, ready to change into in the limo."

"Atta girl. You will totally stand out in activewear next to all those girls in evening gowns. Have you heard anything about the guy posing as Mr. Darcy?"

"Only that he's super rich, super posh and consequently, I will have nothing in common with him."

"Who knows? Opposites attract, Em. Maybe you'll stay

on the show the whole time, wearing our label as you fall in love?"

I let out a sudden laugh. "Not gonna happen. His money aside, a guy who goes on a reality show to fall in love is *so* not my kind of guy."

"But he's *Mr. Darcy*." I can hear the swoon in her voice, like she's all flushed and weak at the knees.

And yeah, I get it. Mr. Darcy is considered one of the most dashing heroes of all time. Many a woman has been known to swoon over him, with that heroic, masculine, man-of-few-words thing he's got going on, not to mention his gallantry and immense wealth.

"Penn? You do know Mr. Darcy isn't real, right?"

"Of course I do. But the guy on the show has got to be like him, right? I bet he'll be gorgeous and confident—"

"And zero fun," I add, cutting her off. "Mr. Darcy isn't exactly the kind of guy to do tequila slammers and hit the clubs."

"Do you want to do tequila slammers and hit the clubs?"

"Well, no," I admit. "We did more than enough of that together in college."

"Those were the days," she replies with a sigh. "Meeting you was the only good thing to come out of that boring business studies course we did."

"You quit it to go to design school after about five minutes, Penn."

"My point exactly."

"Well, *my* point is that if this guy is anything like Mr. Darcy, he'll be all formal and rude and boring."

She sucks in air. "How dare you," she mocks. "Never say never, that's all I'm saying."

"Well, in this case you're wrong. Never means never."

"Okay, okay. Gorgeous fictional characters aside, all you've got to do is make sure you're not sent home in the first three rounds. That way you can promote Timothy and show the American people that you're worth watching."

I let out a sigh. "No pressure, then."

"I know everyone will love you just as much as I do."

"How am I going to achieve that?"

"Just be yourself."

Huh. The most useful advice given *ever*.

"Look, Penn. I'll try to stay for two rounds, then I'll break some rule or something so I get sent home."

"Three."

"Two."

"Come on, Em. It's one more week in TV time. It's probably a couple of days at most for you in real time."

"Are you Emma Brady?" a voice says behind me.

I look up to see a woman about my age, dressed in jeans and a hoodie, her oversized, dark-rimmed glasses balanced on her small nose. "Hold on a sec, Penn," I say into the phone. "Yup, I'm Emma Brady."

The girl smiles. "Cool. I'm Suzie. Mrs. Watson sent me. You'll, ah, need to pass me your phone." She holds her hand out, palm up.

I feel like a prisoner who's wasted their one final call on discussing how I'm not going to fall for a Mr. Darcy imposter and keep my clothes on during parties. "Can I at least say goodbye?"

"Make it quick."

"Penn? I gotta go," I say into the phone.

"Remember everything," she replies sternly. "Ev-er-y-thing."

Pressure much?

"I'll do my best."

"What you're doing could lead to big things for us. I love you, Em." I can hear the crack in her voice.

"I love you, too, Penn. It'll all be okay."

"This show is going to change things for us. I just know it," she says with a sniff. "Your dad would have been so proud of you, Em."

Something twists painfully inside at the thought of my dad. Although I'm not exactly sure he'd be proud of me going on a reality show to promote our new label, I know he'd support me in whatever decisions I made. Running his own business was a dream he never managed during his lifetime. Now, through hard work and sacrifice, I've got a real shot at it.

"Look after Frank, okay?" I say, suddenly fiercely missing my cat.

I glance back at Suzie. Her hand is outstretched, and she's got a mildly panicked look on her face. I say goodbye to Penny, turn my phone off, and reluctantly hand it over.

"Frank?" she questions.

"My cat." I collect my clutch from the counter and ready myself to leave. I glance at the handkerchief. There's no way I'm giving a grown man that thing, I don't care how scary Mrs. Watson is. This is twenty-first century America. People don't give each other handkerchiefs anymore. It's just weird.

I pick it up and discreetly drop it to the floor, where I kick it under the table.

Suzie doesn't seem to notice as she connects a pack inside the back of my dress and a mic discreetly tucked inside the lapel of my top.

This has all begun to feel very real.

Suzie presses her finger to her ear and then says, "It's time."

On sky-high heels, I follow her unsteadily out of the room. As I slip into the back of the long, black, glossy limo parked up at the curb, I know this could be the making of Timothy.

Or the undoing of Emma Brady.

Chapter Two

How on this sweet Earth did I get myself into this position?

I'm not talking metaphorically or spiritually or anything like that here, you understand.

Oh, no. I'm being much more literal.

Right now, I'm all alone in the back of the limo, whizzing through the outskirts of Houston on my way to some ranch out in banjo territory. I've managed to remove my mic, which was a feat all its own, and now I'm wrangling with my Timothy leggings. With an almighty effort, I pull them up to my thighs, my dress bunched up under my chin. Ever bunched up a sequin dress under your chin? Not comfortable.

As the car turns corners, my task becomes increasingly complex. Just when I scoop my butt up off the seat to pull the leggings up, the car turns, and I go crashing into the door. Luckily it's firmly shut or I'd be splattered across the road somewhere.

By the time I'm halfway done, I'm hot and sweaty and panting like I've gone three rounds in the ring with

Muhammad Ali. Or some other boxer from this century. (Fighting's so not my thing).

My leggings finally in place, I heave a sigh of relief. Time for my Timothy top. I pull my sequined dress over my head, only for it to get snagged on my hair.

I tug at the dress. It pulls at my hair but it holds tight. I tug again. This thing is not budging.

The car begins to slow. I peer out the smoky glass window and see a large house at the end of the long drive. It looks like a ranch in the middle of nowhere.

Uh-oh.

Panic begins to set in. I need to get this dress off and pull on my T-shirt over my strapless bra, and I need to do it *now*.

As the car slows to a stop, I yank on the dress, hard, only to cry out in pain as my hair refuses to untangle itself from the many sequins.

I hear a car door thud closed and know the driver is about to walk around to open my door.

No! We can't be here already!

Think, Emma, think!

In just my leggings and strapless bra, my dress acting as some sort of weird hair extension, I'm not only going to be the laughing stock of the nation, but I'm sure the Mr. Darcy wannabe will send me home before he can say "that one was totally cray cray." Penny's and my dream will amount to nothing.

With probably less than about three seconds to go before the driver reaches my door, I ditch the near-impossible hair issue and focus on getting my top on. I grab it out of my clutch and loop one leg through, then the next. With a strength that would impress Wonder Woman herself, I yank the top up over my thighs, and begin to loop an arm through one side. So far, so good. All I've got to do now is loop the other arm through and ...

The next thing I know, the wall I'm leaning up against gives way and I fall backwards out of the privacy of the limo and land with a thud on my butt.

Ooof.

As my butt meets the hard, unforgiving ground, the wind is instantly sucked out of me and the pain sears. Trying to regain my balance, my legs flail in the air like I'm some kind of insect that can't get itself back up. At least twelve different cuss words erupt from my mouth. Cuss words my mother would blush to hear me say.

Everything goes quiet around me.

Smooth, Emma. Real smooth.

"Well, that was quite an entrance," a voice says.

I blink. Everything around me is bright white. I raise my hand to shelter my eyes from the blinding lights and see a silhouetted figure leaning over me. I lift my head from the ground and do a quick tally. Legs still look like, well, legs, both nestled snugly in my Timothy leggings. Thank goodness. My body is mostly covered, but for the straps of my top, which I quickly rectify by snapping them into place. Other than a throbbing pain in my butt, I'm all in one piece. Physically, at least.

"You are very original," the voice continues. "Do you need help getting up or is this all part of the show?" Is that an English accent I hear, or has that Mrs. Battle-axe Watson somehow got into my brain?

I peer up at the figure. "That'd be great. Thanks." I reach out and take his outstretched hands. "Are they filming right now?"

"I believe they are, yes."

Dammit! *So* not the entrance I was going for.

"Do y'all think the Mr. Darcy guy saw?" I ask him in a low voice. I'm still blinded by those dang lights. "I mean, this is hardly much of a good first impression. Am I right?"

"I'm certain you have made an impression," he replies stiffly. "Whether or not it's a good one remains to be seen. May I help you with your, erm, dress?"

My hand flies to the back of my head. The dress! It's still hanging from my hair in a deeply unflattering way. Not that a dress can ever hang from your hair in a flattering way, but you get the picture.

"You can give it a shot, dude, but it's really wedged in there." I turn and the man unhooks the dress from my hair with ease. "How did you do that?" I ask.

"It was very easy, actually."

Is there judgment in that tone?

I shift from the blinding lights to get a proper look at him for the first time. He's a good-looking guy, there's no denying it. He's tall with dark brown hair. His eyes are brown and flecked with tiny chunks of gold that make them appear to sparkle in an unworldly way. Dressed in a perfectly-fitted tux, he positively radiates masculinity in a way I'm sure has made many a woman weak at the knees. The similarities between him and James Bond are not lost on me, particularly with that pompous English accent of his.

He holds the dress out to me. "Yours, I believe."

And then the penny drops. I don't even have the excuse of being slow on the uptake because I bumped my head.

He's Mr. Darcy! This guy. The one with the smooth as silk, aristocratic voice, dressed to kill.

The guy who scooped me off the ground in a state of relative undress is the star of the show.

Humiliation seeps through me and my cheeks flame.

"What I would like to know is why you chose to make your entrance tonight wearing a dress in that most unorthodox fashion? Most women wear them on their bodies, I've found. Not attached to their hair." His lips quirk into a smile, his eyes trained on me.

I narrow my own eyes. He's mocking me, and by the look on his face, he's having a good old time doing it, too.

I lift my chin and grasp at what dignity I have left. Which is not a lot, let's face it. "It was a mistake. A wardrobe malfunction, if you will." I attempt to smooth out what I know must be a bird's nest of a hairstyle and try to salvage the situation. Which is a pretty tall order, I know. I lift my lips into a brave smile as my humiliation reaches all the way down to the tips of my toes.

He cocks an eyebrow. "That was less of a malfunction and more of a complete disaster, as far as I can see."

Mockery does not look good on you, Fake Mr. Darcy.

"Thank you for the dress, even if my ego is a little dented right now."

"As long as nothing else is dented?" he asks, a concerned look on his face.

Faking concern for the cameras after mocking the crap out of me? Oooh, this guy is good. He's reveling in my humiliation, I can tell. As if an aristocratic, publicity-hungry snob like him would be interested in my well-being.

"Nope. Nothing dented. All good." I lean in a little closer to him and do my level best to ignore his scent, a heady mixture of vanilla and musk with woody undertones. He might be a jerk, but he's a jerk I need right now. "Look, dude. I know you've got some sway here." I nod my head in the direction of the production crew, who are standing around us with cameras and notebooks. "Do you think I could get a do-over?"

"A what?"

"You know, a do-over."

"Simply repeating the expression won't help," he replies condescendingly.

Oh, he is so enjoying this.

I decide to spell it out in no uncertain terms. "What I'd like is to get another chance at exiting the limo. You're the big guy around here, right? I'm sure you can pull that off for me if you want to."

"You would like the opportunity to step out of the limousine and meet me at the end of the red carpet, the way the other ladies have this evening? The ones who managed to actually *wear* their dresses?"

I ignore the jibe. "That's right."

"Uh, we don't do that," one of the people standing by the camera operators says.

"Why not?" I ask.

"I dunno," the guy replies with a shrug.

"Because we want to see Mr. Darcy's natural reaction as he meets each of the contestants," a familiar voice says.

Awesome. It's Mrs. Freaking Watson.

"I understand perfectly," Fake Mr. Darcy replies.

I'm sure he does.

"Look, I don't want to be seen falling out of a limo on national television," I say to both of them. "I mean, there's natural and then there's *natural*, you know what I'm saying?"

I look to the Mr. Darcy imposter at my side for back-up, hoping he has at least an ounce of decency in that body of his. I give him the quick once over and try not to notice what a body it is.

"Viewers will love it, Emma. It'll bring a wonderful touch of humor to the episode. Although it would have been much more effective had you worn your microphone," Mrs. Watson replies.

"I don't want to be the 'touch of humor!'" I protest. Not when I'm trying to promote Timothy. Becoming the laughingstock of the nation wasn't exactly the goal when Penny signed me up for this sham of a show.

I look back at Mr. Darcy, my eyes appealing for his help. "Can you help me out here, dude? Please?"

He presses his lips together in a vain attempt to suppress a smile. "What would you do for me in return?"

Is he kidding me right now? I don't know, *not* smother him in his sleep?

"I'll be super nice to you and tell all the other contestants you're a great guy because you helped me out of a tricky situation."

He raises his eyebrows at me. "Will you, now?"

"I will," I reply resolutely.

He studies me for a moment before he says, "It would only be fair."

"You're considering this, Sebastian?" Mrs. Watson asks with a tone of distaste.

Sebastian? I look him up and down. He's got money and privilege written all over him. Yup, that fits.

"And you looked so gallant helping her up," Mrs. Watson continues. "Quite the dashing knight in shining armor." Her stiff upper lip quivers into what I think might be a smile, but it lasts less than a second, so who can really tell?

But seriously. A dashing knight in shining armor, my ass. He did it for the cameras. We all know it. Let's not pretend this is something it's not.

She turns her attention to me. "I don't know what you were thinking, removing your microphone and changing out of that dress into ... whatever *this* is." She raises an eyebrow at me and I cast my eyes down at the painted toes on my bare feet. Shame I couldn't fit sneakers in that clutch.

I look back up at her. "It's activewear by Timothy," I reply with pride. I might have humiliated myself in front of all these people, but I am proud of Penny's and my label.

"Whatever it is, you're meant to be in the dress," she quips.

"Well, I—"

"We're getting off topic here," the so-called knight interjects. "Emma wants you to reshoot her exiting the limousine, just like all the other contestants. It seems reasonable enough to me. I'm sure she'll provide the viewing public with many moments of humor in the coming weeks, if that's what you're looking for, Margaret."

I raise my eyebrows at him, my hands on my hips. What the heck does he mean by *that*? That I'm some sort of accident-prone mess for people to laugh at? And yes, I know they've got the proof that I am. But I'm not. Honestly.

Mrs. Watson pulls her already thin lips into an even thinner line, her features taut with annoyance. Without replying, she turns and walks away. I watch in hope as she mutters something to one of the crew who have been standing by, watching this whole thing unfold.

A woman rushes over to me, a hairbrush in one hand and a lipstick in the other. As she goes to work on me, straightening out my hair and fixing my face, someone else reattaches the mic I discarded in the limo.

I glance at Sebastian. He could very well be Mr. Darcy himself, with his self-satisfaction and obvious pride. His eyes are lit with an inner glow, and I know it's at my expense. But the guy did just help me out. I should say something.

"Thanks," I mumble to him and he gives me a brief smile.

And yes, I know I could be a lot more gracious about it, but this guy has gone on a reality show ostensibly to find love. What does that say about him? Either he's a hopeless romantic with no clue about the world, or he's here for another reason that's got nothing to do with love and everything to do with fame.

Either way, he's not my kind of guy.

"Sebastian? In position, please," one of the crew says, and Sebastian turns his back to me and walks back up the carpet. "And Emma? Back in the limo. We're going to take it from the top."

Relief washes through me. "No problem," I reply brightly.

I slide back into the limo and the driver closes the door behind me. A moment later, he reopens it and I step elegantly out. Well, as elegant as I can be in activewear and bare feet.

I make my way up the red carpet, careful to hold my head high and show off my outfit. When I reach Sebastian, I smile sweetly at him and say, "Mr. Darcy. It's wonderful to meet you. I'm Emma."

His lips twitch in amusement. Is he still laughing at me?

"It's wonderful to meet you, too, Emma." He takes my hand in his, lifts it, and brushes a kiss across my knuckles.

So cheesy.

I bet he's done that ten times tonight already. But then, who knows? Maybe it's a thing in England? Maybe all the rich pompous idiots run around kissing each other on the hand?

I make a face. It's hardly sanitary.

"You decided against a dress this evening, I see."

"I'm wearing activewear by Timothy." I do a twirl, feeling thoroughly self-conscious, but reminding myself the reason I'm here.

He cocks an eyebrow and I try not to notice how attractive he is up close. Fail.

"Activewear?"

"Yes. It's comfortable, moves with your body, and is made of material that wicks sweat away so you can be fresh as a daisy while you work out."

Both brows are raised now. "It wicks away sweat? How charming."

I ignore his obvious sarcasm. "It *is* charming, Mr. Darcy. You are quite right."

"Please, call me Sebastian." He takes my hand in his. "It was truly an ... *experience* meeting you, Emma." He kisses me on the hand once more and I work hard to refrain from rolling my eyes. I am on camera, after all.

Instead, I flash him a smile. "You, too, Mr. Darcy." I toss my hair, hold my chin up high, and walk away from him. As I reach the main doors, a member of the production crew greets me. I look back at Sebastian. He's watching me, his lips curved into a self-satisfied smile.

Against my will, my belly does a flip, as though I hadn't humiliated myself in front of him, as though he hadn't been mocking me this whole time. I know it doesn't mean anything. There's no way I'm attracted to him. It's got to be nothing more than the Mr. Darcy Effect. He is the most adored romantic hero of all time, after all.

Sebastian may be posing as a hero, but he is definitely no Mr. Darcy.

Chapter Three

"**W**hat are you wearing?" a woman in a dress similar to the one I discarded only moments ago asks, a look of shock on her stunningly pretty face.

We're in a room with high ceilings, inviting couches, and large windows, leading out to a pool. There are cameramen lurking around, capturing our every move.

"This is Timothy activewear," I reply. "It's super comfortable."

She looks down at my feet. "But you've got no shoes on."

"Wouldn't fit in my clutch."

I think it's a perfectly acceptable explanation, but she's clearly flummoxed. She pulls her eyebrows together (perfectly plucked, probably by Linda the torturer), and scrunches up her face. "I don't get it."

"There's nothing to get, really," I reply with a shrug. I'm hardly going to tell another contestant on the show that I smuggled my own brand of activewear in my clutch, and came out worse for the wear in a tussle with a sequined dress. Instead, I extend my hand. "I'm Emma, by the way."

She takes it and smiles her beautiful smile at me. "I'm Phoebe."

I glance at her long, straight, blonde hair. "Do you get *Friends* references much?"

She nods, giving a resigned but good natured sigh. "All the time."

"So, you're looking for your Mike, huh?" I say, continuing the *Friends* theme.

She laughs. "As long as his last name is Darcy, right?"

I smile back at her. "What did you think of him?"

"Oh, there's no denying he's gorgeous, and he was very sweet and old fashioned kissing my hand."

Ha! I knew it.

"You got that too, huh?"

Her face drops a fraction. "Oh."

She's so sweet, I feel bad popping her bubble. "I think it's just his thing, you know? Part of being Mr. Darcy or something."

"I'm sure you're right."

"Anyway, how could he *not* have liked you. I mean, you're stunning." And she is. She makes me feel like the poor cousin who's got no clue about anything other than what to feed pigs, how to catch catfish, and how to smile without showing that half my teeth have fallen out. None of which I actually know how to do (and I still have all my own teeth).

Her cheeks blush pale pink, rendering her even prettier. "You're so kind, Emma. Thank you."

I eye her glass of champagne. "Where did you get that?"

"There's a waiter lurking around here somewhere. I'll go track him down for you."

"Oh, you don't have to do that," I reply.

"Emma, on account of the fact that you have no shoes, I think it's my duty to at least find you a drink."

Kind and funny. I can tell we're going to be friends. She'll be the sweetest, kindest, prettiest one and I'll be ... me.

"I'll have a beer, thanks."

She disappears and I survey the room. There have got to be at least ten women here, chatting away animatedly, as though they're already the best of friends. Because there are a bunch of cameras around us everyone's on their best behavior. They're all in glamorous evening dresses, pretty much cookie cutters of one another. It's a lot like that old music video from the '80s where all the women in the band look exactly the same.

"Hey. You look different," says a woman with long dark hair who's virtually orange as she's got so much cheap fake tan on. Her enhanced cleavage is straining painfully against her dress with a neckline so plunging she may as well not be wearing one at all. She's accompanied by another much more normal looking girl dressed in yellow, who beams at me enthusiastically.

"I'm wearing Timothy activewear. It's super comfort-able and—"

"And you stand out from the rest of us," Orange Cleavage finishes for me, gesturing at the room. "Make him notice you from the start."

Is this what's called the pot calling the kettle black? Or should that be orange?

"I've got your number, girl. That's your game," she continues. "It's smart, I'll give you that, even if you look like you should be at the gym."

My game? R*iiii*ght. Like I'd want to have a "game" to win a guy's heart.

I eye her up. There's an undeniable ruthlessness about her you can spot a mile away. Well, that and the oversized orange orbs stuck to her ribcage.

"Well, I'm not the type to—" I begin then stop myself. Choosing a different tack, I extend my hand and say, "Nice to meet you. I'm Emma."

"Hayley," she replies with a tight jaw, her oversized lips giving her more than a passing resemblance to a fish, "and this is Sharon." She nods at the woman in yellow beside her.

"It's Shelby, actually, but that's fine," she says as she pulls me in for a hug.

Hayley waves her hand in the air as if to say "whatever." Nice girl.

"Oh, you smell lovely, Emma. Don't tell me. Lily of the valley? Rose? No, I've got it: grapefruit," Shelby says.

"Err, yeah," I reply, thinking those scents are all quite different from one another.

Her face lights up in a fresh smile. "I knew it."

"Shelby here thinks she's destined to be with Mr. Darcy. She said it's her fate," Hayley says with an obvious note of distaste.

I raise my eyebrows at Shelby. "Which one? Sebastian or the actual Mr. Darcy?"

"Who doesn't exist," Hayley adds.

"Oh, Sebastian, definitely. He's my destiny. I know it in my heart. Why else would we both be here right now? It doesn't make any sense." She gives us a confident smile.

I open my mouth to reply, then close it again. I've got no idea how to answer that. Well, not without sounding like a grown up, anyway.

Hayley rolls her eyes and changes the subject. "So, what

do we think the lay of the land is here, ladies? Who's a contender, who's going home a-sap, and who am I going to have to poison in the dead of night?"

I blink at her. Is this woman for real? "Poison?" I ask.

Shelby rubs Hayley's arm. "Oh, she's only kidding. You'll realize that as you get to know her."

Hayley doesn't look like she's kidding to me.

"You two are friends?" I ask.

"We were the first ones in this room tonight," Shelby replies. "Us and Camille, whom I know you'll love as much as we do. We've bonded. The three of us are going to be besties for the whole show. Right, Hayley?"

Hayley harrumphs. "Sure." She fixes me with her stark blue eyes, and I try my best not to wither.

"Here you are, Emma," Phoebe says as she returns with a drink. "No beer, sorry."

I take the glass of wine, thank her, and take a grateful gulp.

"Whoa!" a woman in a strapless hot pink taffeta gown exclaims as she comes to a stop beside me. "What look are y'all goin' for there, darlin'?" she asks as her eyes glide over me.

"Not a look exactly," I begin.

"Her game is to stand out from all of us," Hayley says with her arms crossed. "It's smart, even if she forgot her shoes and has ended up looking like she belongs in a yoga studio."

"Oh, I love yoga," Shelby gushes.

"Of course you do," Hayley replies.

"Well, whatever you're doin', it's workin'." The girl grabs my arm. "Oh, I got it. I know who you're trying to be."

"You do?" I ask in surprise.

She nods, a triumphant look on her face. "Sporty Spice!"

"Sporty Spice? Oh, you mean from that '90s band, the Spice Girls?"

"That's right," she replies. "You're the feisty one who could actually sing."

She and the other girls look at me in expectation.

I decide to give in to it. "Sure. Why not." I punch the air. "Bring back Sporty Spice, that's what I say."

"You go, girl!" Pink Taffeta replies. "It's good to stand out from the crowd."

"Oh, she's doing that all right," Hayley harrumphs with a disapproving look.

Well, I didn't stand out so much as *fall* out, but there's no need to share my limo exit with anyone, is there?

Pink Taffeta gives me a light hug. "I'm Reggie, and wow, do I want your butt."

I shift my weight, feeling self-conscious, my admired-butt still throbbing with pain from its unfortunate collision with the tarmac a short while ago. "Had it all my life," I quip.

"Ha!" Reggie exclaims so loudly I fear for my eardrum's health. "Abbi, Camille, Kennedy. Y'all have got to come meet this one. She's a real hoot!"

Within moments, I'm surrounded by a gaggle of women, all of whom look like they stepped out of the eveningwear section of a beauty pageant, only they forgot to put on their sashes. At five foot three in my bare feet, they tower over me, and good butt or not, I feel like a prepubescent child.

"Didn't you get the dress code memo?" a woman with expensively highlighted blond hair in an elegant silver dress says. She stands out from some of the other women around us in that she screams class—well, class and cattiness, that is.

"It must have gotten lost in the mail," I reply.

She looks me up and down, clear she doesn't like what she sees. "Right."

I ignore her judgmental tone and instead smile at her. "I'm Emma. It's nice to meet you."

"Camille," she replies as she continues to look down her nose at me. "It's an interesting move to turn up today in this." She gestures at me. "Do you really think someone as cultured and educated as Sebastian will be interested in a woman who dresses like ... you?"

I blink at her. Wow. Just wow.

"I guess we'll find out," I reply sweetly, taking an instant dislike to her and imagining the TV audience will, too. Has she forgotten everything we say and do is being filmed right now? But then, maybe she's just doing her.

"Hmmm. My guess is we'll find out pretty soon," Camille replies as she turns her back to me.

I totally catch her drift. She means Sebastian is going to send *me* home tonight.

Well, we'll see about that, Camille.

I feel a hand on my arm and turn to look at who it is. It's a pretty girl with shoulder-length brown hair, wearing a gorgeous white gown that shows off her curves.

"I envy you," she says. "This dress may look good, but it's making it hard to breathe." She extends her hand. "I'm Kennedy, and please be as normal as you look. There are some total freakshows here."

I smile at her. She's a girl after my own heart. "I'm Emma, and I'm pretty sure I'm normal."

"Do you think you're destined to marry Mr. Darcy?" she asks and I shake my head, thinking of Shelby.

29

"Did you sign up for the show because your boyfriend kicked you out and now you've got nowhere to live?"

"There's seriously someone here who did that?"

"I'm not naming names. Let's just say there are a lot of stories out there."

"Well, personally, I'm beginning to wonder what the heck I'm doing here."

She grins at me. "Oh, I'm with you. My well-meaning sister made me do this because she thought it would help me get over my ex."

"How's that working out for you so far?"

Kennedy rolls her eyes. "So well."

I snort with laughter.

"There's nothing for it but to take advantage of all this free champagne," she says, holding her glass up and taking a sip.

"Because being drunk on national television is always such a great idea. Right up there with wearing activewear. I've been told I'll be going home tonight."

Kennedy's eyes flick to Camille. "Oh, I wouldn't worry about her," she says to me quietly. "She thinks she's better than everyone because she comes from some wealthy New York family. Apparently, Sebastian is going to be able to tell straight away she's one of 'his kind' and rush her down the aisle."

"So, you're saying we may as well give up right now?"

Kennedy grins at me, and I think I've found my reality TV bestie. "Clearly," she replies.

An hour passes, maybe more, and then the atmosphere around us suddenly changes and a hush descends over the group. I look up from a comfy seat I've been happily nestled into with Kennedy for the last half hour as the man himself, Sebastian, the Mr. Darcy wannabe, saunters into the room.

He has a drink in hand, a relaxed smile on his undeniably handsome face, and every eye in the room is trained on him.

My bet is it's pretty good to be Sebastian right now.

He's accompanied by another man. He's about the same height, age, and build, with dark blonde hair and a flash of white teeth. The fun conversation of only seconds ago has completely dried up, and the women around me begin to flick their hair, sit up straighter, and simper, and nearly all the cameras are trained on him.

No wonder this guy's ego is the size of this ranch.

The man with the dark blonde hair begins to speak. "Ladies. You all look wonderful tonight, and I would like to thank you personally for being here." He's so upper class English, he sounds like Queen Elizabeth—only a lot younger and a lot more masculine. Obviously. "My name is Johnathan Bentley, and I have the dubious honor of being Sebastian's best friend." He grins at Sebastian.

I nudge Kennedy in the ribs. "He's probably his lover."

"They both do dress extremely well," she replies.

I glance at the camera filming us. I should probably keep my opinions to myself.

"Now, you might be wondering what I'm doing here. Well, one of the things you were required to do before coming on the show was to read Jane Austen's *Pride and Prejudice*. If you did, you'd know that Mr. Darcy's best friend is Mr. Bingley." He gives a bow and the women around me titter with excitement. "Unlike Bingley, however, I'm not looking for my Jane. I'm simply here to support my good chum and help him find his Miss Elizabeth Bennet." Johnathan flashes his grin at us all, and I'm certain several of the women swoon.

"Does that mean he's up for grabs, too?" Kennedy says out of the corner of her mouth.

"He is very attractive," Phoebe, who is next to us, replies.

"The show's not called 'Dating Mr. Darcy *and* Mr. Bingley,' so, my money's on 'no,'" I respond.

"Pity," Kennedy says with a sigh.

"And now, without further ado," Johnathan continues, "I give you the man you're all here for and, I'm quite sure, eager to get to know better: Sebastian, your Mr. Darcy." He stands back and gestures at Sebastian, who waves and smiles as the women applaud. Somewhere behind me I hear a catcall followed by a couple of *woots*.

"Ladies," Sebastian begins in his equally 'I'm-related-to-the-Queen-of-England-and-lead-a-life-of-total-luxury' voice, "I am truly honored to be Mr. Darcy. I only hope I can live up to your expectations of such a beloved character."

More titters among the women.

"I look forward to getting to know each and every one of you over the coming weeks."

I scoff. I *bet* he is.

And yes, I know, I'm being harsh, cynical, and unchari-table. Take your pick.

Who knows? Maybe this Sebastian guy is actually genuine? Perhaps he really has come on the show to find love? Maybe he's been out there on the dating scene, hoping to find his Mrs. Darcy, and keeps getting knocked back by the good women of England. Because, let's face it, us women hate good-looking rich guys with sexy English accents, don't we?

As if! With his Henry Cavill good looks and his air of cockiness, it's so obvious he doesn't need a TV show to find love.

Which begs the question: why is he here?

I chew on my lip. Publicity, sure. That's a given. But to

what end? Is he a narcissist, wanting to see himself on TV getting chased by a bunch of gorgeous women? Is his multi-million dollar inheritance from Daddy not enough to keep him in Lear Jets and private islands?

"But for now, I think a drink is in order," Sebastian continues with that smile of his pasted across his face. "Would any of you care to join me?"

There's a rush of excitement, and as women scramble to reach him first, I'm elbowed in the face and kicked in the shin with a spiky heel.

"Ouch!" I rub my injured shin.

"What's the rush?" Kennedy says, leaning back against the cushions beside me. "The guy's not going anywhere, girls."

"And he's not getting any less self-satisfied, either," I add.

She turns to look at me. "Oooh, you don't like him."

"It's just that I've got the champagne and the comfy seat and you. I'm all set."

"Good call," she says with a laugh. "There's plenty of time to get to know him."

We sit back against the soft linen cushions and watch the games begin. Sebastian is already surrounded by a horde of eager participants, and I'm quite sure his ego is swelling to the size of Jupiter.

"You know we'll need to talk to him at some stage if we don't want to be sent home first," Kennedy says.

"I figured I'd wait until things calm right on down." I watch Camille, the one with the expensive hair from a wealthy New York family, as she holds onto his arm and coos in his ear. "I see Camille's moved in straight away."

"I wonder if he's already realized how appropriate a match she is for him?"

"Undoubtedly. Maybe we could all go after that guy Johnathan instead? He seems a lot less like he's got a stick up his butt than Mr. Darcy."

"He is a little formal, isn't he? I just figured it's his English way."

"Oh, I think he's got an ego so big he's got to pay extra luggage allowance to schlep it all around with him."

Kennedy giggles. "Can't you take as much luggage as you like in First Class?"

"I would have no clue. I'm strictly a coach girl, and I wish I meant the purses."

"Well, coach or not, we both need to get in some face time with Mr. Darcy tonight."

I watch as Camille throws her head back in laughter. After my humiliating entrance on the red carpet, I'm pretty sure Sebastian knows exactly who I am—and definitely not in a good way.

But they say being memorable is half the battle in the first few days, and I guess I've got that covered, even if he only wants to keep me around to see me make a fool of myself again.

I watch as he makes his way around the room, stopping to chat with a bunch of different women, many of whom openly flirt, some of whom actually fawn over him.

It sure wouldn't be bad to be Fake Mr. Darcy right now.

Chapter Four

K ennedy disappears to talk to some of the other contestants and I lean back against the cushions and start to fantasize about escaping to some quiet corner to be on my own, preferably under my duvet at home in front of a movie with Frank.

As I think of my cat, snuggling up to Penny and her husband, I feel a pang of jealousy, followed quickly by a wave of nostalgia for my old life (and yes, I know I only left it this morning. But still.)

"Have you fallen out of anything else since I last saw you?" a deep voice says beside me.

I snap out of my Frank-induced reverie to see Sebastian looming over me as a couple of photographers hover nearby. He looks down at me with questioning eyes.

I push myself up against the cushions and try not to openly wince as my butt protests. "Nope. I've taken the caution of sitting here on this very safe couch, as you can see."

"That sounds sensible to me," he replies in his sexy English accent which I refuse to be moved by, even if it does make me think of Henry Cavill, Jude Law, and Colin Firth, all wrapped up in one handsome package.

"You can't be too cautious, I always think."

"As long as you don't try to remove any more of your clothing."

I raise my eyebrows at him. Is he flirting with me? That sounded a little suggestive. "I'll try to do my best."

To my surprise, he sits down next to me, a collection of cameras around us, focusing on his every move. *Don't look at the cameras*, they said. *Act natural*, they said.

Sure, if you're a Kardashian.

Sebastian leans his elbows on his knees. "While you've been sitting here and working hard at *not* falling off the couch, I've been having an illuminating evening."

"You mean you're being followed around the room by a bevy of eager beauties, all wanting to flirt their skinny butts off with you?"

His lips curve into a small smile. "Something like that."

I give him a fake concerned look. "That must be so hard for you."

"You have no idea, Emma."

"You remembered my name," I say in surprise and instantly regret it. I sound like one of his sycophants, thrilled to clutch at any crumb of attention he deigns to offer me.

"You, Emma, are hard to forget."

I think of my initial limo exit and cringe. "Yeah, I can see that." Eager to change the subject I ask, "Tell me what's been so illuminating about your evening so far."

"The different ways the contestants have tried to stand out."

"Like what?"

"There's you, of course, with your entrance and your sweatpants."

"Activewear," I correct.

"Then there's that woman over there who read me a poem she'd written about how we are destined to be together."

"Fun."

That's got to be Shelby.

"Then there was the contestant who tried to give me a vial of her blood."

I stare at him, too stunned to remember I decided not to like the guy before I even met him. "Are you serious?"

"I am serious. She tried to give it to me on the red carpet and asked me if I could furnish her with a vial of my own blood in return."

"Which you just happened to have on you."

"Well, naturally," he replies with a smile that sets off a couple of misguided butterflies in my belly.

I take a mallet to them straight away.

"I've got a vial for every contestant," he continues. "I thought that was part of the show."

"No, you don't."

"You're right, I don't. The production crew said it was against the rules."

"But if it wasn't?"

"Well, you'd all have little bottles by now. Clearly." His delivery is totally deadpan, and I've got to suppress a smile.

Mr. Darcy, it turns out, has a wry wit.

"Who knew you were Billy Bob Thornton in disguise?" I say.

"I'm sorry, who?"

"Billy Bob Thornton. He was married to Angelina Jolie

37

about a hundred years ago. They famously wore vials of each other's blood around their necks."

"How delightful."

"Not the word I'd use, dude."

He gives me a questioning look before he leans back against the cushions with a sigh and, despite everything I know about him, those dang butterflies start up again. I deal to them swiftly once more, this time using a blowtorch to make sure they're dead and gone. I refuse to fall for this guy and his charms, even if half the women in the room here probably already have.

He's a means to an end. Nothing more.

Anyway, I bet he thinks he's better than everyone else, just because he's aristocratic and rich and has a family tree that reaches back to the Romans or something. I'm sure he and Camille will make a wonderful couple, surrounded by their collection of gold bars and wads of cash and family seals.

Some of us don't have the luxury of family money behind us. Some of us need to make it on our own. And when I say "some of us," I mean me, of course.

"Have you met many of the contestants?" he asks me.

I take a sip of my wine. "Some."

"So, you'd know if there was anyone I should know about?"

"Even if I do, I'm not going to tell you." I punch my fist against my chest. "I'm all about sisterhood."

"Does that sisterhood extend to the mildly insane?"

"Oh, yeah. Especially the mildly insane."

"I see." He seems to size me up for a moment before he says, "You're not as tough as you make out, are you?"

"Excuse me?"

"You've got a soft side. And I don't mean the one you

landed on earlier tonight. Although that was entertaining. Well, more for me than for you, I imagine."

"Entertaining is not the word I would have used."

I know I've got to be nice to this guy so he doesn't boot me off the show for a few rounds. But by bringing up my humiliation, he's making it a tall order.

"So, tell me, Emma. Why are you here?"

The question throws me. I know why I'm here. Penny knows why I'm here. But I'm not about to tell him it's got nothing to do with him.

"To fall in love," I say as convincingly as I can.

He holds my gaze for a beat or two, and then, to my surprise, he erupts into a low, rumbling laugh.

"What?" I ask, totally nonplussed. Is it so hilarious that I could fall in love with this guy?

On second thought, don't answer that.

"Nothing. It's nothing," he replies as though it's *so* got to be something.

I turn the tables on him. "Okay. Why are *you* here, Sebastian?"

"Same reason as you, Emma. To fall in love."

"Well, we're both here 'for the right reasons,' then, huh?" I reply, using the expression every contestant on every dating show *ever* uses to ensure the viewer knows they're genuine.

"It would certainly appear so," he replies in that terribly grave English accent of his, like he's from *Downton Abbey*. Only he's from his own, real manor house, with real servants and everything. "Now, if you'll excuse me, I really must circulate some more."

"Sure. Go ahead. Circulate away. Your gaggle is waiting for you." I gesture at a group of eager women, hovering nearby.

He gets up from his spot next to me, and the cameras follow him as he moves away.

I lean back in my seat. It wouldn't take a rocket scientist to work out that a guy with a freaking castle is doing a reality TV show for something other than what we're all led to believe.

And I find myself wanting to know what that reason is.

Chapter Five

At some point during the evening, right about the time Sebastian has spoken to all of the contestants (not that I'm keeping an eye on him, of course, I'm only interested to see how this all unfolds), there's a *ding ding ding* of silverware on glass. A hush falls across the room.

"Ladies," Johnathan begins as Sebastian moves to stand at his side. "I trust you've had a wonderful evening getting to know not only Mr. Darcy, but also one another, as well. Some of you have stood out to him already, and as he leaves to deliberate, you must ask yourselves whether you are one of them."

I spy Hayley standing near me, and she shoots me a look I can only read as pure aggression. I smile at her and shrug, the human equivalent of a dog lying prostrate on the ground to show it's no threat. But all she does is shake her head at me and look away.

What is with that girl?

"And with that said, it's time to leave here to assemble

for the very first card ceremony. We will see you all shortly."

The two men turn to leave the room, leaving us to wonder what's about to happen.

"The card ceremony?" I ask Reggie beside me.

"Your guess is as good as mine, darlin', but it looks like we're rollin' out, so we best follow the herd."

I find Kennedy nearby and we walk out of the room together.

"How was your talk with Mr. Darcy?" she asks me.

I think about it before I reply. "Weird."

"Weird how?"

"I don't know. Weird in that I didn't expect him to have a sense of humor, I guess."

"Why not?"

"Because he looks all serious and stiff and James Bond-y."

"Maybe there's more to him than meets the eye?"

"I doubt that," I scoff.

"Well, he talked to you longer than anyone else, and he sat next to you, which he didn't do with anyone else either."

"So the guy is fond of standing. So what?"

"So nothing. Hayley and Camille noticed, that's all, and they are not happy about it."

That explains the glare.

We enter another huge room, this one devoid of furniture other than a lone table.

"What else did you two talk about?"

"He told me I'm not as tough as I think I am. Whatever that means."

She lets out a light laugh. "Random."

"I know, right? What did you talk about with him?"

"The weather and where I'm from."

"How riveting for y'all," I deadpan.

A good half an hour later, we've been arranged and rearranged by the production staff in a bunch of different ways before they seem to be happy. I find myself stuck at the back, standing on a platform on my tippy toes so I can see over the heads of the other contestants.

I feel a twinge of regret for the heels I left behind in the limo.

"What do you think this card ceremony is?" Shelby asks. She's the one who's apparently destined to be with Sebastian. You know, the really balanced, sane, non-crazy one.

"I think it's to eliminate one of us," sweet Phoebe says on my other side.

As Mr. Darcy arrives in the room, accompanied by Stuck-By-His-Side-Johnathan, I reply, "I guess we're about to find out."

With the cameras trained on both us and him, we watch the men with expectation.

"Ladies. Mr. Darcy has a set of invitational cards on this table." Johnathan gestures to a wooden table which is indeed covered in envelopes, complete with red wax seals from the olden days. "Each card represents an invitation to stay here at the ranch, which of course is an invitation to secure Mr. Darcy's heart."

I stifle a scoff. "Too cheesy," I mutter under my breath to entirely the wrong audience. Phoebe shushes me, Shelby looks at me as if I've just said "I am the devil's servant," and I receive several annoyed looks from other women around me.

Tough crowd.

"Eleven of you have named invitation cards on this table which, I'm sorry to say, means that one of you is going home tonight."

Virtually all the contestants strain to see if their name is on one of the invitations, but it's all in vain. Of course they won't put them close enough to us to read. That would ruin the moment, which is designed to amp our nerves up to maximum, all in the name of good television ratings.

Not that my nerves are amped in the least. I don't care what Mr. Pompous thinks of me.

"The contestants who are invited to stay for another week are called The Lizzies, a nod to Elizabeth Bennet from Jane Austen's *Pride and Prejudice*," Johnathan says. "We thought it would add a touch of fun to the proceedings."

The Lizzies? Jane Austen must be raising a deeply disapproving eyebrow in her grave right now.

"Now I ask Sebastian, our Mr. Darcy, to step forward to hand the cards out. Sebastian?"

And so the process begins. It's a process I've seen enacted before on countless dating shows. I know, because Penny has made me watch them plenty of times before, always tempting me with free takeout and wine in exchange for girl time.

This time, it's different. This time, as the names are read out and more and more girls collect their cards, thoughts run through my head, my palms getting sweaty, my heart beginning to thud: Have I done enough to stay here? Has Sebastian decided against me, thanks to that humiliating entrance of mine? Am I going home?

Could this mean the end for our new, precious activewear label?

"Emma. Please come and join The Lizzies."

I heave a sigh of relief. There are only four of us left up here, so that was a pretty close call.

I step down from my position and collect the card with my name from the table. I glance at Sebastian as I do so, a mixture of emotions bubbling inside. He shoots me an impassive smile, one that doesn't meet his eyes, and I pad on my bare feet to the other side of the room to join the others.

The names are read out until a woman whom I barely spoke with is sent home. She doesn't look overly bothered by it all.

The experience has shown me I need to try a little harder to ensure I stay for at least the next round or two. Otherwise, Timothy won't get the promotional boost it so desperately needs to stay alive—Penny's and my dreams along with it.

Then I can be home free, back to Frank and my couch, and put this whole weird experience behind me.

As the dismissed contestant, Sebastian, and Johnathan all leave the room, one of the production staff tells the rest of us to stay put. We look at one another questioningly. Seriously? It's got to be about three in the morning, and after the weirdness of the day—and possibly the amount of champagne I drank tonight, but who can say?—I, for one, am in desperate need of my bed. And I don't even know where it is yet.

The cameras are still rolling, so this has got to be part of the show.

Penny reminded me there are all sorts of twists in reality dating shows. Maybe they're going to announce we're all hopping on a plane to the Bahamas? Maybe a second bachelor? One *without* a stick up his butt.

We don't have to wonder for long. Mrs. Watson walks into the room and we turn and stare. There's something about her that makes my eyes bulge. Something so out of place in a sea of plunging necklines, long flowing hair, and sky-high heels, that it makes me almost laugh out loud.

"What the—?" Kennedy mutters.

Mrs. Watson is wearing old fashioned clothes, and I don't mean flared jeans and platforms from the '70s. I mean *old* old fashioned, like from a couple of centuries back, when flashing a bit of ankle was considered risqué, skirts touched the ground, and women wouldn't be seen dead without a pair of long gloves.

There's a general titter among the contestants as she comes to a stop in front of us, her clipboard and pen from earlier today replaced with a scroll of yellowed paper and what looks like a quill.

Seriously. A quill.

Has this woman flipped out? Has she taken the whole Mr. Darcy thing a step too far? The answer is yes, people. Yes, she has.

"Ladies. You may have noticed my attire," Mrs. Watson begins. "You might be wondering why I'm dressed like this."

I glance at the women around me. *Uh, yeah.*

"Let me explain. I am wearing what the women of Jane Austen's social class would have worn in the year *Pride and Prejudice* was published. In fact, this is how Miss Elizabeth Bennet would have been dressed once she married Mr. Darcy."

Poor Miss Elizabeth Bennet.

I glance at Kennedy with a look that says "WTF?" and she returns it twofold.

"Who's Miss Elizabeth Bennet?" someone says behind me.

Seriously? We're on a show called *Dating Mr. Darcy* here, people, one of the most famous works of literature of all time.

"You would know who she was if you had read *Pride and Prejudice*," Mrs. Watson scolds, and rightly so. "Miss Elizabeth Bennet, for those of you who are unfortunate enough not to be familiar with Jane Austen's classic story, is the young lady who captures Mr. Darcy's heart. She is who the winner of the show will be. She is Mr. Darcy's love. That's why the contestants who receive an invitation at each card ceremony will be referred to as 'The Lizzies.'"

There's more tittering among the contestants, but I'm too busy taking in Mrs. Watson's getup in all its glory to pay much attention to what they're saying. She's in a cream Empire line dress that reaches the floor, with cap sleeves. It's cut low enough to show off what my Nana would call her "bosom," which is something I didn't expect I'd ever think about when I met Mrs. Watson earlier this afternoon. She has on long white gloves that reach above her elbow, and her hair is arranged in a simple bun, except for the ringlets around her face. The entire look is topped off with what appears to be a frilly white shower cap standing proud on top of her head.

"Ladies, as you know, this is *Dating Mr. Darcy*, not dress up time." Her stony features melt a fraction as she gives a half-smile at her joke. "I assure you, there is a method to the madness. Forget your Millennial way of dressing. Forget your splits, your bare backs, your stretchy pants." She looks pointedly at me.

Stretchy pants? How insulting.

"From now on, you are all going to dress as though it were 1813."

Wait, *what?*

I stare at her, wide-eyed.

1813? Is she kidding right now?

I take in her smug expression, her chin raised as she looks down her nose at us all, and I know this is no joke.

"Have we all got to dress like you?" Marni, one of the contestants asks.

"You do."

No no no no no! No!

This cannot be happening.

If I've got to dress like that I can't wear Timothy. If I can't wear my label, what's the point in being here?

Penny's and my entire game plan for this show has been vaporized by Mrs. Watson and her Lizzies.

The contestants burst into a variety of responses, from the shocked to the excited and everything in between.

My head begins to pulse.

"Ah, ma'am? Mrs. Watson?" I say loudly over the chatting. "Do we have to dress like you all the time?"

"Only while you're on camera."

"So...all the time," I clarify.

"You'll have your leisure time, of course. You can wear your *comfortable* clothes then, Miss Emma, but you'll be wearing Regency dresses appropriate for ladies the rest of the time. We aim to make this show as authentic as possible."

"Authentic? Mr. Darcy is a character from a book!" I exclaim in exasperation.

"Ah, yes, Miss Emma, but Jane Austen was very real, and he is her creation."

As if that's an actual answer.

"What do the dresses we're going to wear look like?" Abbi, one of the contestants, asks, and Mrs. Watson's attention is diverted away from me.

I slump my shoulders.

That's it. Game over.

There's nothing for it. I can't achieve what I set out to on this show.

I may as well pack my things and go home.

Chapter Six

I don't go home. Don't get me wrong, with that little bombshell last night, I *want* to go home. There's no point in being here if I can't showcase Timothy. End of story. What's more, staying here will be daily torture, thanks to the fact we've got to wear old fashioned dresses and that I'll be forced to watch smug Sebastian pick and choose between the contestants.

Memories of my dignity are becoming more and more blurred.

Why not go home right this minute and collect that dignity at the door as I leave, you ask? The sad fact of the matter is that when I came on the show I signed a contract that says very clearly I can only leave when I'm sent home, I break the rules, or if I do decide to simply walk out, I'll get slapped with a fine I just can't afford right now—or at any time, for that matter.

When I signed the contract, although pretty harsh, none of it seemed too bad to me. I knew from the outset a guy who would go on a show like this to find love was not my type, so I figured he'd send me home pretty fast, and all I had to do was make sure it wasn't on the first night.

Now? Well, now I'm forced to take things into my own Regency gloved hands. That means "Operation Make Sebastian Send Me Home" is well and truly on. Either that, or break some rules.

Speaking of the man himself, the fact that he singled me out by sitting next to me last night before the "dress like it's 1813" bomb was dropped, has really raised some of the contestants' hackles, just as Kennedy said it did. Which is ridiculous. It's not as though I asked him to come sit with me, and our conversation lasted all of five minutes, during which he poked fun at me for falling out of the limo and tried to get me to snitch on the other contestants.

Nice guy.

Nevertheless, it would seem I've been labelled as a front runner by some, and deserve to be treated with disdain, suspicion, or all of the above.

Lucky me.

One of the contestants, a cute girl from Nebraska called Amy, asked me what my secret was, to which I had to reply I had none. Because there is no secret! Another, Abbi, accused me of using witchcraft to lure him in (I kid you not). With that one I simply nodded and moved to another table to eat my toast. I don't need to be around that level of crazy before my morning coffee.

But they're the harmless ones.

Several of the contestants have totally blanked me, including, of course, Hayley, the unnaturally orange looking girl with the stick-on cleavage. She and her cronies moved away from me when I sat down next to them to eat my breakfast, and they've continued to shoot evil glares in my direction ever since.

It's so *Mean Girls* meets a good old fashioned Salem witch hunt right now.

So much fun.

Some of the contestants seem nice enough, like Kennedy and Phoebe. But really, I don't know these women, and I couldn't care less what Sebastian thinks of me.

The sooner I'm out of here, the better.

And now I'm in a room with blacked out windows, sitting in front of fancy gilded wallpaper with a huge bunch of white roses on a table. Bright lights are trained on me as I'm peppered with questions by a member of the crew on camera.

"What do you think of Sebastian?" a woman called Cindy with spiky peroxide blond hair asks.

Many words spring to mind, but instead of being honest, I reply, "I think he's just great," as I give her my most winning smile.

"What in particular do you like about him, Emma?"

"His accent. I like it a lot. It's a really, really great accent."

She looks at me in expectation. Clearly I need to add more.

"You know it's all English and stuff, which is nice. It reminds me of *Downton Abbey*, actually, but only the family's accents, not the servants. Oh, and not the guy who was the chauffeur who ended up marrying the daughter that died. I think he was Irish or Scottish or something?"

"What else did you like about him?" Cindy asks, cutting me off. I'm not sure she's vibing with my *Downton* angle.

I wrack my brain. "His suit. Yeah, I liked his suit. It was very James Bond-y, and I like that about him."

Cindy is clearly unimpressed with my responses.

"Honey, what we're looking for here is more personal detail. Did you feel anything when you met?"

A sore butt?

I shake my head. "Sorry, not really, no."

"No sexual tension? No desire to touch him, to kiss him?"

I think of the way he made me feel when he came to sit next to me on the couch and swiftly push those feelings away. "Nothing. I will try to feel something, though."

"You do that." Her tone is not exactly genuine. She glances at her notes and then looks back up at me. "How about you tell us about the other contestants. Who do you think has a shot with him, who do you see as your competition, who do you want to be sent home next? That kind of thing."

There's no way I'm going to get drawn into dishing the dirt on my fellow contestants. I've watched reality TV. I've seen how that plays out on these shows, and the person dishing the dirt is never portrayed in a good light.

"Kennedy is terrific. She's smart and funny and super pretty. I really like her."

"So, you see Kennedy as your competition?"

"No. I mean she would be a good choice for Sebastian, that's all." If Sebastian weren't a total douche, that is.

Cindy looks at me like I've told her I'm a Martian who sucks people's brains out through their ears. "You don't see yourself as a good choice for Sebastian?"

"Well, of course I do," I reply hurriedly. "Who wouldn't? He's got the sexy accent that I mentioned before and the suit that makes him look like James Bond. It's a winning combo."

Cindy gestures for me to elaborate.

"Of course I find Sebastian attractive. I mean, he's Mr. Darcy, right?"

Either she's satisfied with my responses or she's completely despaired of me, but the next thing I know I'm being thanked and excused and I head to the dining room for some much needed caffeination.

I'm pouring a cup when Phoebe appears beside me. She's just as pretty as she was last night, despite the lack of makeup and styled hair, and I give her a smile, genuinely happy to see her again.

"Hey, Emma. How was your night? Sleep well?" she asks as she collects a fresh coffee mug from the collection on the table.

"It was fine," I answer without a hint of truth. You see, I've got roommates. Two of them: Reggie and Lori. Between Reggie's snoring and Lori's sleep talking (all mumbled, nothing of interest), I think I grabbed only a handful of hours of sleep. "How was yours?"

"I slept so well," she replies with a beaming smile. "I've got the nicest roommates. We talked for a while and agreed to be friends no matter what happens with Sebastian."

"You did? Who are your roommates?"

"Hayley and Camille," she replies, naming the two worst possible girls she could.

"I'd be careful with them," I say under my breath.

"Why?"

"Just trust me on this one."

"Okay. Want to sit with me?"

"Sure thing."

We find a free couch over by the window with a view of manicured lawns and the fields beyond and sit down. We could almost be in Mr. Darcy's Pemberley, if it weren't for the fact everything in this ranch was made in China.

"Have you done your first interview?" I ask her.

"Oh, yes. I got called in early. It was fun to get to talk about Sebastian and all the wonderful people I've met so far on this show."

I take a much-needed sip of my coffee. "Why did you enter the show?"

"I don't know," she replies with a shrug. "It seems so romantic, you know? Meeting the love of your life on somewhere as crazy as a TV show? It's worked for others, so I figured, why not for me?"

"I'm not sure it's worked for many others, exactly."

"It has for some, though."

"Really?"

"Definitely."

Phoebe is relentlessly positive, I'll give her that.

"Do you think Sebastian's the guy for you?" I ask.

She bites on her lip for a moment as she looks out at the view before replying, "I think he could be."

"Personally, I think the chances of one of us finding love with this guy are about as likely as the Pope wearing a tutu to his next public event."

She giggles. "I'd like to see that."

"Yeah, me too."

She takes a sip of her coffee and asks, "Why do you think he won't fall in love with one of us?"

I shrug. "I dunno. He's this great looking, super rich guy who lives in an English castle, right? Why would he need a dating show to help him find a girlfriend?"

"Maybe he's a romantic, like me?"

I try not to scoff. Chances of that are as likely as the Pope hula-hooping in his tutu at his next public event.

"Can I join you?" Kennedy is standing in front of us, holding a plate and mug.

"Definitely," I reply as she takes a seat opposite me.

"How are things? Survive the night?"

"Barely," I reply as Phoebe says, "Totally."

"We were just talking about why we think Sebastian is doing this show," I say.

"To find his one true love, surely," Kennedy remarks with a twinkle in her eye.

"See?" Phoebe says, missing the glint altogether. "We're not all hardened cynics like you, Emma."

"What's your theory?" Kennedy asks me.

"I've got a couple. I think either he lost a bet, or the Mafia's after him and he needs to hide away somewhere for a while."

"The Mafia?" Phoebe shakes her head at me. "Emma, really?"

"Okay, so maybe hiding from the Mafia isn't plausible, but he could have lost a bet."

"Oh, I think you were totally right about the mafia thing," Kennedy replies. "He looks the type to get chased around the globe by gangsters."

I giggle. "There's a type that's got to hide from a gang of angry Italians?"

"Oh, yeah. Definitely."

"Isn't love a good enough reason?" Phoebe protests.

She's so sweet I half expect chirping cartoon birds to fly around her head like she was Snow White.

I make a face to show her exactly what I think of her hypothesis and slide my eyes to my comrade-in-arms. Kennedy laughs and shakes her head.

"No matter what you say, I think Sebastian is here for the right reasons, and you'll eat your words when you see him fall in love with one of us," Phoebe says.

"We'll see," I reply. Not that I have any plans to be here

at the end to see him fall in love—or, more likely, *not* fall in love. I'm out of here just as soon as I can wrangle it.

"Keep your head down," Kennedy says before she raises her mug and literally hides behind it.

"What? Why?" I ask.

She hooks her thumb in the direction of one of the tables, where Camille, Hayley, and Shelby are now standing.

"Which one?" I ask quietly.

Kennedy nods. "Camille. She's a nightmare. She told me I've got the dress sense of a blind turkey. Whatever that means."

I skim my eyes over Kennedy's t-shirt and shorts combo and decide she looks perfectly normal. "How do blind turkeys dress, exactly?" I ask.

"Not in Prada or Gucci, like Camille over there. She tells anyone who'll listen that she's from some super rich New York family and only came on this show because she's bored."

I glance back over at Camille. She's flicking her hair, and laughing prettily at something one of the girls is saying. "Nice for some."

"I know, right? I had to give up my job and sublet my apartment to be here."

"Me too," Phoebe chimes in.

I think of my own current lack of funds. If Timothy doesn't begin to show some sort of serious profit soon, Penny and I will have to quit our dream.

"What do you think of this whole Regency thing?" Phoebe asks.

"Regency?" Kennedy asks.

"The era we've got to dress in. It's called Regency

because the Prince Regent was ruling Britain for his father at the time."

"Look at you with the knowledge," I say.

She shrugs. "History major back in college."

I scrunch up my nose. "Well, whatever y'all want to call it, I'm not exactly thrilled about it, that's for sure. Not unless we get to kill zombies, of course."

"What are you talking about?" Phoebe asks as Kennedy questions, "Zombies?"

"You know that movie based on *Pride and Prejudice* where the Bennet sisters are all trained assassins who kill zombies?"

They look at me as though my brain just fell out of my head and landed with a splat on the table.

"It's a book and a movie? Super popular?" When they continue to stare at me blankly, I say, "Forget about it."

"Well, I for one am excited to wear these dresses," Phoebe says wistfully, just as I expected she would. "I think wearing Regency clothes will add to the romance of the whole thing. The long dresses, the gloves, the up-dos with the ringlets around your face."

Kennedy shakes her head. "Nuh-uh. I'm not doing ringlets."

I shudder as I think of Mrs. Watson's hair last night. "The ringlets are the worst part. That's what hair straighteners are for."

"Actually, I think the worst part is that weird hat Mrs. Watson was wearing," Kennedy says.

"Oh, you mean the shower cap?"

Kennedy shudders.

"Only married women and older spinsters wore those, so we won't have to," Phoebe explains.

"Thank goodness for that," Kennedy says.

Phoebe collects my hair in a ponytail and pulls a few strands out around my face. "You'll totally rock the look, Emma. Don't you think, Kennedy?"

"Definitely."

"Half nun, half poodle?" I suggest.

Phoebe drops my hair and resumes drinking her coffee. "Do you think Sebastian and his friend will be dressed in Regency clothing, too?"

"Probably," I huff. "I mean, the show's called *Dating Mr. Darcy*, so it figures."

I picture Sebastian dressed like Colin Firth as Mr. Darcy in the BBC adaptation my mom used to watch. Wow, did I have a crush on him! I mean, who didn't, right? In tight pants and knee-high boots, that jacket with the long tail things and a white shirt to show off his dark hair? Not to mention the wet shirt clinging to his muscular frame when he got out of that pond ...

"He'll look hot," Kennedy says. "Don't you think, Emma?"

"I don't *hate* the idea of him dressed as Mr. Darcy," I admit in my Colin Firth-induced haze.

Camille and the delusional Shelby arrive at our table.

"Well look at you. If it isn't Sporty Spice, the Disney princess, and," Camille looks at Kennedy with disdain, "your nondescript friend."

"Nice, Camille. Real nice," Kennedy says.

"There's no need to be rude," Phoebe says. "Kennedy is gorgeous, and I'm no more a Disney princess than any of you."

Camille harrumphs.

"Good morning, y'all," I say breezily. "You both look lovely today." Mom always told me to kill the enemy with kindness, so I lather it on.

Shelby smiles and thanks me as Camille replies, "Well, you look the same."

I glance down at my Timothy top and pants. Although she's wrong in that they're not the same as last night's ensemble, because *ew* that would be gross, they are from the same line. But I doubt that's what she means. "Actually, I do have shoes on today, so I think I've got a totally new look." I raise a foot and wave it in the air.

Camille harrumphs. "You tell yourself that, honey. You'll be kissing those sweats goodbye soon, anyway. I've heard we're being called for fittings."

Fittings? How fan-freaking-tastic.

"I wonder if we'll get any choice?" Shelby says excitedly. "If we do, I want yellow. I love yellow."

"I think I'd want pink, because it's so girly and cute," Phoebe says.

"What color would you want, Camille?" I ask, acting all innocent. "Black to match your soul?"

Kennedy stares at me. "You did not just say that."

"Oh, yes she did," Shelby says as we watch Camille for a reaction.

She opens her mouth to reply when the door swings open and Sebastian strolls in, instantly grabbing everyone's attention. Which is probably a good thing for me, since I just insulted Camille.

He smiles at us all. "I thought I'd pop in and say a quick hello after my workout. I trust you all slept well?"

I run my eyes over him, like every woman in the room, and probably the serving staff to boot. If I thought he looked good in his tux last night, it's nothing in comparison with how he looks right now. He's wearing shorts and a tank top, his face glowing with exertion, his tan, muscular arms and legs on show for all to admire. In good shape? Heck, yes. But

I'm sure he knows it, and dropping by to see us fresh from the gym is doubtlessly a calculated move to make us swoon.

"Oh, we did sleep well. Thank you for asking, Sebastian," Abbi says for us all. Inaccurately, in my case, however.

"That's good to hear. I'm looking forward to seeing you all later in the day. I understand you're going to look quite different then." He flashes his smile and the women around me seem to melt. Not that I'm entirely impervious to his charms, because *hello*, he's a hot guy, even if he is a stuck up snob. But melt? No thank you.

"How's the food? Is the coffee good?"

"Would you like a cup, Sebastian?" Camille says as she twists her hair around her fingers. "I'd be happy to fetch you one."

"I thought she'd have servants to do that," Kennedy mumbles to me under her breath.

"She probably brought one in her suitcase. I bet he's called Jeeves."

Kennedy snorts with laughter and instantly covers her mouth with her hand. Sebastian looks our way and I give him a little wave to say "Hi," and instantly regret coming across as one of his simpering sycophants.

He shoots me an uncertain look. "Thank you so much for the offer, Camille. Maybe later. Right now, I think I should take a shower before my fitting."

I'm sure every female mind in the room is picturing him in that shower.

"Enjoy your morning." He turns to leave and several of the women call out goodbye.

I let out a puff of air. I'm glad I'm not "here for the right reasons" and have got to deal with a bunch of women thinking they're half in love with the guy already.

As the production crew begins to pick us off individually and herd us to other rooms for fittings, I sit and wait with Kennedy until it's my turn.

"Are you really here because your sister signed you up after a breakup?" I ask her.

She nods her head. "Yup. She thought the experience would get me out of my head."

"And?"

"I haven't thought about my scumbag ex since I walked down the red carpet. Too many other dramas here, I guess."

"He's clearly a man with poor judgment if he dumped you."

She taps her mug against mine. "You are so right, babe. I am moving on."

"Good for you."

"Emma," Trudi, one of the production crew, calls from the doorway. "Time for your fitting."

"Wish me luck," I say as I stand to leave.

"Don't forget to channel your inner Lizzie Bennet," Kennedy says. "Not so hard for me, considering my last name actually is Bennet."

"You are the obvious choice for Mr. Darcy, then."

"Not if I value my life," she replies, looking at Camille across the room.

I shoot her a sardonic smile. Even though I've known Kennedy for less than a day, I know she'll be the only thing I'll miss about this insane asylum when I leave.

Chapter Seven

I trudge behind Trudi down the wide corridor with its long Turkish runner carpet and black and white photographs of horses lining the walls. We reach a white painted door, and as she pushes it open, I spot Reggie in front of a wardrobe, filled with Empire line dresses. She grins at me, looking like she stepped off the pages of *Pride and Prejudice* itself.

"Don't I look cute, Emma?" She does a twirl.

Her skirt is ivory, her top a pale lilac, and with her dark hair arranged like Mrs. Watson's last night—but without the hideous shower cap—she does indeed look cute.

"You totally do, Reggie."

"Why thank you, darlin'. Now, if only I had my phone I could post it to my followers."

"Missing social media, huh?"

"Like I lost my right arm. Up until I arrived here, my entire life was catalogued on Instagram. My followers must be missing me somethin' wicked."

"But you'll have a great story to tell them."

"I'd better. That's all I'm sayin'." She does another twirl.

63

"Dressing up is fun. Well, other than the undergarments piece."

"The undergarments?"

She glides past me toward the door, followed by Trudi. "You'll see, darlin'. You'll see."

With the door closed behind them, it's just me and an older woman I've never seen before. She peers over the top of her bright red glasses at me. "You must be Emma."

"Yes, ma'am."

"I'm Mable Richardson, Head of Wardrobe. Let's get started on this." She's got a no nonsense tone and a briskness about her.

I eye the pile of weird looking corsets piled up on a chair.

"I'll need you to take everything off, and that includes your bra and underpants."

My jaw drops. "All of it?"

Mable flicks her wrist. "There's a modesty screen if you want it, but I've been fitting people for costumes for thirty-five years and I very much doubt you have anything I haven't seen before."

"Yes, ma'am."

I step behind the screen and begin to slip off my things. Before I've reached my bra—super supportive and soft sports bra by Timothy, naturally—her hand appears around the corner of the screen, thrusting something at me.

"Put this on."

I take it from her and examine it. It's a pair of underpants so big and roomy, it puts my nana's to shame. And my nana had some pretty big underpants in her time.

I look from the garment up at her. "You have got to be kidding me."

"Put the bloomers on, please."

Bloomers? Dear sweet Lord, help me now.

"Historian's aren't certain absolutely what underwear Regency women wore, but bloomers were popular in the second half of the nineteenth century, so we felt it was fitting for you to wear them now."

I eye the bloomers. "Can I skip this part on account of them not being historically accurate?" I couldn't care less about historical accuracy, but what I do care about is *not* wearing these bloomers.

"It's part of the rules."

I pull the huge garment up with a resigned sigh and tie it at my waist. It reaches down to my knees and is easily the least sexy item of clothing I have worn in my life. How anyone is going to feel like flirting with Sebastian while wearing these is beyond me.

"Traditional bloomers didn't have a gusset," Mable explains helpfully. "We thought the contestants would be more comfortable if we broke with that tradition, so you'll find your bloomers do."

"Comfortable" doesn't begin to describe wearing these things. Did I mention they're huge?

"Right. Got it. Thank you so much," I mumble.

The original crotchless panties, and they're as voluminous as a pair of curtains.

Mable delivers the next item of clothing around the screen. This one looks like some kind of oversized smock, the sort you'd see the French artist Monet wear with his beret as he paints his masterpieces. I slip it on over my head and, assured that I'm now fully covered, I take a tentative step out from behind the screen.

"Next is this." Mable holds up what looks like an old fashioned and deeply uncomfortable bra type of contraption.

"What is it?"

"It's called stays, and it's the Regency era's answer to a corset. Turn around."

I do as instructed, and she hoists me into the "stays," pulling on strings so tight my usually modest boobs spring up toward my chin in shocked protest. I glance down at them in alarm. The Regency answer to the push-up bra is about as comfortable as wearing a tight wooden barrel around my chest.

"Is this good for me?" I ask.

"You'll survive," Mable replies, dismissing my concern. "Now, it's time for a petticoat."

"Another layer, ma'am? But it's 90 degrees out."

She ignores me as she fastens the floor-length petticoat with hooks. It's ivory, just like Reggie's, and it's trimmed with lace.

I glance in the long mirror. So far, I look like a vaguely pornographic fairy without the wings. *So* not my preferred look.

Mable brandishes a pair of long white things in my face. "Stockings."

"Yes, ma'am."

There's no point in fighting it.

I sit down and pull them up, holding them in place below my knees with the garters she hands me.

Then, she helps me into an ivory dress, which feels like another layer of petticoat. Thank goodness it's light.

She points at the cropped jackets on the rack. They're all in pastels and look like they've been cut too short for adult women to wear. "These are spencers, and you'll be wearing one of them over the top of your petticoat. Choose your size and preferred color."

I run a hand across the "spencers" and settle on a pale

blue version with puff sleeves. I know it's very Elizabeth Bennet in the BBC adaptation, but I figure I'd may as well go for it in the short time I'll be wearing these clothes.

Mable helps me pull it on and do it up, and hands me a pair of ballet slippers. I slide my feet into them.

Then, she tells me to take a seat on a hard, wooden chair. She yanks my hair back, twisting it into what I can only assume is a bun like Reggie's, then pulls some strands out around my face and curls them with a hot iron.

"You'll need to learn to do this yourself for the soirées. This is just to show you how to do it."

As she leans over me, I notice her chin hair poking through her thick foundation. I look down at my lap. Man, I hope she doesn't singe my hair.

"After we're done here, go to the living room to join the others for your training."

"Training?"

"Of course. You need to learn how to be a nineteenth-century lady."

"I'm sure I can manage."

"It's compulsory."

Oh, how terrific.

Mable stands back and assesses me. "You're all set."

I can't resist the urge to look in the mirror. The transformation is surreal. As I look at myself, a young woman from 1813 England peers back. It's like I've stepped off the pages of Austen's novel and into this Texas ranch, the spitting image of Lizzie Bennet herself.

And if I'm Lizzie Bennet, then Sebastian must be my Mr. Darcy...

The door bursts open and in sashays *Mean Girl* Camille, accompanied by Trudi. Although she gapes at me for a moment before she remembers I'm a nobody and certainly not worth her time, it pulls me back to the current century—and the fact this is merely dress-up for the audience.

I force myself to shake off any silly, romantic ideas I might have of being an Austen heroine. I'm being ridiculous. Put one costume on me and I turn into a little girl, fantasizing about another life, another time.

I turn away from the mirror and leave the room, giving myself a stern talking to as I return to the dining room.

I'm Emma Brady. Single. Co-owner of Timothy. Parent of Frank the smug, but lovable, tabby cat. And, most importantly, a girl who needs to get the heck off this dating show before it does any more weird things to my head.

Chapter Eight

I walk down the corridor toward the living room, my feet kicking my petticoat with each step. Despite being determined not to, I feel like a heroine of a period drama. To add to that feeling, when I waltz into the living room, it's like a scene from *Pride and Prejudice* itself. About three quarters of the contestants are already dressed in their Regency outfits, and they're sitting on the couches and chatting, appearing like they belong in the fancy looking room. All of them have their hair in buns, with curled tendrils around their faces, just like me. It suits most of them, but especially Phoebe, who looks like she was born to be the perfect Regency lady.

I plunk myself next to her and Reggie. "Hello, ladies of the Regency era," I say with a grin as I take in their costumes. Although Phoebe is dressed identical to me, right down to our matching cornflower blue spencers, somehow she manages to look ten times better than me and ten times more beautiful. "Wow, you two. What a transformation."

"Who knew we'd be doing this, right?" Reggie says. "It's kinda fun, but kinda weird, too, don't y'all think?"

"Weird in what way?" Phoebe asks.

"Do people really want to see us contestants dressed up like we're in some movie?" she asks.

"The production crew clearly thinks they do," I reply. "Maybe there's a market for this kind of thing."

"Perverts," Reggie says and I can't help but giggle.

"Is it considered perverted to get a bunch of women to dress in Regency clothing with their cleavage hoisted up to their chins and film them vying for the attention of one lone man?" I tap my chin. "Hmm. When you put it that way..."

Reggie's eyes light up. "See? Like I said, it's perverted."

Phoebe shakes her head at us. "It's not in the least. It's perfect."

"Let me guess, Phoebe. You think this is super romantic and we all look like elegant ladies from yesteryear."

"Well, yes," she admits. "Haven't you always wanted to be Lizzie Bennet, winning Mr. Darcy's heart and living happily ever after? I know I have."

"How do y'all know they lived happily ever after?" Reggie says. "The book ends with their weddin'. They could have had a miserable marriage, divorced, had affairs. Who knows?"

"He might have turned out gay," I offer. When Phoebe blinks at me, I add, "He was very close to Mr. Bingley and he was always perfectly groomed."

Reggie grins. "Good point, darlin'. Good point."

Phoebe lifts her chin in defiance. "I don't care what you two say. Lizzie and Mr. Darcy *do* end up living happily ever after, and nothing either of you can say will change my mind."

"I can't believe we didn't know about this. I think we should've been told upfront that this was gonna happen," Reggie says.

"Heck yes," I agree. "I wouldn't have come onto the show if I'd known."

"I bought an entire new wardrobe of sexy dresses and the like, and now I can't even wear them," Reggie complains.

I think of my suitcase, packed to the brim with Timothy activewear and I let out a heavy sigh. I have got to get Sebastian away from the cameras so I can get him to send me home soon. "I know what you mean."

We spend the next hour sitting together in the large living room, waiting for everyone to get their fittings and for this "training" we've been told is about to begin.

One thing I've noticed in my short time on this show is that there isn't a whole lot to do when we're not filming. Like nothing. No Internet, no social media, no Netflix. Not even a book to distract us. It's like cramming for finals: all you're allowed to think about is the show. It's almost impossible not to get wrapped up in the world they've created.

What all this free time does, however, is give me time to devise an exit strategy. Despite secretly enjoying the costume—and I'm not going to delve too deeply into that little gem—I know there's no point in me hanging around now that I can't get my label on TV. The best thing I can do now is to get back to work and hope the small amount of TV time I might be given will help us promote Timothy once the show goes to air.

Better that than sitting around here in stays that are digging into my ribs and making my boobs look like a couple of baseballs.

My plan is simple, really, and that's the beauty of it. I'm going to get Sebastian away from the cameras tonight at the soirée and ask him to send me home. No messing around with breaking the rules and no silly games. Just a straightforward request. I'll explain to him that I made a mistake coming on this show, and now I need to be sent home.

I know it'll work. I don't think he likes me, and I sure as heck don't like him. I'm the girl who fell out of the limo and embarrassed herself. I'm the girl who had to talk him into letting her get a do over to avoid national humiliation. I'm the girl he thinks is a total pushover, the one who's not tough in the least.

I'm probably as much of a pain in his butt as he is in mine.

And he's got so many contestants to choose from. What's one less?

The cameras are wheeled into the room, which must mean someone is about to turn up to train us to be Regency ladies.

I try to contain my unbridled excitement at the prospect.

The chatting amongst the contestants comes to a sudden halt as someone unexpected walks into the room. It's Johnathan. No sign of Sebastian.

The cameramen aim their lenses at him.

"Good afternoon, ladies. You really do look quite something," he says. "I know you're about to start your training, but I am here to deliver a message from Mr. Darcy himself. He would like to invite one lucky lady to attend an afternoon picnic with him today."

The women around me give excited squeals.

"She has been chosen based on last night's soirée. Phoebe, would you care to accompany me to your date with Sebastian?"

"Me?" she says, her face flushing as her hand flies to her chest.

"You," Johnathan confirms with a grin.

72

She glances at Kennedy and me as she stands up and straightens out her skirt. I shoot her an encouraging smile and she returns one tinged with nerves.

Maybe Phoebe will be the eventual winner? On the other hand, she's so kind and sweet; she's too good for someone like Sebastian.

"Have fun, Phoebe," Kennedy and some of the others call out as she leaves on Johnathan's arm.

"Take five, girls," Toni, one of the crew says. I notice the cameras are still rolling.

"Why *her?*" Hayley complains with a pout of her over-sized lips.

"Maybe he goes for the passive, easily manipulated type," Camille replies snidely.

Hayley harrumphs, making her fish lips protrude even further. "She's so *nice.*" She shudders as though being nice is the worst thing in the world to be. I guess for a girl like her, it is.

"Oh, I hear you. All that unicorns and rainbows crap. It's enough to make me puke," Camille replies.

Rushing to Phoebe's defense without thinking the potential consequences through, I say, "I bet that's exactly why he chose her, because she's so nice."

"I agree," Kennedy adds. "Good luck to her. Who knows? She might win his heart today over cucumber sandwiches."

I giggle. "Ah, cucumber sandwiches: the ultimate sexy food."

"Why would you say something like that?" Camille throws her hands on her hips and glares at us. "Are you trying to upset us all?"

"Because cucumber sandwiches are deeply *unsexy?*" I

offer. I know I'm being facetious, but seriously, what's she getting so riled up about? It's just a date.

"Not that, you idiot," Camille dismisses with a scowl.

Really, she's quite lovely, and I challenge anyone to think otherwise.

"Why would you say they'll end up together? Don't *you* want to be with him?" she asks.

All eyes in the room turn to Kennedy and me, like the Eye of Mordor itself, locking onto The Ring.

We share a look between us before I attempt an appeasing reply.

"I guess the most important thing to us is that Sebastian is happy, and if that happiness comes in the form of Phoebe, then I've got to be glad for them both." I smile sweetly.

Eat your heart out, Miss America.

Although I could give two hoots about Sebastian's happiness, it's greeted in the room with a deafening silence.

Shelby is the one to break it. "You are such a kind person, Emma. To think that when your own happiness is at stake."

Puh-lease. As if Sebastian could be responsible for my happiness.

"Oh, I just try to think the best of everyone," I reply, which is sadly not the truth. "Kennedy does too. Don't you, Kennedy?"

Kennedy smiles impassively. "Oh, I try to."

Camille arches a perfect eyebrow at us as Hayley scoffs. Those two are the Laurel and Hardy double act of the *Mean Girls* set.

"We'll all get a chance to get to know him," Shelby says. "My attitude is to be open to the possibilities as I wait patiently for my time."

Hayley gives a condescending shake of her head. "Yeah, you do that, Shelby."

Camille giggles.

The scene is broken up when Mrs. Watson arrives, dressed as she was last night, right down to that shower cap balanced on top of her 'do.

"Ladies. You look magnificent," she says with a dramatic sweep of her arm. "What you're dressed in now will be what you'll wear during the day. For the soirées, you will wear a pelisse, a long garment worn in place of the spencer."

"The what?" someone questions under her breath beside me.

"The jacket thing," someone else replies.

"Well, why didn't she say that?" she whispers back.

"You have each been allocated a pelisse, which you can collect later. Now. This afternoon we are going to learn how to act like a lady in 1813. If we all focus, this will only take a few hours."

A few hours?

"First on our list is how to sit."

"Oh, good Lord." I roll my eyes.

"This is insane," Kennedy mutters beside me.

"In terms of insanity, it's right up there with the bloomers," I reply and she stifles a giggle.

As we're all made to stand up and copy as Mrs. Watson demonstrates how to sit with an unnaturally straight back on the world's least comfortable chairs, my resolve hardens to stone.

Tonight, this ends. The girl drama, the Regency dresses, the whole Mr. Darcy mess.

Tonight, I go home.

Chapter Nine

After losing time I will never get back learning such useful things as how to curtsy, sit, walk, and talk like a Regency lady, we're given a measly hour to do some much-needed lounging around before we're due back downstairs for the next soirée.

Now, we've been told to get changed into our "pelisses," which are basically long versions of our cropped jackets but without the long sleeves, which we wear over the ivory dress and petticoats we wore during the day.

I'm beginning to wonder how often the Regency ladies washed their clothes, because getting in and out of them isn't exactly easy. Let's just say my roommates and I don't need to go to the gym today after all the straining and pulling and wrestling with spencers and garters and all things I never expected to wear in my life, let alone on national television.

And women dressed like this back then every freaking day! No wonder they spent half their time breathless or fainting.

Once we're downstairs on the terrace, I thank a server as

I take a glass of wine from his tray and look around. It's a balmy Texas evening, and there are fairy lights hanging from the palm trees around the pool, stretching across to the oversized pergola. I take a moment. It's breathtaking in its beauty, and filled with the contestants in Regency dresses as it is right now, it's quite surreal.

Hayley shoots me a withering look. With her distinctly orange fake tan and her cream petticoats and lilac pelisse, she looks like an Oompa Loompa in period drag.

And that does it. Now, I've got the Oompa Loompa song stuck in my head.

I scan the room for someone I actually like. I spot Phoebe by one of the palm trees and head over to her.

"Emma, you look amazing," Phoebe breathes as she pulls me in for a hug.

"Not as amazing as you, babe. You are beautiful. Mr. Darcy would be insane not to choose you. You're beautiful on the inside and the outside."

Color rises in her cheeks, making her even more gorgeous. When I blush, I look like I've been dipped head first in glowing red Easter egg dye. So not pretty.

"Oh, I don't know," she replies. "There are so many great women here, and anyway, I've only been on one date with him. I don't really know much about him yet."

"How was the date?"

"It was great. We sat on these comfortable chairs on a beautiful lawn and talked."

"And?" I lead.

"And he's a really nice person."

I try not to scoff. Sebastian is a really nice person? Maybe she knows more about him than I do, but I suspect she's had the wool pulled well and truly over her willing eyes.

"Anything juicy to share?" I ask.

"There was no kissing, if that's what you mean."

"Shame."

"Why?" she asks with a light laugh.

"It would really annoy a couple of people if you did."

She looks down. "Oh, I wouldn't want to do anything like that."

Could this girl get any sweeter?

"Of course you wouldn't. Maybe next date." I nudge her with my elbow and her blush deepens.

"Are you talking about the date?" Shelby asks as she and Reggie join our little group.

"You've gotta tell us, darlin'. We're starved of male attention here," Reggie says.

"Reggie, we've only been here for twenty-four hours," I point out.

"A woman has needs you know, and twenty-four hours is a long time in my books," she replies with a wink.

"There's not much to say," Phoebe says. "We talked and ate. It was nice."

I clutch her arm dramatically. "Tell me you got to eat cucumber sandwiches."

Phoebe laughs. "No cucumber sandwiches. It was cheese and crackers with grapes and a glass of wine."

"Bliss." Reggie sighs. "I wonder who'll be next?"

"Oh, it'll be me, for sure," Shelby says with confidence.

I cock my head. "How do you know?"

"On account of the fact they're destined to be together," Reggie says. "Remember?"

Kennedy arrives, drink in hand. "How's it going, girls?" she asks.

"We're talking about who Sebastian is going to take on a date next," I say. "Shelby is sure it'll be her."

"You are?" Kennedy asks her. "How do you know?"

"Because I do," she states simply.

"Ok*aaa*y." Kennedy widens her eyes at me.

'You know, I can tell by looking in his eyes he's got a wise soul," Shelby says randomly. "You can tell a lot by looking in someone's eyes, you know."

"Like what color they are?" I offer.

Kennedy's face shines and Reggie lets out a giggle as she drapes her arm around Shelby's shoulder. "What Shelby means is he's totally hot and she'd go there in a flash. Right, Shel?"

"It's so much deeper than that, I can't even," Shelby protests.

"How long do you think Sebastian will be here tonight?" Phoebe asks, changing the subject.

"Well, if it's anything like last night, it'll be as long as it takes to talk to all of us before we get to be picked off in the line-up," I reply.

"You make it sound like a shooting range, Emma," Kennedy says.

Phoebe makes a face. "It kind of is. It's brutal for the one who gets sent home."

Not if they want *to go, it's not.*

"I've heard somethin'," Reggie says as she leans in closer to us and we automatically follow suit. Funny how that happens. "Apparently, one of the girls is gonna fake faint in front of him tonight."

"Why?" I guffaw.

"So he'll get all chivalrous and the like and catch her as she falls, I suppose," Reggie replies. "Oldest trick in the book, darlin'." She rolls her eyes as though it's something every woman has considered at least once in her dating life.

"Isn't a damsel in distress play taking this whole '1813' thing a little far?" Kennedy asks.

"Not to mention that it's insulting to womankind," I add. Plus, his pompous demeanor aside, doesn't Sebastian deserve someone better than a contestant who thinks it's perfectly fine to fake faint to get his attention? Not that I care, of course. It's the principle of the point, you understand.

"She might hurt herself, too," Phoebe adds. "And that would be horrible."

"Oh, I'm sure she'll faint at just the right time, and in front of the cameras, too. The nation will feel sympathy for her, and watch as sparks fly between their hero and potential heroine," Reggie replies.

I give a sardonic smile. "If there's no one to record it, did it really happen?"

Reggie replies, "Stop! Y'all are makin' me miss my phone." She gets a faraway look in her eye. "My pretty, pretty phone."

"Sebastian would be a total gentleman if some poor girl actually did faint," Shelby states with confidence based on nothing but thin air. None of us know this guy.

"Either that or the girl will land on her tush," Reggie says with a laugh.

I try not to think of my own recent experience with that.

"I want to know how she would be confident that he'd catch her," Kennedy muses.

"Because he's a gentleman," Shelby repeats with total assurance.

I eye her suspiciously for a moment. And then the penny drops. "It's you, isn't it, Shelby? You're the one planning to faint on him."

Shelby's eyes widen. "He'll catch me. You'll see."

We all gape at her. Is she serious?

"What if he doesn't catch you?" I ask.

"Oh, he will," Reggie replies for Shelby. "He's her destiny."

"Right. I forgot about that." I chew the inside of my lip.

Kennedy cocks her head to the side. "But if he's your destiny, why have you got to pull out a trick like that to get his attention?"

It's a good point. We wait with interest for her reply.

"Because even destiny needs a helping hand every now and then," she replies with a wistful glint in her eyes.

This girl is on another planet.

I feel Phoebe's hand on my arm as she says, "Oh, look. Here he is."

"Be still my beatin' heart," Reggie says, her voice breathless. "Would you look at that."

I turn around to see Sebastian, framed by the double doorway leading out to the terrace. He's dressed in a pair of tan pants, tucked into knee-high boots that show off his long, muscular legs, a white shirt and one of those short black jackets with tails, buttoned up to show off his slim waist. On his head is a top hat, which he removes, a broad smile on his face.

He looks ... well, he looks like Mr. Darcy.

Every female pair of eyes in the room are trained on him, and I'm sure many a pulse is racing. Mine? Well, if it is —and that's a big "if"—it's only because he's dressed as one of the most famous heroes of all time. The Mr. Darcy Effect, *hello?* Don't judge me. I'm only human.

"Good evening, ladies," he says with that English accent of his.

"Good evening," most of the women reply, all with the same level of breathlessness Reggie had moments ago. It's like every woman has lost the ability to take anything but extremely shallow breaths, and their already pushed up cleavages are bobbing up and down like some sort of weird, orchestrated street performance.

"I must say, you are all looking quite enchanting this evening in your new clothes," he says. "I look forward to speaking with you all as the night progresses."

He's super formal. I wonder if that's him or the role he's playing?

I watch as he strides across the room, his hat tucked under one arm, and strikes up a conversation with a couple of more than eager contestants.

"Well, that was quite an entrance," Phoebe exclaims with a smile.

"He nailed the whole Mr. Darcy vibe, that's for sure."

"Did he *ever*." Reggie fans herself with her hands again. "Oh, my."

"I'm going to go talk to him," Shelby says and turns to walk away.

I grab her arm and say quietly, "Please don't do it, Shelby. You could hurt yourself."

"Oh, Emma. He'll catch me. You'll see."

I force out a breath as I watch her make her way through the throng of contestants, making a beeline for Sebastian.

"She's going in?" Kennedy asks as she takes a sip of her drink.

"She's got game, that's for sure."

We watch as she approaches Sebastian and he turns and acknowledges her. They begin to chat, and I can tell she's flirting by the way she toys with one of her curly tendrils.

"This is better than Netflix," Kennedy says.

"We need popcorn."

My least favorite humans right now, Hayley and Camille move closer to us.

"What are you all looking at?" Hayley asks.

"Sebastian," we reply in unison.

"Is she doin' it?" Reggie asks, a fresh glass of wine in her hands.

"We think she's gearing up for it," Kennedy replies.

"Who's gearing up for it? And what is 'it?'" Hayley asks.

"Shelby is going in for the kill, darlin'," Reggie explains.

All our eyes are riveted on Shelby and Sebastian. It's like watching car crash television as it unfolds, which I guess is exactly what this is.

"She's making a play for him, isn't she?" Hayley snarls through gritted teeth.

"Heck, yeah," Kennedy replies.

As the words leave her mouth, we watch Shelby raise her hand to her chest and her legs crumple, as she slow-falls perfectly, right into Sebastian's arms. He instantly wraps them around her and holds her up as she lolls her head back in total diva fashion.

"She's fake fainting?" Camille squeaks in disbelief. I bet she's angry she didn't think of it.

"Oh, she's good," I murmur.

"And don't forget completely insane," Kennedy adds.

Camille is fuming. "I cannot believe she just did that."

"She's smarter than I thought," Hayley says.

"I'm not sure I'd call it smart," I say to her.

Next thing we know, Sebastian has cleared a space for Shelby on a nearby couch, much to the disdain of the contestants who had been sitting there before, and is gently placing her limp body down. After a beat—not too quickly as to create suspicion, and not too slowly so the moment passes—she opens her eyes and looks up at him. She says something we can't make out and he crouches down next to her, playing right into the palm of her dainty hands.

I feel as though we should be applauding the performance.

In one fluid movement, she pushes herself up on an elbow, hooks her other hand around his neck, and plants a kiss on his lips.

I'm not going to deny it, seeing her kiss him makes me feel ... weird. I can't explain it. All I know is, I don't think I like it all that much.

Which is insane, I know. This is a dating show, and he's the only guy in a sea of women. We're all meant to be vying for his love, and so far, Shelby's the only one to take a bold step.

Why should I care when all I want to do is get the heck out of this place?

"Would you look at that," Kennedy says as we continue to watch. "The first to kiss Mr. Darcy, and it's the girl who thinks she's destined to be with him."

"I guess there's a certain poetry in that." I reply.

"She is an inspiration to us all," Reggie says. "Watch and learn, girls."

"She isn't an inspiration," Hayley spits. "She's manipulating him with science."

I press my lips together to stop from laughing as I tilt my head to look at her. "With science?" I ask.

"You know, the thing that happens when someone cares for someone else and they fall in love? The nurse and soldier thing."

"The Florence Nightingale Effect," Kennedy says.

I shoot her a questioning look, and she adds, "Psych major."

Hayley is clearly enraged. "That's it. That's what she's

doing. She's Florence Nightingale-ing him. It's unbelievable."

"And so degrading," Camille adds, and for once, I've got to agree with her.

I give a shrug. "I'm just glad she didn't crack her head open on the coffee table."

Hayley looks at me as though I'm speaking a foreign language.

"She could have really hurt herself pulling that stunt."

The look on her face tells me she still needs an interpreter.

I try a different approach. "Oozing blood from your head isn't very romantic, Hayley."

"Oh." She taps the side of her nose. "Got it."

Where did they *find* these people?

Shelby is now propped up on some pillows, surrounded by a gaggle of contestants, with Sebastian sitting right next to her as a crew member checks her over. Sebastian is cradling her hand in his, looking genuinely concerned for her.

Huh. If he's dumb enough to fall for that kind of nonsense, I know beyond a whisper of a doubt I will not miss a single thing about him when I'm gone.

Chapter Ten

An hour later and Shelby has miraculously "recovered" and has either been clinging to Sebastian's arm and gazing up at him as though he were her knight in shining armor, or whispering in corners with the other contestants.

I, on the other hand, have decided that escape can take but one form: alcohol. Good thing it's on tap. With my fourth glass of wine—or quite possibly my fifth, but who's counting?—I find myself propped up against some cushions, chatting with a group of women I've not talked to much before, discussing the ins and the outs of our new costumes.

"It's the bloomers that get me," I say as I take another sip of my wine.

"Oh, me too," agrees Lisa, a tall, slim girl from Southern California who doesn't appear to be one of the crazies. "They're so long and roomy!"

"I miss my Spanx," says Marni, a shorter, more voluptuous girl. "These things give no control to anything whatsoever. I've got lumps where I don't need lumps."

"Oh, I hear you, babe," Lisa replies, and I shoot her a

look. There's not an extra dash of fat on her frame, other than her lifted cleavage that sits perfectly rounded above her top.

"You know, we could cheat and wear our regular underwear under these petticoats. No one would know," I say.

Spanx-loving Marni screws up her face. "I guess."

"It's not like they're checking or anything, because that would be a total invasion of our privacy," I say. When the girls don't reply, I get concerned. "They're not checking, are they?"

"How could they?" Marni asks. "It's not like there are cameras in our rooms."

I cock an eyebrow. "You sure?"

They wouldn't do that, would they?

Her response is reassuringly decisive. "I'm sure. I checked. Not my first rodeo, ladies."

"It's not?"

She shakes her head. "This is my third dating show, but I've acted on *Vets in the Wild*, too," she replies, naming a TV show I've heard of but never seen. "Only a walk-on part, but it's TV, you know? It all helps to keep my profile up."

Well, Marni's clearly "here for the right reasons."

"You're an actor?" I ask.

"Actor, model, social media influencer. All of the above."

Lisa scoots her butt off the seat and makes a face as she reaches up inside her skirt. I know what she's doing because I've already had to do it a couple of times myself tonight.

"Did your butt eat your bloomers?" I ask.

"It's so annoying. How can something so big and roomy work its way right up in there?"

"Oh, I hear you," Marni says empathetically.

"I suggest we revolt," I say. "Ditch the clown-like bloomers and snap on our Spanx. What do y'all say, girls?"

"This sounds like an interesting conversation," a deep, velvety voice with a distinctively clipped English accent says behind me.

Oh, no.

I squeeze my eyes shut for a moment before I open them and look up into a pair of brown eyes with a mischievous glint, trained right on me. The last thing I want to talk to Sebastian about is our underwear. He was probably the one who insisted we had to wear the bloomers in the first place.

"It's nothing, really. Just, you know, girl stuff." My cheeks flame and I try to think of cold things like icebergs and swimming pools in winter. Glowing red Easter egg dye, remember?

"'Girl stuff' sounds interesting to me," he replies.

I hear the whirr of the cameras around us, which makes my blush go nuclear.

"Spanx," Marni says without preamble. "We were talking about Spanx and how we hate having to wear bloomers."

His lips twitch. "Bloomers? I had no idea."

Well, there goes that theory.

"Oh, we're full-on authentic here, mister," Marni says.

His laugh is deep. "That is good to know. Other than the, err, bloomers situation, how are you finding the new clothes?"

"I love them," Lisa says, moving her shoulders from side to side.

I watch as Sebastian's eyes drift down to her pert cleavage and linger for a moment too long.

Ha! So much for being Mr. Darcy. *He* would never eye

up a girl's assets in such an obvious way. *He* would be a complete gentleman.

Sebastian might have loads of money and come from some stuffy, upper-class background, but at the heart of it all, he is just your standard, lecherous guy.

Lisa seems quite happy with the attention, and even goes on to toy with the ribbon on her bodice to keep it on her. "I feel really feminine and pretty in it, especially next to you, *Mister* Darcy." She looks up at him through hooded eyes, telegraphing her message loud and clear.

Subtlety, thy name is not Lisa.

Sebastian seems to be working hard to raise his eyes from her chest. "I'm pleased to hear it, Lisa."

I raise my eyebrows in judgment at him. Get a grip, dude. They're only boobs.

"Sebastian, tell us. Are you sending someone home tonight?" Marni asks.

He wins the battle and manages to raise his eyes. "I have to, I'm afraid. Those are the rules of the show."

"But you've barely spent any time with any of us," Lisa protests. "How can you know who to send home?"

"That's why I'm trying to talk individually to a number of women I'd like to get to know a little better tonight, just as I did last night. And on that note," he looks from Lisa, to me, to Marni, and back to me again, "would you care to take a stroll with me, Emma? I have a rather nice little secluded spot set up in the garden."

I blink at him in surprise. "You want to talk to me?"

He shoots me a look that questions whether I'm right in the brain. "Well, yes. That is the general idea."

I glance at Lisa and Marni. They're putting a brave face on it, but I can tell Lisa, especially, is disappointed. She probably feels knocked back, despite going all in with her impressive weapons of mass distraction.

I smile sweetly at Sebastian. "Sure. I'd be more than happy to talk with you, Mr. Darcy."

This is my chance. I need to get him away from the cameras, explain the situation to him, and within the next few hours, I could be home free. And I've got a little plan up my sleeve to do it. Well, strictly speaking it's down my top as my sleeves are miniscule, but you get the idea.

"Have fun, you two," Marni says as we turn to leave.

We walk together past the contestants on one side, the pool on the other, and I'm sure Camille isn't the only one weighing up whether to push me in right about now. Sebastian leads me down a path with low lighting to a pretty gazebo with a cushioned loveseat, and candles lining the edges.

"Please, take a seat," he offers, and I do my best imitation of Mrs. Watson sitting down on the edge of the seat beside him with a ram-rod straight back. I probably look ridiculous, but at least I look the part.

He quirks an eyebrow, but says nothing.

I concentrate hard on not looking at the cameras, as we've been drilled, and instead gaze out at the dark night sky. I take a steadying gulp of my wine. "How—"

"What—"

We both begin to speak at the same time.

"What were you going to say?" he asks.

"I was going to ask you how things are going, I guess. This is, what, day two? And we're already playing dress up."

Well, that came out a whole lot flirtier than I'd intended.

The outer edges of his mouth curve into a small smile, and I know he took it that way.

"I mean, we're in costumes. Me in this," I claw at my petticoats, "and you in your jodhpurs and whatnot."

"Breeches."

"Sorry, what?"

"They're called breeches. Jodhpurs are what one wears when one rides a horse."

"Forgive me," I say in mock apology. "I grew up in the 'burbs, not in some massive castle knowing what the right pants are to wear on a horse. In fact, there weren't a lot of horses on my street for *one* to ride."

His smile is now fully formed. "I imagine not if you grew up in the 'burbs, as you put it. By which I assume you mean the suburbs."

I look at him out of the corner of my eyes. "Are you for real?"

He pats his chest. "I believe so, yes."

I roll my eyes. "And a lame comedian at that."

"I do try. The boys at Eton were pleased with my efforts, I recall."

I throw my hands in the air. "You see? That's what I'm talking about here. 'The boys at Eton' and 'one wears jodhpurs on a horse.' You're from a totally different world from me. From all of us."

He nods, a thoughtful look on his face. "And that's bad in your books?"

"No. Not necessarily. It's a thing, that's all."

He cocks an eyebrow. "A thing?"

"A thing."

"Well, I'm glad we got *that* cleared up."

I flick my eyes up to his and see the amusement written

across his face. This guy has got such a stick up his butt, I'm surprised he can even sit down.

He smiles, and it's hard not to warm to the guy a little. Not a lot, of course. He's still a toffee-nosed, over-privileged, castle-owning Mr. Darcy imposter whom I morally object to on so many levels I could form a high-rise in my mind. But still. A little.

And right now, this particular pompous snob is standing between me and going home. Although I hate to admit it, I do need his help.

I've never been a girl scout, but I thought ahead and I've come prepared. I wrote a note that says, *We need to talk, just you and me. NO CAMERAS,* and I was forced to put it in the only place I knew it would be secure. No pockets, you see.

It's time to dig it out.

I avert my eyes from his as I fish around inside my top for my piece of paper. I check one side of my ... "obstacles," and then the other. Dang it, it's not where I put it. How could it have moved? It's not like I've been exactly active while wearing this outfit, unless you count dodging Camille and Hayley's evil glares, that is.

Chewing on my lip, I dig deeper, and finally, with a rush of relief, I locate my note. I pull it out and give a sigh of relief.

Sebastian is looking at me as if I'm some kind of freak.

"Duh. No pockets," I explain, which is, like, so obvious.

His lips curl up in that sexy smile of his. You know, the one to which I'm entirely impervious.

Okay, I admit to a little wave of tingles, but it means less than zero.

"No pockets. I see."

With the warm and slightly damp (*ew*) note in my

hands, I glance out of the corner of my eye at the camera. It's trained on us, as I totally expected it to be, of course— this is a reality TV show, and I'm sitting alone with Mr. Darcy. Like the non-girl scout that I am, I knew there was no avoiding the cameras while I did this. So, I've got a cover story.

"Look, Seb. Can I call you Seb?"

"No."

See? Stick. Butt.

"I've written you a note to tell you how much I, err, like you." I try to retain eye contact with him, but it's beyond my capabilities right now. Like this guy? Ha! Never gonna happen.

He blinks at me a couple of times. "You have?"

"Yup. You're my type. Totally my kind of guy."

"Well, that's ... reassuring." The sarcasm oozing from him is not lost on me.

Whatever. I'll be gone tonight, and we will never have to see one another again.

I barely manage to keep the sarcasm from my own voice when I reply, "I thought you might think that. So," I lead as I angle the note away from the camera so only he can see it.

I watch as he takes the note, reads it, and then looks back at me. "Well, that's a lovely note, Emma, thank you." He slips it into the top pocket of his Mr. Darcy jacket. "It is against the rules to invite me to your bedroom, though, I am afraid."

My bedroom? What is he talking about?

"That said, I do look forward to spending a lot more time with you, too. Although, it is a little soon to be speaking of love, don't you think?"

I stare at him, agog. Love?

"I'm sorry, what now?"

He places his hand on mine, and adds in a heartfelt tone, "Let's just take it one day at a time, shall we, Emma? Let things progress at a natural pace."

I glare at him and notice that irritating smile of his has returned full-force. I'm itching hard to pull my hand away. But, like a cat with a mouse, he's toying with me, and he's loving every moment of it.

"Thank you, *Seb*," I say with a Phoebe-like simpering smile. "That's very understanding of you." My eyes throw a series of pointy daggers right at his stupid face.

I cannot believe he's made out that I've written him a love letter on national television!

"Just to set the record straight though, I said I *like* you and did not mention my bedroom."

"Oh. I think you did."

I shake my head. "Uh-ah. Didn't."

"Don't be ashamed, Emma. It's only natural."

Oh, the cheek of this man! Problem is, he may be a self-absorbed jerk who apparently likes to make jokes at my expense while being filmed, but he holds all the cards. I've got to get him on my side if I stand any chance of getting out of here.

I control the urge to throw my drink in his face, *Real Housewives* style, and instead smile at him and say, "Thank you for our little chat. I hope you take what I said in the note into consideration. I'm going to go now." I stand up, my eyes not leaving his. "I. Need. To. Go. To. The. Bathroom."

"I see." He stands up slowly, and I notice his impressive height, my Regency slippers no better than bare feet in the "give Emma a much needed three extra inches" stakes.

He calls me closer to him with his index finger, and hope springs inside. He's going to meet me! This nightmare will be over soon!

I wait in expectation as he leans down toward me and whispers in my ear, "I'm certain the American people don't need to know about your toilet habits, Emma, but thank you so much for sharing that information with them, and with me."

He straightens back up, looking very pleased with himself, and it's all I can do not to stomp on his foot in sheer frustration and storm off like some reality TV star diva. Which would be childish and very poorly thought out, I know, but ... *argh!* The man is beyond infuriating.

To add to the infuriation (is that a word? If not I'm making it one because it is perfect for Sebastian), he then proceeds to smile at me and offer me his arm as though he hasn't just embarrassed me on national television and completely ignored my plea for help.

I stare at his outstretched arm in disbelief before I lift my eyes back up to his smarmy, arrogant, condescending (but still handsome, dang it) face. I know I could say something cutting. I've been known to have a quick wit. I could bring him and his arrogant game playing down to size. Instead, I choose to rise above it. I'm the bigger person. I don't play games.

And I need him to help me out.

"Well, I guess I'll be seeing you around, Seb." I pat him on the arm, flash him a smile, and turn on my slippered heel and walk away.

"It's Sebastian," he calls after me, but I'm already out of the shot, so I hold my head high and trudge up the path as my fury bubbles up inside.

Chapter Eleven

With my head held so high I'll need a chiropractor to snap me back into place before too long, I trudge down the path, crunching gravel beneath my flimsy ballet flats, as I head back to the terrace.

Well, that was a big fat waste of my time. What was I thinking appealing to his sense of decency? The guy didn't even give me a chance! He cut me down to size with his ridiculous line about me professing my love for him in my note, making me look like some sort of prepubescent school-girl with a crush.

Oooh, I'm so angry I could scream!

That man is beyond exasperating. He's so arrogant and I can tell he thinks so much more of himself than he does anyone else. Save perhaps for Johnathan, even though he's probably some actor being paid to pretend he's Sebastian's friend.

I can tell you one thing for free: that little exchange between us back there makes me even more determined to get out of here as soon as I can. Between the cast of *Mean*

Girls and Snobby Sebastian, I cannot stand another minute here.

I've got to come up with another plan. This feels so much more than simply a lost opportunity to market Timothy. It feels personal. And I for one am—

I feel a hand on my arm and look up in surprise to see Sebastian standing right behind me.

"Move. Quickly."

He cups my elbow and steers me off the path in between some bushes. My petticoat snags on a branch and rips, and I hoist it up around my knees. How did women in 1813 manage to do anything physical while maintaining "decorum," as Mrs. Watson puts it?

We reach the other side of the bushes, and he drops his hand. "This way."

"Where are we going?" I hiss.

"You'll see."

I follow him as we enter the house. I rush down the corridor behind him, and into an area of the house I've not been.

"My living quarters," he says by way of explanation as he closes the door behind us.

I cock an eyebrow. "So, you diss me in front of the cameras, then whisk me away to *your* bedroom?" I ask, incredulous.

Who the heck does this guy think he is?

Yeah, I know: Mr. Freaking Darcy.

Well, he's not Mr. Darcy. He's just a pompous English stiff who thinks he can take what he wants, when he wants.

"You and I both know you're jumping to entirely the wrong conclusion, Emma," he says sternly.

I eye the bed. It's the hugest bed I've seen—and I live in Texas. "We're in your bedroom."

97

"I assure you, you are perfectly safe with me."

I shoot him a look. Is that meant as an insult?

I give a short, sharp nod. "Good." I take in the room. Other than the big bed, there's a spacious seating area, a large TV (he's a guy, so *duh*), and a door leading through a closet to an *ensuite*. It's the opposite end of the accommodation scale the contestants have got to put up with, with three single beds to one room and shared bathroom facilities.

He sits down on one of the couches and looks up at me. "We've got a couple of minutes. I suggest you take full advantage of it."

He gestures at the couch opposite.

"Look. After what you pulled out there—"

"I thought it was quite funny."

I cross my arms. "I bet you did."

"We've got one minute and thirty seconds now." He gestures at the couch once more and I give in and sit down.

"Okay, here's the thing."

"Another thing? You Americans and your 'things.'"

"Don't you talk that way in England?"

"We tend to use actual, descriptive words instead of relying on 'thing.'"

I give him a false smile. "Well bully for you." I lean in, my elbows on my knees. "The *thing* is," I begin, emphasizing the word for effect, "I can't do what I intended to do on this show if I have to wear this." I tug at the fabric of my petticoats.

He raises his eyebrows at me. "You don't want to wear clothes? Because if that's the case, Emma, I would say you're on entirely the wrong kind of show."

"*These* clothes. The Jane Austen stuff."

"So not clothes per se, then?"

I make a face. Does he think I'm some kind of exhibitionist nudist? "No! Of course not. I wear clothes like everyone else. Every day, in fact."

"Including your Spanx."

I pull my lips into a thin line. "That was Marni, not me and ... oh, forget it." I cross my arms and sit back in my chair. "I'm asking you for your help here, dude. You being all smart and smarmy isn't helping."

"My apologies. I will refrain from being smart or smarmy from now on."

"You do that."

"I will."

"Good."

We glare at one another for a moment and I wonder if I might break my jaw, I'm clenching it so tight.

"So, Emma. Let's start again, shall we? You were telling me about your intentions on the show, correct?"

"I was about to, yes."

"I can only assume your intention is what it is meant to be: to fall head over heels in love with me. Because why else would you come on a reality dating show if not to fall in love?"

Thrown momentarily off my game, I mutter, "Well, there's that—"

"And now you're telling me you can't fall in love with me because you've got to wear a Regency period costume. Please tell me if I've got this wrong."

He is exasperating, infuriating, irritating. All the "ings."

"I'm not talking about *that* intention, and let me tell you something," I brandish my finger at him, "there are some women out there who I bet are only here for the fame."

"How shocking," he deadpans.

So I guess he knows about that.

"And some of them are certifiably insane."

"I am also deeply shocked by that information," he replies in the same tone.

I let out an exasperated breath. "I'm gonna be straight with you."

"Please do."

"What I wanted to do—other than fall in love, of course —was to showcase Timothy, the activewear label I co-own with Penny, my best friend. Who, incidentally is the reason I'm on this stupid show in the first place."

He raises his eyebrows. "Stupid show?"

"Well, it is, isn't it? You can't tell me you're actually here to find love."

He shifts in his seat. "I already told you that is exactly what I intend to do. Why else would I be here? I don't have an activewear label to promote. Or a friend called Penny, for that matter."

I eye him up and decide to drop it. He's sarcastic and enjoying this. And anyway, does it matter to me whether his intentions are genuine or not? Not at all.

"Well, I have both an activewear business and a friend called Penny, and like it or not, the fact I can no longer wear my label on camera because I'm forced to wear Regency stuff means I can't stay here any longer."

"I see."

"But I do genuinely, *genuinely* hope you find your princess or duchess or whatever she'll be, and you both live happily ever after with your fifty servants in your posh English castle."

"Whomever I marry will be called 'Lady.' And I don't have fifty servants."

"But you still live in a castle."

"It's what we refer to as a manor, even though there once was a castle on my family's land."

Potato pot-*ah*-to.

I raise my hands in the surrender sign. "My bad. I really should brush up on the homes of the English aristocracy."

"You may find it quite educational."

I narrow my eyes at him. I think I detect a hint of snark in his voice, but I could be wrong. "Anyway, now you know I can't wear my label while I'm dressed like Elizabeth Bennet every time I'm on camera, so—" I lead.

"Why not simply leave? You are able to do so, you know."

"I, ah, I can't do that."

He raises his brows at me.

"There's a fine, and cash is a little short right now."

The understatement of the decade.

"I see. I'm guessing you need *me* to help you."

I tap the side of my head. "Handsome, rich, and smart. You're the triple threat, Seb."

He chortles. "So, you definitely weren't dragging me off to have your wicked way with me."

Right on cue, those dang tingles twinge. "Puh-lease! *Neither* of us wants *that*." I frame it as a statement, but a small part of me wants to pose it as a question.

A part that needs to be stamped out immediately.

His lips quirk. "Indeed."

"And anyway, we both know you're not interested in the likes of me."

He raises his eyebrows. "Do we?"

"Heck, yes. Y'all could have drowned in Lisa's cleavage back there on the terrace."

"Drowned, you say?"

"Oh, yeah. Dogs drool less over a juicy bone than you did."

"Is that jealousy I detect in your voice, Emma?"

"Jealousy?" I scoff. "Do you think no woman is capable of resisting you?"

"Oh, I'm certain there are some who can."

I shoot him a sardonic smile. "Like women related to you, right?"

"And don't forget the lesbians."

I let out a surprised laugh. It ends in an embarrassing snort, and he looks at me with a dash of smug amusement in his eyes.

"Endearing laughter aside, without the ability to promote your designs on the show, you want me to send you home. Is that correct?"

I give an emphatic nod. "Yes."

He stands up and smooths down his pants. "All right."

Hope rises inside. "Is that 'all right' as in you'll do it?"

He gives a short, sharp nod. "I'll do it."

I'm so ecstatic, I leap out of my seat and throw myself at him, gushing, "Thank you, thank you!" As I press up against him I do my best not to notice how big, firm, and muscular he feels. Which I do an absolutely terrible job of, truth be told.

Smooched up together, he looks down at me and our eyes lock. My heart rate kicks up and those tingles make a reappearance, only this time they've brought back-up, so they're more like a jolt.

The thing is, despite the long list of things I dislike about this guy—and it is a very, very long list, believe me—there's something alluring about Sebastian.

Something I most definitely do not want to explore.

I pull away from him and instead stick my hand out. "It's a deal."

He takes my hand in his and we shake. "It can't be

tonight, though, I'm afraid. I've already made my decision to send the blood vial contestant home."

My heart drops a fraction. Jessie, a girl with wide, starey eyes I've managed to mostly avoid so far. I can understand why he'd want her to leave. She's pretty intense. "Oh."

"Next elimination?"

"Sure."

"With that agreed, we'd best get back to the others."

"Of course. You've got love to find, and that's not going to happen for you tucked away here with me."

"My sentiments exactly."

We walk to the door.

"Have you got any clue who you're going to choose? Because I've got someone in mind for you."

"You do?"

"Kennedy. She's gorgeous and fun and super nice. Oh, and her last name is Bennet. Wouldn't it be cute if Mr. Darcy ended up with Miss Bennet? The viewers would die for it."

"Perhaps, if my surname really were Darcy."

"What is your last name?"

"Huntington-Ross."

Oh, yeah. That *so* fits.

"Of course it is."

He arches an eyebrow. "What does that mean?"

"It means your name is perfectly suited to you, that's all."

"What's your surname?"

"Brady. As in Bunch."

"*The Brady Bunch*? That show about the blended family from the sixties?" He arches an eyebrow. "How old *are* you, exactly?"

"Don't you need to get back to your adoring women?"

103

"I do."

I pull the door open and turn around to face him. "Thank you for this, Seb. I'll look forward to being dumped by you at the next card ceremony."

"You're welcome, Brady Bunch," he replies with a smile.

Brady Bunch? That definitely sounded a little flirty.

"And it's Sebastian."

I pat him on his lapel. "Whatever you say, Mr. Darcy."

Chapter Twelve

As if being stuck for another round in this place isn't torture enough, the production crew have crafted a new and wonderful way in which to humiliate the contestants on national television. It's a singing competition.

Yup, you heard it right, people. We all get to sing for Mr. Darcy.

How perfectly terrific.

Jessie, the contestant who tried to give Sebastian a vial of her blood, was sent home last night, just as Sebastian had told me she would be. I can't say I blame him. She was definitely a little unhinged, even if she did take my spot.

So, now our numbers have dwindled to ten, and I'm forced to endure at least another few days here until Sebastian delivers on his promise.

But before the singing contest, we all have to be interviewed once more. Unlike some of the other girls, I do not relish my time on camera. I've got to watch what I say and walk the line between coming across as though I'm into Sebastian, but not delusional. I don't want to seem like I'm totally into him for him to then dump me at the next card ceremony.

"Tell us about you and Sebastian," Cindy asks once I'm settled in the usual spot in my Regency finery (bloomers included, but don't get me started on *that* again).

"Oh, we're good. We had a chat about things and he's been very nice to me."

"Do you mean the conversation you had when you handed him a note telling him that you loved him and invited him to your room?"

Dang it! Of course they had to bring that up.

"It wasn't like that."

"Oh? How was it exactly? I'm sure our viewers would love to know, and please start your statement with 'I gave Sebastian a note because.'"

I've got to think, and fast. "I gave Sebastian a note because I wasn't sure we would get the chance to spend much time together. All the note said was that I was looking forward to getting to know him."

"But he said you invited him to your room."

"He was kidding about that. One thing I can tell you about this Mr. Darcy: he's a kidder."

"So, you're telling me that you didn't invite him to your room."

I reply firmly, "I did not invite Sebastian to my room." I feel like President Clinton declaring he didn't have an affair with Monica Lewinsky. Only in my case, it's the truth.

"Did your note tell him you loved him?"

"It said I liked him. That's all. He just made that part up."

"Why?"

"For fun."

"Was that fun?"

"Sure. It was hilarious."

"You seemed quite annoyed at the time."

"I guess I didn't get the joke."

"But you do now?"

"I do now."

Cindy takes a long, hard look at me, and I squirm in my seat.

"Is there anything else you wanted to ask me?" I say weakly.

"There is, actually," she replies and my heart sinks. "I guess the viewers would probably want to know why you told him you liked him in a note, like the type of note you might pass a boy in middle school, when you'd already said you hoped Kennedy would win his heart."

Double dang it! Why does this woman need to be so astute?

I word my response carefully. "Kennedy would be a good match for Sebastian, and so would I. We would both be good matches for him."

I hold my smile in place for what feels like a year before she says, "What about Phoebe? Do you like her?"

"Who wouldn't? Phoebe's sweet and kind and all things wonderful."

"Is that a note of sarcasm I detect in your voice, Emma?"

"What? No. Phoebe's great."

"But a little too sweet, right? Between you and me, I wonder whether she's for real, she's so nice."

I chortle. She's right. Phoebe is super sweet, but Cindy's not going to catch me out quite so easily. "I disagree. Phoebe is lovely and totally genuine. She's totally here for the right reasons."

I cringe a little inside.

"Awesome," Cindy replies with a shovel-load of sarcasm.

"Are we done here?"

She waves me off with her hand. "Sure. Go."

I make my way back to the living room where Mrs. Watson is loving every moment as she dishes out the rules on what is and is not acceptable for today's super fun task in front of the ever-present cameras.

Lucky for us they've served up some drinks, presumably to give us all Dutch courage. Or make for better TV, more like.

Mrs. Watson is holding court with her usual sunny disposition that lights up the room. "It goes without saying that dancing, clapping, or anything considered too modern will attract an instant elimination from today's competition. That will mean you won't be in contention for dinner tonight with Mr. Darcy."

Yippee. We are literally singing for our supper.

"If you play the piano, you may perform your song accompanied. Ladies often played the piano to an audience at Regency soirées. If you don't play, you will need to sing unaccompanied."

Sitting beside me, Kennedy is looking about as thrilled about this new development as I am. She puts her hand in the air as though we're back in school, which is what this feels like. You know, if we were in school in the nineteenth century. "Mrs. Watson?"

"Miss Kennedy."

"Just so we're clear, you're saying there's no electric guitar allowed?"

I work hard at stifling a giggle.

Mrs. Watson shakes her head. "No electric guitar."

"Harmonica?" Kennedy inquires.

By now I'm sure I'm bright red with my efforts to stop my laughter from bursting out. I'm deeply thankful I swallowed that last sip or the woman in front of me would be wearing a healthy smattering of Eau de Chardonnay by now.

"No harmonica, either."

"What about the bongos?" I ask, getting into the swing of things. "I'm feeling like I could channel my inner Matthew McConaughey for this thing."

Some of the contestants laugh. Mrs. Watson does not.

Marni sticks her hand up in the air.

Mrs. Watson glares at her. "Is this a serious question, Miss Marni, or are you going to be facetious as well?"

"It's a serious question, I promise," Marni says in a serious tone. "What about an autotune mic? I don't know about you all, but I could really do with one of those."

There's a murmur of agreement among the contestants. Mrs. Watson is not swayed. She twists her face with annoyance. With her weird shower cap on top of her head she looks like Smurfette in a bad mood. Only she's not blue. Clearly.

"There will be no autotune microphones, no six-piece bands, no backing vocals," she replies tersely. "Just you, your voice, and the piano, if you can play it. And Miss Kennedy and Miss Emma? I suggest you put your efforts into your performance rather than into asking questions in order to entertain your fellow contestants." She shoots us a look that states very clearly that she's in charge and we need to stay in our place.

Have I mentioned already how much I love being here?

Undeterred, Mrs. Watson continues. "Singing is the cornerstone of every young lady's accomplishments in Regency society. The men of the day would fully expect to be entertained by ladies of their acquaintance at soirées."

"I bet they would," I mumble under my breath to Kennedy.

"Now, you have two hours in which to practice, after which you will return and perform for Mr. Darcy. Go and find a quiet spot. We will meet back here at six."

When no one moves, she adds, "What are you waiting for? Go!"

As she turns and leaves with a swoosh of her long skirt, the room erupts into chatter around us.

"What were you thinking of performing with an electric guitar and a harmonica?" I ask Kennedy as we make our way from the room.

"Tom Petty. I thought that was pretty appropriate for 1813 England."

"*Refugee?*" I ask, naming one of his hit songs.

"Obviously."

"Tom Petty totally screams Regency parlor music to me."

"You get it." She grins at me before she adds, "I cannot believe we've got to do this. I mean, can any of us even sing?"

"I bet Sebastian doesn't care whether we can sing, anyway."

"I'm not sure many people list 'parlor singing' on their online dating profile."

I snort with laughter. "As if being paraded around in these clothes isn't undignified enough."

"I like wearing these clothes," says someone behind us.

We look back to see Phoebe. Of course.

"Don't you think it makes this all feel like we've stepped back in time by two hundred years?" she asks.

Kennedy cocks an eyebrow. "Sure, if in 1813 people were being incessantly filmed for all of America to see."

"And don't forget that we are all competing for one man's attentions," I add.

"You two are so negative," Phoebe replies with a shake of her head. "Why not let yourselves enjoy this amazing experience?"

"You're right, Phoebe. I'll drop Tom Petty and go for some heavy rock instead," Kennedy says.

"Much more appropriate," I agree.

"You two," Phoebe gently scolds with a shake of her head.

We walk through the double doors and out onto the patio. The hot Texas sun is beating down, and in our layers and restrictive stays we don't want to get anywhere near that, so the three of us find some shade on the grass below a tree and flop down.

"Who knows what they're going to perform?" Phoebe asks.

"I bet you already do," I say without a trace of malice. With her positive approach to all this Regency insanity, she probably worked out her song before Mrs. Watson had even finished bossing us around.

Her face lights up in excitement, just as I thought it would. "I'm going to sing *Loving You*."

"*Loving You*?"

"It's a classic. It was sung by Minnie Riperton back in the '70s. Big hit. My mom used to sing it to me when I was little and it always made me smile."

"Wait. Is that the really high one?" I've got a vague memory of the song.

Phoebe gives an enthusiastic nod. If it's the one I'm thinking of, that is one super high song. I hope she can actually sing, or we're all in for an eardrum splitting experience.

"What about you, Emma?"

"Nothing, if I have my way. Me and singing are not well acquainted. Well, other than in my car. I do my best work there, but it's strictly for my ears only."

"What do you sing in your car?" Kennedy asks.

"Rihanna, Katy, Beyoncé, Taylor. Maybe a touch of Miley, if I'm in a crappy mood." I raise my hands in the air. "I know, I'm a total pop diva wannabe, but I've made my peace with it, so you should too."

"I think they're great choices, Emma," Phoebe says. "Not exactly Regency, but that doesn't matter."

I shake my head. "I'm not going to sing any of them."

"Whether you like it or not, you've got to, babe," Kennedy points out helpfully, "or you'll miss out on a chance to have dinner with Sebastian. And you never know what could happen over a bottle of wine at a romantic candle lit dinner for two with the luscious Mr. Darcy." She waggles her brows at me suggestively.

"Dinner with Sebastian, huh?" I tap my chin in the internationally recognized sign for thinking. "Somehow, I think I could sacrifice that to hold on to what dignity I've got left."

Although I don't want it to, my mind goes to the way he looked at me in his room last night, and I know I'm not telling the whole truth. Despite the fact he's the total opposite of the kind of guy I go for, dinner with Sebastian might be ... nice. Maybe more than nice.

Wow. I *so* need to get out of here.

"I'm going to try my best. I'd be more than happy to win that dinner," Kennedy says.

"Me, too," Phoebe adds as her face flushes Santa-suit red. "What? He's hot."

"He is hot," Kennedy agrees. "A little pompous maybe, but the guy's got the goods, that's for sure. And that sexy accent of his?"

"Yeah, okay," I admit, "I agree about the accent. But it makes him even more stuffy, don't y'all think?"

"I think it makes him even more attractive," Phoebe says. She hops up to her feet. How she does it in her floor-length petticoats is a feat of major dexterity. "Okay, girls. I'm going to go practice my song. And Emma? You've got to sing, so choose something good. You'll just have to pretend you're in your car."

"How about I bust out *All the Single Ladies*, Regency style?" I say with zero intention of doing so.

Kennedy bats me lightly on the arm as she too gets up to leave. "Hey, that's my jam, girl."

I rub my arm theatrically. "Okay, you can have it. No need to beat me up over it."

She flashes me a gorgeous smile before she and Phoebe make their way to quiet corners of the garden to practice. I reposition myself up against the large, old tree, rearrange my petticoats that were rising scandalously high, as Mrs. Watson would no doubt inform me in that friendly way of hers, and lean back. I take a deep breath of the warm, fresh air. I can hear contestants around me practicing different songs to varying degrees of proficiency. It's weirdly relaxing, kind of like listening to the squawks of unharmonious tropical birds.

I'm not going to practice anything. Besides the fact my singing voice sounds like a chimpanzee with a sinus infection, there's absolutely no point. Winning today's little game of humiliation will only take a dinner date away from one of the other contestants. And anyway, wouldn't it look weird if I won, went to dinner, and then got booted off the show at the next card ceremony?

It's all about the optics, people.

As I take another deep breath, my eyelids grow heavy. After my deal-making with Sebastian last night, I didn't get nearly enough sleep. I could catch a few z's now and no one would be any the wiser ...

"Sleeping on the job, are we?"

Oops. I must have dozed off in the heat. I open my eyes a crack to see Sebastian peering down at me. Dressed as Mr. Darcy once more, he looks achingly handsome, and his presence quickly wakes me up.

I sit up straighter, smile, and try not to look at the camera hovering nearby. "Sebastian. How long have you been standing here?"

"Long enough to see a little line of drool make its way down your chin."

I quickly wipe my face. It's perfectly dry. I snap my eyes to his. "You're messing with me."

He shrugs. "Perhaps I am. You did look very angelic, though."

"I am angelic, don't you know?"

His lips quirk. "I must have missed that part of your personality." He gestures at the ground beside me. "May I?"

Despite the insult, I nod. The cameras are on us, after all.

He sits down next to me. "I've come to check how the practice is coming along, but it looked to me like you were catching up on some sleep, instead. Late night last night, was it?"

I shoot him a look. Having not left his room until the

small hours, he knows exactly how late my night was. "I'm fine, thanks."

"That's good to hear. We don't want you missing out on your sleep, now. Do we?"

"Err, no," I reply uncertainly.

What is he playing at?

He tucks a finger inside his cravat and pulls. It shifts about a fifth of an inch. "Is it always this hot in Texas?"

"Yes. Well, other than when we get a shock of cold from the north in winter. Then we Houstonians all stay home and wonder what happened to our seventy-five degrees."

"Seventy-five in winter? That's warmer than a summer's day where I'm from." He collects a twig from the ground and toys with it in his hands.

"Maybe you should lose the jacket," I suggest, then realize how flirty that may sound. "You know, to keep cool," I add, so there's no confusion that I'm simply trying to help his internal temperature regulate.

Which is all I'm trying to do, of course.

"Now, why didn't *I* think of that?" he says with a glint in his eye. He leans in closer to me, and I can't help but breathe in his heady scent. "You are so wise, Brady Bunch," he says quietly.

Right on cue, those tingles kick back to life, and I've got to remind myself that I'm here under duress—and not for him.

I try not to watch as he stands back up and unbuttons his double-breasted jacket. I try. Really, I do. But I fail. Miserably. Please don't judge me. *Mr. Darcy is taking off his jacket right in front of me*. Only the superhuman could manage to avert their eyes, and I'd put money on the fact they'd sneak a peek, anyway.

His jacket off, he folds it neatly over his arm and then

places it on the ground. As he sits back down, I try not to notice the way his cream shirt falls from broad shoulders, tucked into a slim waist.

Yup, you got it: another fail.

Why does this guy have to be so hot? Doesn't he know it's distracting me from disliking him?

"Now, Emma. What will you be delighting me with this afternoon?"

I shoot him a look. Is that a flirty lilt to the way he said "delighting?" "Oh, I won't be delighting anyone, I can tell you that right now."

"Are you certain? I, for one, find you quite delightful." His eyes are trained on mine in some kind of challenge.

Yup. Definitely flirty.

"I—" I begin, only to stop. I'm not sure what to say. What is this guy playing at, coming over to sit next to me, smelling all yummy, taking off his jacket, and looking the way he does right now? He's not playing fair, that's what it is.

But there's a small part of me that doesn't want him to stop.

I pull my face into a smile. "Thank you."

His own smile stretches across his face and his eyes linger on mine. "Whatever it is you decide to perform this afternoon, I must tell you, some of the contestants have hidden singing talents. The competition will be stiff."

A lot like you.

I don't say it. It's just his way. He's upper class *and* British. The guy never stood a chance.

"I can say with confidence right now, I won't win any singing competitions. Not today, not any day."

"That's a shame. I rather enjoyed our conversation last night. Dinner won't be the same without you."

Seriously, dude! What are you playing at?

"Now, before I forget, I have something for you."

"You do?"

He reaches into the inside pocket of his jacket and pulls out a folded piece of paper. "I responded to that very sweet letter you wrote for me."

I search his face for a clue as to what he's doing. "You did?"

"I thought if Mr. Darcy received a letter from a lady, he would certainly reply. It would be considered ill-mannered not to."

I take the paper from him and turn it over in my hand. "Okay."

"Enjoy reading it," he says with a fresh twinkle in his eye. "I need to do my rounds with the other contestants. I'll see you in the living room for the performances." He stands back up and collects his jacket from the ground. I watch as he walks across the grass toward another contestant, followed by the cameramen. In his tight breeches, long boots, and white shirt, most of the contestants stop their practicing and simply gaze at him. He really is quite something to look at.

I slump back against the tree and exhale. Well, that was confusing with a capital "C."

I check there are no cameras on me and then open the folded piece of paper and read his letter. It's one line.

I'm sorry to see you go, Brady Bunch.

I fold it back up again and slip it down my top. (No pockets, remember?)

I chew on my lip, a bunch of emotions springing around inside of me like bouncy balls on a caffeine high.

Sebastian is sending me home. This is what I've been waiting for. I'm going home to my regular life, my regular clothes, normal people, and no more reality TV. Well, not on this side of the cameras, anyway. Penny is still borderline obsessed.

I want to go home. I don't want to be here. I'm not interested in Sebastian. When I leave, I'll never see him again, and never seeing him again will be ... what? Great? What I want?

I let out a heavy breath.

Part of me wants to go. No question.

And the other part? That's the part of me I'm keeping hidden from everyone, the part of me that's changing in an unexpected and alarming way.

It might be small, but it's the part of me that wants him to ask me to stay.

Chapter Thirteen

The moment of reckoning has arrived. Well, for everyone else, that is. I'm choosing to sit this one out. No one needs to be subjected to my singing, and it's not like I've got a shot at winning.

And anyway, what are they going to do about it? Send me home?

We're sitting back in the living room in rows facing a makeshift stage. This time we're joined by Mrs. Watson, Sebastian, and Johnathan.

I catch Sebastian's eye and shoot him a conspiratorial smile. He knows I'm not going to perform. He lifts his lips a fraction and nods his head in response.

Johnathan stands up to address our group. "We are so looking forward to hearing you sing this afternoon, ladies. As you know, the winner will be chosen by Mr. Darcy, and she will be invited to dine with him at a romantic, candlelit dinner for two."

There's a throb of excitement among the contestants.

"You should definitely pick me," Hayley calls out, and Sebastian shoots her his stiff smile.

"We'll just have to wait and see, Hayley," Johnathan replies. "We have an order for the performances. It was decided when Sebastian pulled names out of a hat earlier today." He holds up the top hat Sebastian wore that first evening of Regency dress-ups. "Literally." He collects a piece of paper from his pocket and brandishes it in the air.

I look around the room at the eager faces. Is it just me or is this super demeaning? A bunch of women literally performing to gain one man's attention. I know, it's the way of these dating shows—Penny always loves this part—but when you're involved in one it feels ... wrong.

Johnathan looks up from his list. "Your wish is a reality, Hayley. I'd like to invite you up to perform first."

Hayley doesn't need to be asked twice. She leaps out of her seat with a squeal of delight and rushes over to the stage.

At least someone's enjoying this.

"I'm going to sing one of my favorite songs of all time," Hayley says. "I think you're all going to love it."

Well, you've got to admire her confidence.

She bursts into that famous song from the kids' movie, *Frozen*, telling us she needs to let something go. To my surprise, she's actually quite a decent singer. Not that I didn't think she could sing. I figured she was more about the fake tan, the fake boobs, and the highly competitive edge driving her to win at all costs. But then again, perhaps I've judged her too harshly? Perhaps she's more than a caricature of a mean girl?

When she finishes her song, she curtsies to the audience, throws me a triumphant look, and mouths, "suck it."

Yeah, I think I'll stick with my initial judgement.

She turns her attention to Sebastian and beams at him. "I hope you liked it, Mr. Darcy," she coos, all sweet and bashful as she looks at him through her lashes.

"That was wonderful. Thank you, Hayley," he says.

Satisfied, she sits back down with her cronies, who pat her on the back and tell her how amazing she is.

"Surprisingly good," I mumble to Kennedy.

"Meow," she replies.

"I'm not being catty. She's horrible to me."

"Only because she sees you as a threat, Emma. You should take it as a compliment."

I harrumph. "Some compliment."

"Emma," Johnathan says, snapping my attention away from Kennedy. "We would love to hear your performance. Please, take to the stage."

I wave my hand in the air. "Oh, I'm going to sit this one out, if it's all the same to you. But thanks for asking."

His eyes shift to a crew member and back to me. "All the contestants need to perform, I'm afraid."

"As much as I may want to perform—and believe me I do so, so much—I'm afraid I'm no singer. I told Sebastian that already and he seemed cool with it. Believe me, I'm doing all of y'all a big favor here."

"She doesn't want to have to follow *my* performance. Do you, Emma?" Hayley says with the fakest sweet smile ever.

"I can well understand that," Johnathan replies, "but the rules are the rules. Aren't they, Mrs. Watson?" He's looking for back-up now.

Mrs. Watson rises to her feet and glares at me. "You. Stage. Now." Gone is the firm but polite language. It seems she's going for straightforward orders now.

I chew on my lip as I look around the room. "Do I have to?" I ask, and yes, I know I sound like a whiny kid being made to eat her broccoli.

"You do," Mrs. Watson replies.

I let out a defeated sigh. "Okay." I make my way over to the stage like I'm walking the line. I don't want to perform, and I haven't practiced anything either.

I scramble around in my brain, searching desperately for a song in my range. Which is basically about four notes, all of them flat, if my car singing skills are anything to go by.

"Miss Emma? We're waiting," Mrs. Watson says tersely.

All eyes are on me. Johnathan is watching me warily, Sebastian is looking somewhere between concerned and amused, and there's no way I'm going to look in Hayley's or Camille's direction right now.

I've got to think of something, *stat!*

When I don't do anything, Mrs. Watson barks, "Sing!"

Out of pure shock, I open my mouth and begin to sing the first song that comes to mind. It was playing in the car as I was driven here what feels like a lifetime ago, even though I think it was only a matter of days. Days? Really?

Lil Nas X's voice is in my head, and I sing along with it. I'm taking my horse down to an old road, and it takes all my willpower not to bob on the spot as though I'm on that horse myself. When I get to the Billy Ray Cyrus part, I notice a few of the contestants go from controlling their mirth to openly sniggering. It puts me off my game. Not that I had much of a game in the first place.

I fudge some of the words and replace others with the word "horse," which seems appropriate, given that it's a song about riding one. Or is it a metaphor? All I know is this is about a gazillion miles from being my finest hour, and I wish more than anything it was over.

When I finally get to the end of the song, I stop abruptly, clamp my mouth shut, and wait for the inevitable laughter to roll around the room. I'm not disappointed.

Camille is doubled over, shaking with laughter, Hayley has tears rolling down her cheeks, and even Phoebe and Kennedy are snickering, although I can tell they're working hard to hold it in.

I glance at Sebastian. His face is alight with amusement, but his eyes are surprisingly soft. "Nice work," he mouths, and I shoot him my most withering look, which is a little hard to muster when you're up to your neck in a lake of humiliation, your cheeks hot enough to scramble eggs.

"Thank you, Miss Emma, for that, uh, very interesting song about a horse," Johnathan says. I can tell he's also working hard at keeping a straight face. "It was quite, err, unique."

"In my defense, I never said I could sing," I say as I take my seat next to Kennedy.

"We all have our talents," Johnathan replies kindly, and I shoot him a small but grateful smile.

Next up is Camille. When she stands on the stage she looks intensely nervous, and as she begins to sing *Amazing Grace*, her voice wobbles like it's a bowl of Jell-O in an earthquake.

We work our way through the list of contestants, and I learn that Kennedy can actually sing when she performs an Adele song, that Marni's voice is very sweet, and that Reggie is so good, she could have fronted a band.

The final to perform is Phoebe. As she said she would, she sings the impossibly high and utterly kitsch *Loving You*. Her voice is so angelic and sweet I half expect the room to fill with puppies and kittens and all things adorable.

Finally, Johnathan thanks us all for our efforts and hands over to Sebastian to make his decision on who has won. As he stands, I catch Hayley bristling, fully expecting to win. Which she should, really, if this were an actual singing competition. She was easily the best, with Reggie, Kennedy, and Phoebe as runners up—and me an extremely distant last.

But this is a dating show, not a singing competition. We all know Sebastian will choose the contestant he wants to spend the evening with.

"It was a very hard decision today, ladies," he begins. "I want to thank all of you. For some, singing is clearly a talent you possess, and for others," he looks directly at me and I want to shrink into my chair, "less so, shall we say?"

No need to rub it in, dude.

"But all is fair in love, war, and reality television, so for tonight's romantic dinner for two, I choose Kennedy." He beams at her.

Kennedy?

I turn to look at her. Her gorgeous face is alight with happiness, a grin spreading from ear to ear.

"Thank you so much, Sebastian," she breathes. "I would love to have dinner with you."

Something unpleasant twists inside.

As Sebastian takes her by the hand to lead her to their date, I feel odd. Unsettled.

Which is crazy, right? I didn't want him to pick me. I want to go home.

And yes, I know I told him to go for her, plus I told the production crew she was the girl for him. And let's face it, choosing Kennedy over the loathsome Camille or scary Hayley is a much better decision. But Kennedy's my friend, she's not insane, in fact she's a great girl.

I know she could win his heart.

And I'm good with that. Really, I am. She's an amazing

woman, she deserves every happiness, and if that happens to be with Sebastian, then she's got to go for it.

But I can't help feeling deep down that I've done something I might grow to regret.

Chapter Fourteen

C attle. That's what we are. Fancy cattle in our Regency period clothing. Well, without having to wear cowbells and live in fields, that is, but you get the point. Like cattle, we're rounded up, herded, and constantly told what to do. How to sit, how to stand, how to pour freaking tea into delicate china cups. Give me my large café mocha with extra whipped cream any day of the week.

And now, here we are once more, herded together for the next card ceremony. We're squished in like sardines in a can, awaiting the verdict as Johnathan and Sebastian face us.

At least it's not all bad. This may be my third card ceremony, but I'm also pretty sure it will be my last. Two contestants are long gone, so it's got to be my turn to get to leave the insanity of reality TV far behind.

It feels great, but also ... odd.

Don't get me wrong, I'm more than happy to be leaving, particularly after those unexpected feelings surfaced when Sebastian chose Kennedy for the date.

It's just ... nope. Forget it. I don't care to delve into

whatever it's about. FOMO, maybe? But Fear Of Missing Out with Sebastian, a guy I don't even particularly like? It doesn't make sense.

This place is messing with my mind.

The sooner I get out of here the better.

As the contestants are being picked off and sent to the other side of the room, clutching their cards to their chests as though they were a large wad of cash, I can't help feeling a little wistful. Yes, this whole process is like being back in high school, waiting to be picked for a game of basketball. But the excitement and anticipation in the air is palpable, and a small part of me (infinitesimal, really) will miss a few things about the show. Phoebe, Kennedy, even Shelby with her deluded sense of destiny. In their way, they're all interesting women, and I'll be sad to say goodbye to them.

And the clothes. Sure, the stays are tight and annoying, and I've added bloomers to my list of least favorite things, but there is a certain romance to dressing like Elizabeth Bennet and living in a Jane Austen world.

I glance at Sebastian. He's all rigid and formal in his Mr. Darcy outfit, his jaw locked as Johnathan calls out each name.

Will I miss Sebastian?

His eyes meet mine for a second before he looks away. I chew on my lip. No, I will not miss him and his pompous game-playing. He's flirty one minute then all formal the next. It's confusing as all get out. And I do not need confusion in my life right now, not with trying to get Timothy off the ground.

"Hayley," Johnathan says.

She squeals with delight and bounces up and down on the spot, clapping like a seal at a zoo before she pushes through the now small group of us left, directing a purposeful kick in my shin as she passes by. I wince with pain.

Classy, Hayley.

She collects her invitation from the card table and blows a kiss at Sebastian. He smiles at her as she joins The Lizzies.

Johnathan announces the next contestant, and the next, until it's just me and a girl from New York called Mandy. We step together and the place falls silent, a bunch of cameras trained on us.

This is it.

"Ladies, you are the final two. I regret to inform you that one of you will not receive an invitation from Mr. Darcy to stay. You will need to leave tonight, and return to life in twenty-first century America."

Warmth radiates through me at the thought of my old life. No more stays, no more cameras, no more boredom, surrounded by the borderline insane (yes, Hayley, I'm looking at you). Work and Penny and Frank and, ooh, one of those chocolate chip cookies with the big chocolate chunks from Cardinelli's to go with my large café mocha with extra whipped cream followed by my all-time favorite, mac and cheese ...

"Emma."

Wait, *what?*

I snap my attention back to the room. Did Johnathan just say *my* name? I knit my brows together. No, I must be hearing things. My subconscious is messing with me. Sebastian and I have got a deal. He wrote me that note telling me he's sorry to see me go.

I'm going home tonight. End of story.

"Emma," Johnathan repeats with a firm voice, looking right at me.

I glance from him to Mandy, standing at my side. She's

got her chin lifted in an attempt to seem as though she's not upset, but the telltale glisten in her eyes is a giveaway of how she truly feels.

I turn my attention back to Johnathan. "Did you mean to say 'Mandy?' Because it sounded like 'Emma.'"

He shoots a crew member an uncertain look before he says, "I said your name, Emma."

"But—"

He's got it wrong. *I'm* the one who's meant to be bowing out graciously tonight. *I'm* the one who should be pretending I'm doing okay about it all when I'm actually gutted. Well, fake gutted, anyway.

"Mr. Darcy has placed you on the invitation list, Emma. Please collect your card from the table and join The Lizzies."

I glower at Sebastian, willing him to look at me. He doesn't meet my gaze. Instead, he seems to be concentrating very hard on his shoes.

The yellow-bellied coward! He betrayed me. He went back on our deal.

I grind my teeth, my heart beginning to pound.

How could he?

"Ah, Emma?" Johnathan says. There's a hint of desperation in his voice now as he gestures hopefully at the table.

Resigned, I glance at the final card, with its cursive handwriting and red wax seal. That's it. I've got no choice. I can't simply storm out and leave the show, no matter how much I might want to. I'd be up that well known creek without a paddle, that's for sure. I'll have to pay a big fine and Timothy will go under and all of this will be a waste of my time.

Not that it isn't a waste of my time already.

Fuming, I stomp over to the table in the most unladylike

129

manner, snatch up my card, and join The Lizzies. Some of them shoot me questioning looks. Camille openly glowers at me.

"Mandy, I regret to inform you that you have not been given an invitation to stay. You may pack your bags and leave," Johnathan says in a grim announcer-ish sounding voice.

I watch through my red-tinged anger mist as she bites her lip and nods before she turns and leaves the room. I feel a twinge of pity for her. Although I've got no idea if she's "here for the right reasons," she looks genuinely upset to leave the show.

Something else to add to the rapidly increasing list of reasons to despise Sebastian Huntington-Ross.

I feel a poke in my back and turn to see Phoebe and Kennedy shooting me questioning looks. I shake my head at them.

"Ladies." Johnathan is facing the group once more. "Congratulations to you all. You are The Lizzies, and we are delighted you accepted your invitation to stay here as Mr. Darcy's guests."

Ha! Like we had a freaking choice.

"Mr. Darcy has a few words he would like to say to you."

Sebastian, otherwise known as The Slippery Lying Double-Crossing Jerk, smiles out at us as though he hasn't just broken his word to me and kept me here when he should have sent me home.

I will him to look at me so that I can throw an arsenal-full of poisoned daggers at him. He doesn't meet my eyes.

"I'm delighted that you accepted my invitations to stay here with me."

I scoff.

His eyes find mine for a second before he averts his gaze once again. "Tomorrow, we have something special for everyone, of which I think you will all be absolutely delighted."

The contestants bristle with excitement. I, on the other hand, continue to seethe.

"I hope you all sleep well, and I shall look forward to seeing you again tomorrow. Until then, I bid you all adieu."

I bid you something a whole lot less pleasant than "adieu," you double crossing back stabbing non-keeper of promises.

The women around me all say goodnight and goodbye to him while I fume. I watch as he leaves the room with Johnathan without a backwards glance, and I squeeze my fists so tight, I'm surprised when I don't draw blood.

Ten minutes later, we're in our rooms, getting ready for bed. Well, my roommates are. I'm getting ready for warfare.

I heave a sigh of relief as Reggie unlaces my stays and I pull it off. "Oh, thank goodness for that."

"Too tight, darlin'?"

"Too everything." I pull off the petticoats and chemise, collect one of my Timothy tank tops with an inbuilt bra out of my suitcase and slip it on.

Reggie eyes my open suitcase. "Y'all should unpack. You're the only one here still livin' out of your bag."

"Yeah, sure." I remove my bloomers, otherwise known as the world's largest pair of underwear. I replace them with a thong about one hundredth its size, followed by a pair of leggings.

As I lean down to tie on my sneakers, Reggie says, "Why are you puttin' on shoes, darlin'? It's night time. Aren't you tired? I know I am."

"I'm going for a run."

She knits her brows together. "It's two in the mornin'."

Right.

I need to make this plausible.

"I won't be long. Just a jog around the grounds. It'll clear my head. I do it all the time. Go to sleep." I throw my eyes at our other roommate. She's already tucked up in bed, breathing steadily despite our noise.

Reggie shoots me a look that tells me she's concerned for my sanity, but nods anyway.

I close our bedroom door behind myself with a click, and on light feet, dash down the corridor to the other end of the house. It's dark and still but for the muffled conversations between the contestants behind closed doors.

I reach my destination and knock lightly. A moment later, Sebastian opens the door. He's still in his Mr. Darcy clothes, but he's lost the jacket and cravat and his shirt is open at the neck, revealing a hint of upper pec curve.

"I've been expecting you," he says.

What is he, a villain in a movie? He'll pull out an evil looking cat and begin to stroke it menacingly in a minute as sharks circle threateningly in a massive tank below our feet.

"What a dick move," I spit at him without preamble. Because he's not a movie villain, there is no cat, and there are no circling sharks. It's just Sebastian, going back on his word.

He glances up and down the hallway and then takes me by the hand and pulls me into his room.

"Hey, what the—?"

He muffles my words with his finger over my lips, shushing me as he closes the door behind me.

What is with this guy and pulling me around?

He removes his finger. "I see you're being your usual charming self."

"Whatever. This isn't the Dark Ages, you know, dude. You can't just pull women into rooms and expect them to be okay about it. Have you heard of the 'Me Too Movement?'"

"Of course I have. But do you really want everyone to know you're here with me, or just the people within a square mile radius?"

I huff. I know he's right, but I've got a bone to pick with this guy. I balance my hands on my hips and glare at him. "We had a deal. Y'all were going to send me home tonight. You even gave me that note."

"I know."

I raise my eyebrows in expectation. "Well?"

"Let's sit down."

"No. I don't want to." I know I sound childish, but I'm so mad right now.

"Well, I'm going to." He takes a seat on one of the couches.

"Do whatever you want," I say. "You could even renege on our deal, if you felt like it. Oh, wait. Silly me. You already did that."

He raises his eyes to mine and the look on his face tells me he's barely tolerating my presence. "Emma, please. Sit."

"I'd rather stand."

"So I can admire your Timothy activewear?" he asks.

"Don't get cute with me."

"I'm only trying to lighten the mood."

I cross my arms and glare at him—something I've been making a habit of lately. "Explain yourself."

"I'd planned on sending you home tonight as you'd asked. The problem is, I need to keep contestants around who, well, entertain the audience."

I scrunch up my face. "Entertain the audience?"

"This is a television show, in case you hadn't noticed. Cameras, lights, mics, that kind of thing."

Who does this guy think he is?

"You know you really should be more observant, Brady," he says with a small smile.

Oh, the gall of this man!

I keep my voice steady when I reply, "What has entertaining the audience got to do with our deal?"

"You, Emma, are entertaining," he explains as though I'm some sort of simpleton. "Well, at least, that's what the production crew have told me. I'm of another mind on the matter."

"What does *that* mean?" On second thoughts, I can imagine: my less than stellar singing performance this afternoon. I wave my hand in the air. "Forget it. I don't want to know. What I do want to know is what happened to our deal?"

"Contrary to popular belief, I do not make the rules."

I slip down onto the facing couch. "Are you telling me you told them you wanted me to go home and they didn't let you?"

"That is precisely what I'm telling you."

I let the news sink in. "Oh."

"Oh indeed. Now, perhaps, you can understand why I couldn't follow through with our arrangement. I wanted to, believe me."

You and me both, dude.

"I guess," I reply distractedly. "What have I done that's been so entertaining? I mean, I know my singing isn't going to win me any competitions."

"Ah, no," he replies. "You really are a terrible singer."

"I did warn everyone."

"I think you should have been more forceful with that warning. I'm not sure I'll ever fully recover."

"Oh, ha-ha. Very funny. I bet you can't sing either. No, wait. I've got it. You can sing and you were a choir boy at some fancy school, weren't you? I can picture it now. Your red and white robes, your little halo gleaming as you sing so high only dolphins and dogs can hear you."

"Actually, when I was a child I was an alto, not a soprano."

"I was right!" I cry with glee. "Sebastian the choir boy." It's an endearing image, and my heart softens a fraction. But only a fraction. "What else have I done that's considered 'entertaining?'" I ask. And then it hits me. "No! They're going to use the footage of me falling out of the limo, aren't they?" I look at him, wide-eyed, my mind whirring. It might very well have been my only opportunity to get my label on camera, but such a humiliating entry can't do either me or Timothy any good. In fact, it could be disastrous.

I bury my head in my hands. This cannot be good. This whole thing is quickly becoming one huge mess. And not only that, it's a mess I cannot escape from.

To my surprise, I feel the cushions beside me move and, startled, I look up to see Sebastian next to me. He's got a look on his face I haven't seen before. Can it be ... sympathy? No, it can't be. This is the pompous Sebastian we're talking about here, the over-privileged, smug aristocrat who likes me as much as I like him.

"Hi," I say awkwardly, not really knowing how to take this strange turn of events.

"Now she says hello."

"What does that mean?"

"You stormed in here without saying hello earlier. It was rather rude."

"No, *you* dragged *me* in here."

"Semantics, Brady Bunch. Semantics." The edges of his mouth quirk into a hint of a smile, and unlike his public smiles out there with the contestants, this one reaches his eyes.

I smile briefly back at him, my heart softening a fraction. If this thing really is out of his hands, then he didn't actually break our deal. Maybe I shouldn't be so hard on him? "I thought you got to decide. I mean, this is meant to be all about you falling for one of us, right?"

"Of course," he replies formally, just like Mr. Darcy himself. "I do choose. Ultimately, anyway. However, this is reality television, as they keep reminding me. They need the ratings, and apparently contestants like you help with that."

I let out a defeated puff of air. "What am I going to do?"

"Well, if you still want to leave," he pauses and I give him an emphatic head nod, "then I suggest you try your best *not* to be entertaining."

"You mean not sing."

"Emma, if you do only one thing, please promise me that." With his eyes trained on me, his smile broadens.

I can't help but return it. I know he's mocking me for my musical performance, but at least he's doing it in good humor.

"Or I could break the rules and get kicked off the show."

"There is that."

"What could I do, I wonder?" I chew on my lip. "Ooh, I know. I could get caught on camera in a passionate embrace with one of the production crew."

"Do you want to have a passionate embrace with one of the production crew?"

Between the cameraman with a face full of acne like a

pepperoni pizza and the one who likes to show the contestants photos of his pet lizard dressed up in Scottish kilts, the pickings are slim to say the least. I let out a sigh. "No."

He pats my knee. "Well, maybe you're stuck here with me for a while longer."

"I guess. I'll just have to work on not being entertaining."

"That could be your best bet, Brady Bunch."

"What's with the Brady Bunch nickname?"

I try not to let on how much I like it. I mean, it's not exactly original, but it's unexpected from a guy like Sebastian.

"You call me Seb, so I thought I'd repay the compliment."

"Okay," I reply warily as I notice how the gold chunks in his brown eyes seem more pronounced tonight. I become increasingly aware of him sitting close beside me, and my body begins to respond. Looking like Mr. Darcy doesn't help, especially this version. He's sexy, casual, off-duty Darcy, chilling on the couch at home. *If* Mr. Darcy did that sort of thing, which seems completely unlikely, really.

I know it's only the Mr. Darcy Effect, toying with me once again. It's perfectly natural, and nothing for me to take seriously.

I mean, it's not like I'm attracted to Sebastian or anything.

Feeling uncomfortable, I hop up off the couch to my feet. "Right-o," I say, sounding as English as him.

He raises his eyebrows at me from his seat. "Right-o?"

"Yes, right-o," I repeat. "It's a common phrase here in Texas. It means ... right."

Smooth, Emma.

He rises to his feet. "Interesting. 'Right-o' means right. I will have to fit in as many Texan lessons as I can from you before you leave, shan't I?"

"Ah, sure. Yeah," I mutter.

He wants to spend time with me?

"Good. I'll look forward to my next lesson. Will it be focused on other British expressions used in the Texan vernacular?"

Got it. He's teasing me.

"The what?" I ask.

"The vernacular. The language."

"Oh, right. Sure. I knew that."

"I wonder whether 'jolly hockey sticks' and 'poppycock' are in common use."

"Oh, sure. Me and my friends always talk about hockey sticks and poppycocks."

"Do you indeed?" His lips quirk. "How fascinating."

His gaze is intense, and I feel it right down to my toes. This is beginning to feel very flirty. Time I refocused the conversation.

"I really need you to insist that I get to leave next time. Okay?"

"I will do my best for you."

I nod. "Good. Thank you."

"What about if I asked them to allow some time on camera when the contestants aren't dressed in Regency clothes?"

"You could do that?" I ask in surprise.

"I can't promise anything, but I can try."

Hope begins to ping around inside my chest. "That could seriously change things for me."

"I imagine it could."

My mind races. "I could do what I came here to do. Maybe I could get some of the other contestants to wear my label too, that way it'll get even more exposure." I look back up at him. "Oh, that would make such a huge difference! Thank you."

"Thank me if I manage to pull it off."

"Okay, I won't count my chickens. But if you could help me out, it would totally make my life."

He gives a single head nod and says, "I'll let you know. Off camera, of course."

"Of course."

With nothing else to say, and with a weird feeling in my belly, I head to the door. I hold it open a crack and check to make sure no one is lurking around outside. The coast is clear. I look back at him and whisper, "Thanks, Seb."

"It's Sebastian," he whispers back.

"Not in Texas it's not. Take that as Lesson Number Two."

His smile lingers with me as I quietly make my way back to my room, slip into my bed, and drift off to sleep.

Chapter Fifteen

With the prospect of being able to wear my label on camera, my mood lightens and I even find myself enjoying some of the aspects of life on a reality TV show.

In fact, I've made a list. Don't judge me. There's not a lot else to do around here. Here it is: Things I like about being in here:

1. Free drinks. All. The. Time. Don't get me wrong, I'm not an alcoholic, but I'm also not one to turn down a glass or two of free wine, either. Because, duh, it's free wine.

2. Some of the girls, the non-crazies, have become my friends. Like Kennedy. She's helped me keep my sanity here, and Phoebe, the sweetest person I've ever met. She keeps me from falling into a snarky, cynical hole. Reggie is a heap of fun and always up for a laugh. I can totally see the four of us remaining close on "the outside," as we've begun to call it (and yes, I know that

makes it sound as though we're in prison. But it's not. I refer you to point #1).

3. The lack of noise is pretty dang fantastic. And by noise, I don't mean the chatter or the laughter around here, because there is plenty of that, believe me. I mean no emails, no social media, no phone calls, no endless to-dos. It's weird, because I never thought I'd be happy to live my life without them. But still, here I am, content to live in a pre-electronic world. Most of the time, anyway.

My mind turns to Sebastian. Is he on my list of things I like about being here? If I were honest with myself, maybe I would include him. I mean, the guy's not what I thought. Sure, he's pompous and formal and quite standoffish at times, and I'm sure he looks down his nose at me. But there's a side to him I'm catching glimpses of that I admit I like. And I don't just mean he's hot, because that's a given. The man is "smokin'," as Reggie puts it. It's more that I'm seeing the real Sebastian, not the guy playing Mr. Darcy for TV.

And the real Sebastian is captivating.

That said, I hate that he's got all the power. Well, him and the production crew, that is. Keeping me here to "entertain" the viewers is enough to make me want to pull my hair out, strand by strand. Whichever way you look at it, the net result is the same: we, the contestants, most certainly do not have the power, and I challenge anyone to say they enjoy that feeling.

You know what can make that feeling of utter powerlessness even more fun? You guessed it: Regency clothing. Why they can't let us wear normal bras instead of these stays things, I do not know. I mean, it's not like the audience is going to see what we've got on underneath our clothes. And yes, I do clearly recall Penny coming up with the ludicrous idea of "whisking off" my clothes at the soirées to show off our label underneath, but believe me, there's no "whisking off" when it comes to these outfits. More like painstakingly unravelling. Not that I was exactly on board with Penny's idea in the first place.

"Holy crap, Reggie. Could you tie those *any* tighter?" I gasp as my ribs snuggle up together in a wholly unnatural way.

"Hold still, darlin'. Nice and tight and your puppies'll pop."

With my favorite pastime I like to call "breathing" severely restricted, I reply, "I don't need my 'puppies to pop,' as you put it, but I would like to avoid a trip to the ER."

"All done." Reggie steps back and examines her handiwork.

I, on the other hand, am still trying to recover. I look up at my reflection in the mirror. "I look like I'm serving my boobs up on a platter."

"You are. Now, help me with mine." She thrusts her stays at me and I reluctantly take it from her as she turns for me to fit it. "Pull as tight as you like. I'm not afraid of a little bolstered puppy action."

I laugh. It hurts. "You're not afraid of a whole lot, Reggie." I slip the stays over her head and begin to pull.

"Tighter."

I pull some more.

"Tighter," she repeats, her voice strained.

"Are you sure?"

"Yes," she squeaks.

I give one final pull on the cords and tie them up. Reggie examines herself in the mirror. "I'm thinkin' of keepin' this when I leave."

"Because you're a masochist?"

"Because they make me look hot, darlin'."

"To each their own." I finish off my outfit and then set about styling my hair.

Reggie settles onto her bed and pulls out a notebook and begins to scribble.

"Whatcha writing?" I ask.

"I record everythin'. I plan on vloggin' my entire experience on the show when it goes live." She sighs. "Oh, how I miss my phone."

"I quite like the calm."

"Calm? You're insane if you think the girls here are calm." She finishes what she's writing and says, "What's your plan?"

I cock an eyebrow. "Plan?"

"Yeah, you know, how you're gonna get yourself noticed."

"By Sebastian?"

"Sure."

I think of Penny's advice the day this all began. "Be myself, I guess."

"Be yourself," Reggie repeats as though I said "eat Brussels sprouts." Side note: I hate Brussels sprouts.

She gives me a look like I'm being completely dense. "You've gotta get yourself out there, darlin'. That's why we're all here: for after the show is done and dusted."

"Right. For the follows."

"The follows, the endorsements, all of it." She glances around the room, even though we're alone. "This is our moment. We have got to grab it by the balls and not let it go."

Reggie might be here for promotion in a way I'm not, but we do share a common goal: use the show to get ahead. Now, I need Sebastian to deliver on his offer to help get Timothy some air time.

"I hope it works out for you, Reggie. Now, we'd better get down there." I stand up to leave. "We don't want to upset Mrs. Watson."

She hops up off the bed and collects her spencer from the closet. "Heck, no. That woman scares the livin' crap out of me."

We are the last to arrive in the living room, and we try to sneak in without being noticed. But you can't pull a fast one on Mrs. Watson, as we find out pretty quickly.

"Ladies, how nice of you to join us," she says with a disingenuous smile.

"Sorry we're late," we both mumble as we try to merge into the background.

"Since you're here last, you have the honor of going first in today's activity."

"Okay," I reply worriedly. "What is the activity, exactly?"

"Horse riding." She pauses, and then adds, "Side saddle," before she shoots us a triumphant smile.

Horse riding? *Side saddle?* I blink at her in disbelief. Is she freaking kidding me right now? I may be Texas born and raised, but the full total of my experience with horses is owning a yellow My Little Pony I called "Matilda Horsie" when I was five. Not so helpful in riding an actual, live horse.

I flash my eyes to Reggie's. She's a city girl through and through. I bet she's as freaked out as I am.

I clear my throat. "Mrs. Watson, neither of us have any experience of riding horses. Can't one of the other girls go before us? Someone who knows about them?"

"Miss Emma, after your remarkable rendition of that song about a horse in the singing competition, I felt quite certain you would leap at the opportunity to ride one."

Sebastian in all his Mr. Darcy regalia appears at the door, and the cameramen turn to capture him. They were clearly not expecting him.

"I'd be more than happy to assist you," he says.

For some inexplicable reason, I blush.

The women in the room begin to gush their greetings, and there's much toying with hair and battering of eyelids as he steps further into the room.

"Oh, my," Reggie says beside me. "I have said it before. This guy is smokin'."

"Oh, it's only because he's dressed as Mr. Darcy," I explain knowledgeably as I think of the way he made me feel last night in his room. "He's one of the most romantic heroes of all time. It's The Darcy Effect."

"Sure, darlin'. If y'all say so," she replies, obviously unconvinced. "I'd prefer to call it The Super Hot Guy Effect, but maybe that's just me."

I open my mouth to respond as I watch Sebastian greet the contestants in his riding boots and snug-fitting jacket with the long tails (I really should find out what those are called). It's true, he does fill that Darcy costume pretty dang well, but I'm beginning to realize it's more than just that. He's got an air of confidence to him that's very appealing, and as his eyes find mine and he offers me a hint of a smile, a sudden jolt of electricity shoots through me.

Much like The Force in Luke Skywalker, The Darcy Effect is getting stronger in me.

"Sebastian, how kind of you to join us," Mrs. Watson says as her eyes dart to Toni, one of the crew who gives her a shrug and gestures for her to continue. "A lovely surprise. We weren't expecting to see you until we were at the stables with our top four riders."

"And miss out on all the fun, Mrs. Watson?" he replies with a cheeky smile. "But please, continue."

"All right," she replies dourly.

"Come sit next to me, Sebastian," Camille simpers as she pats the couch beside her.

"Thank you, Camille," he replies. In a handful of strides —which I don't want to refer to as "manly," but they totally are—he's across the room and sitting between Camille and Shelby, much to both women's unadulterated delight. Camille places her hand possessively on his forearm on one side, and Shelby scoots over so she's pressed up against his other arm.

He's a Mr. Darcy sandwich, stuck between two adoring slices of womanhood. (Too far? I thought so, too, but you get the picture.)

"Mrs. Watson, please pretend I'm not here," he says.

As if.

"In that case, since you're staying," Mrs. Watson begins, looking a little ruffled, "we'll get back to our planning. Miss Emma and Miss Reggie are our first volunteers. They'll be riding side saddle around the paddock, after some tutoring."

Sebastian quirks an eyebrow in my direction. "Will they indeed? I am glad I came."

I bet he's remembering how I fell out of that limo. But just because I fell then doesn't mean I'll fall off a horse. At least, I hope not. I lift my chin and shoot him a defiant look, but my heart's not really in it.

"Who would like to take their turn after our first volunteers?" Mrs. Watson asks.

Every hand in the room stretches up to reach the ceiling, and Mrs. Watson busies herself assigning everyone to groups.

Meanwhile, I notice Sebastian talking with Camille and Shelby. He looks relaxed and more than happy to be in their company, and I get a weird feeling inside, much like I did when he chose Kennedy for that date. It feels like, well, I can barely admit it to myself, but it feels a lot like jealousy.

Which is totally ludicrous. I mean, it's not like he and I are in a relationship or anything. In fact, he's the one who's helping me leave this reality dating fiasco. He wouldn't be doing that if he felt anything for me, would he?

It's just the Darcy Effect, making me think things I shouldn't.

Much flirting with Sebastian by the contestants and bossing by Mrs. Watson later, and Reggie and I are ushered down to the stables, followed by a group of contestants who are next on the list.

We're met by a man in a check shirt and a ten-gallon hat, holding the reins of two huge horses that are snorting and huffing as they stand beside him. And when I say huge, I mean *freaking* huge. Surely they're larger than your average horse. They've got to be as tall as a building!

I try not to panic.

"Howdy, ladies. I'm Russell, and today I'm gonna teach y'all how to ride side saddle," the man in the hat says with a broad grin.

"Hi there, Russell," Reggie says pleasantly.

I grunt my hello, my mind filled with horror scenarios, all of which involve oversized horses trampling me to death.

Matilda Horsie did *not* prepare me for this.

"This here is Marilyn," Russell says, petting one of the horses, "and this here is Monroe."

"Marilyn and Monroe, huh?" Reggie says.

Russell shrugs. "The boss is a big fan."

Casually, she walks over to the horses. "Can I pet one?"

"Sure can," Russell says.

She smiles as she pets the side of the horse. "She's gorgeous. Which one is she?"

"That's Monroe. You can ride her, if you like."

"It's nice to meet you, Monroe. I'm Reggie. I'm sure we're gonna get along just fine."

I look at Reggie with wide eyes. She's not at all afraid of these creatures. Quite the opposite in fact: she's a freaking horse whisperer.

Russell turns his attention to me. "Would you like to meet Marilyn?"

"Oh, I'm fine here for now," I reply, not shifting an inch. "I'll say hi to her when we're, you know, side saddling together later."

Side saddling? Is that a thing?

I feel a hand on the small of my back. Startled, I look up into a familiar face.

Sebastian.

"I grew up with horses. Would you like me to help you?"

"I think I know how to pet a horse," I sniff. I don't add, "only if they're made of plastic and small enough to pick up and put in my pocket." Minor detail.

"Do you?" he asks.

"Yes."

"Really? Because you look terrified," he says quietly.

"I'm not terrified," I reply unconvincingly.

His lips stretch into a smile. "Come with me."

With his hand still on my back, we step over toward the horse. My heart rate kicks up a notch—or ten—but I hold my resolve and stand rigidly at Marilyn's side.

"You stroke her like this," he says as he pets the horse on what I guess must be her shoulder. "Don't touch her face, at least until she knows you. Despite what you see in movies, horses don't like strangers doing that."

I reach out and tentatively touch her coat. It's coarse and warm, and not quite as terrifying as I imagined.

"There you are," Sebastian says. "You are now friends."

I let out a nervous laugh as I eye the saddle on her back. "Let's hope."

"You'll be fine. Just do as you're taught, and don't let the animal sense your fear."

"Well, that'll be easy," I reply with a sardonic smile.

"Okay, ladies. It's time to get you on these here horses," Russell announces.

Sebastian rubs my shoulder. "You'll be fine."

"I know. I got this," I reply with about three thousand percent more confidence than I feel.

"I'm glad to hear it, Brady Bunch."

I look up and see how soft his eyes are, how his smile lights up his entire face. And this time, when the feelings hit me, I don't even try to fight them.

I've totally misjudged Mr. Darcy.

And I am *so* in trouble.

Chapter Sixteen

Far too quickly, Russell hands me a helmet to wear and places a set of steps in place for me to climb up onto Marilyn's back. Which might be a less daunting experience if I were wearing some sensible Timothy leggings and a pair of shoes designed in this century. In my full-length gown and ballet slippers it is utterly terrifying.

I secure the helmet under my chin and eye Marilyn. Her liquid brown eyes seem unfazed, and she lets out a huff as if to tell me to get on with it.

It's now or never.

"Come stand on these here steps, Miss," Russell instructs.

Tentatively, I climb the steps until I'm in position. I give myself a little pep talk, trying to think of all the women I've seen riding side saddle. I land on one. A fictitious one at that. Lady Mary from *Downton Abbey*. Well, if she can do it, then so can I.

And there's no way I'm going to "entertain" the viewers by embarrassing myself once more.

I glance back at Sebastian. He throws me an encouraging smile.

Russell pets the side of the horse. "Put your left foot in the stirrup, push yourself up onto her, and hook your leg around the pommel. That's the part that sticks out, in case y'all were wondering."

"Pommel. Got it." I take a breath. "Here goes nothing." I slip my foot into the stirrup and swing myself up onto the horse. My butt in place, I hook my right leg around the pommel and settle into the saddle. My instinct —or maybe simply too much time watching Lady Mary ride her horse—tells me to lean down and collect the reins in my hands.

"You're a natural," Russell declares, and I think I detect a note of admiration in his voice. But then again, all I did was climb some steps and sit on a horse in a fancy dress, so I might be reading too much into it.

High atop my horse, I survey the stables and the rolling fields beyond. "This isn't so bad."

"It suits you," Sebastian says.

I look down at him and reply in my best English accent, "Am I a lady of the manor now?"

"Absolutely." His features soften as he smiles up at me, and I swear my heart skips a beat. "But I suggest you work on the accent."

I feign offense. "Hey! I thought I sounded *exactly* like Lady Mary."

He laughs, and somehow the sound reaches inside and makes my belly do a flip. "You did, if this Lady Mary were an American on a horse for the first time."

I give him my best glare, but can't help but smile. I distract myself by watching as Reggie climbs carefully onto her horse beside me. "Looking good, Reggie," I call out.

"Whoa!" she exclaims as the horse moves back a step. "Can you make it stay still? It's movin' and freakin' me out."

"I'm holding *her* reins, Miss," Russell replies pointedly.

He's clearly a little touchy about his horses.

Reggie has another try, and this time manages to get herself onto her side saddle. Settling herself in, she says, "Hey, it's kinda nice up here."

"I know, right? Just as long as our horses don't decide to break into a run."

"That won't be a problem if you treat her right, Miss," Russell says. "Be confident and relaxed. Your horses will sense your fear if you're not and may take control."

"That does *not* sound good to me, darlin'," Reggie says.

"We're moving out now, so y'all hold on." Russell takes the reins of my horse and another guy in a checked shirt steps forward to take Reggie's.

I glance at Sebastian and he throws me an encouraging smile.

"We're really doing this," I mutter.

As the horses move, I clutch onto the reins as though they're a lifeline. Soon, we begin to get into a slow rhythm, plodding along, and I even begin to enjoy it.

Once we're out in the paddock and have been led around a course, we come to a halt. It feels strange to be stationary once more, and I surprise myself with wanting to move again.

Russell asks if we'd like to try walking unaided. I nod and grin at him, my initial nerves evaporating.

"All right. Y'all are now officially in control."

I hold the reins in my hands and make the clucking noise I've heard people use on TV. To my surprise, Marilyn begins a slow walk, and soon enough, we're back in the clomping rhythm from before, only this time I'm riding solo, and it feels good.

I look over at Reggie. She's busy telling her horse to "gee up" and clucking and bouncing up and down in her saddle. The horse refuses to move. "A little help here?" she calls out. Russell saunters over to her in his casual cowboy way.

"We're good, aren't we, Marilyn?" I say as we walk steadily along. "You and I are a great team."

I hear the sound of hooves nearby and expect to see Reggie and her horse moving once more. Instead, I'm met with the sight of Sebastian atop another beautiful chestnut horse, riding as though he's been doing so all his life. Which he has. So, you know, it makes sense.

As I watch him sitting upright, commanding his horse, my breath shortens. I will not lie. Looking more like Mr. Darcy than he ever has, with his strong legs in their snug pants and riding boots, he's confident and sexy in that total romantic hero kind of way.

Oh, my.

I watch him ride over toward me, and try my best not to show him what's raging inside of me. The last thing he needs is another woman going all silly over him.

He slows to my pace and pulls in beside me, followed by a cameraman. "Looking good, Brady."

"I'm just plain old Brady now, huh? What happened to Bunch?"

"I think we're on a first name basis now. Don't you?"

"Oh, my last name is Bunch, is it?"

He laughs and it sends a wave of electricity through me. "I see you've graduated."

"Oh, I'm a quick study."

"I can tell. How are you finding it?"

"It's easy once you know how, I guess."

153

"We'll have you riding at the Cheltenham Festival before you know it.'

"What's that?"

"It's the most prestigious race meeting in the British National Hunt."

"That sounds too fancy for me. Don't tell me, you go every year?"

"No, I don't. Naturally, I've been a few times, but I prefer riding. Show jumping is incredible to watch, but I never had the temperament or inclination to jump myself. I prefer it to be just me and my horse, riding through the countryside, enjoying the fresh air and the exhilaration." He gets a faraway look in his eye. "My horse at home is called Artemis. I've had her for years."

I watch how his features soften as he speaks about his horse and my heart melts to see the love he has for her. "Is she this sort of horse?" I ask, not having any clue what breeds of horses there are.

"She's a Thoroughbred."

"Of course she is."

He snaps his eyes to mine. "Are you being rude about me or my horse?"

"Neither. It's just you look like a Thoroughbred horse kinda guy. Not one of those workhorse types with the fluffy feet."

He laughs. "Fluffy feet? You really don't know anything about horses, do you?"

"I'm a city girl, loud and proud."

"Isn't everyone from Texas either a cowboy or a cowgirl?"

"Sure we are," I reply with a laugh. "If this were 1813."

"Which it is."

"Right. I forgot."

"Would you like to go for a short ride together?" he asks. "I think my horse would like to stretch her legs."

I glance at Matty, the cameraman out of the corner of my eye. "I don't want to go too fast."

"We can go at this speed."

I gesture at Matty and make a face, hoping Sebastian gets my unspoken message that I would prefer not to be on film right now.

He looks up and says in a louder voice, "Tell me more about your grandmother's embroidery. Did she really teach you all you know about the art?"

"I'm sorry, what now?"

"Your grandmother," he repeats, shooting me a look. "You were telling me all about how she taught you to embroider."

I tag on. "Oh, she did. She was an excellent embroiderer. She could do cross stitch and back stitch, and," I pause. I've exhausted my knowledge of embroidery already and I'm only two stitches in. "All the stitches, really."

"Any you especially like?"

"I like the double looped back flip over."

Totally made up.

"My personal favorite, as well."

I narrow my eyes at him. "You look more like the type to go for the double crosser stitch." I shoot him a triumphant smile. I like the way I've made a conversation about my grandmother's fictitious embroidery abilities into a swipe at Sebastian for not following through on our deal to send me home.

He chortles, and I know he's caught onto my thread, if you'll excuse the terrible pun. "Oh, Emma. The double crosser is not my preferred stitch at all. I prefer the hands tied stitch. It's very tricky and hard to pull off."

"That's what they all say." I eye the cameraman once more and note he's still filming us. "What type of embroidery stitch do you like, Matty?" I ask him.

"Oh, I, ah, don't know anything about it."

"Perhaps we can teach you?" Sebastian suggests.

Matty lowers his camera. "You're not meant to talk to me, guys. Just talk between yourselves, 'kay?"

"So, you're not into embroidery?" I ask.

"I'm sure it's really interesting and all, but I kinda gotta do my job here." He hoists his camera back into position, and points it back at us.

My plan is foiled. Of course they're not going to stop filming the star of the show with one of the contestants, even if they're talking about something as dull as embroidery. They'll just edit that part out.

I guess I'll have to hope I manage to stay atop Marilyn and not "entertain" the audience.

Sebastian and I ride slowly together. He's considerably more at home on the back of his horse than I am on mine. But I'm putting on a good front, and getting into a groove with Marilyn.

"Do you have a job?" I ask him. "Other than being Mr. Darcy, of course."

"I do. I work for a bank in the City."

He works for a bank. A rich guy's job, for sure.

"Which city?"

"It's the name of the financial area in London. It's simply known as the City."

"Because there are so few cities in the world and everyone automatically knows what you're talking about?"

He shoots me a sardonic grin. "I see Emma The Firecracker is back."

I shrug. "Always."

"Tell me about your job. You've got an activewear label called Timothy, is that right?"

I think of Matty filming us, and know I owe Sebastian a big thank you for raising my label on camera. "I sure do. I was wearing my label when I met you on the red carpet, you know."

"I do recall you mentioning it. Something about sweat, I believe."

I don't miss a beat. "Timothy activewear wicks sweat away to keep you feeling dry as you work out. We're only doing a women's line right now, but once we launch a men's line, I'll be sure to send you some."

"That would be wonderful. Why did you get into activewear? Are you especially sporty?"

I shake my head. "My friend Penny is. She's the designer. She was sick of wearing clothes that didn't fit right or felt uncomfortable. The passion she has for what she does is so infectious that the day she told me her plans, I knew I had to start the business with her. But it was scary, you know?"

"Starting a business?"

"Oh, yeah. I hated my job, but at least it was a regular paycheck with medical and dental."

"So, there's a lot riding on Timothy's success." He pets his horse and adds, "Pun intended."

My mind turns to the size of my overdraft and the money Penny was lent by her aunt. "You could say that."

I hear the sound of pounding hooves approaching us. Disconcerted, I look up to see Hayley atop a horse, bounding toward us. She clearly knows what she's doing, confident and at ease on her horse, the orange orbs attached to her chest threatening to hit her in the face with each step.

She pulls on the reins to bring her horse to a stop next to Sebastian.

"Hi there, you two," she says with a bright smile as her horse stomps its feet and makes horsey sounds (sue me, I'm not a horse person). "What are you two doing all the way over here?"

Maybe it's exhilaration from the ride, but I notice her eyes are slightly manic as they dart between us.

"We were just heading back, actually, Hayley," Sebastian says, avoiding her question. He pulls on the reins and his horse breaks into a walk.

"Great!" she exclaims, her voice unnaturally high. "We've all been missing you, Sebastian. Me especially."

"Thank you," Sebastian replies. "Shall we return to the group?"

"That would be amazing." Hayley gives him a broad smile which she drops when her eyes slide to mine. I swear, if looks could kill I'd be dead, buried, and strumming a harp on a cloud by now. She looks back at Sebastian and says, "Ride with me?"

"We should help Emma back. This is her first time on a horse."

"Oh, I'm sure Emma has stolen you away for far too long already," Hayley purrs. "Haven't you, Emma?"

I open my mouth to reply when Sebastian beats me to it. "I would prefer it if she came with us, Hayley."

I get another death stare from Hayley.

"It's fine," I say with a wave of my hand. "Y'all two go. Me and Marilyn are good." I pet Marilyn and she makes a horse-y sound that I decide to interpret as agreement.

"If you're certain?" Sebastian asks, and the look of concern for me on his face has me melting.

"Sure am."

"Come on, Sebastian. I'm sure you've had enough of this learner trot. Let's go for a decent gallop to blow those cobwebs away," Hayley says.

Sebastian darts me a look and I nod and smile at him. He turns back to Hayley, and says, "Let's go."

I watch as they ride off together, side by side. They look like Mr. Darcy and Lizzie Bennet, out for a romantic ride together.

As I make my way back to the stables alone, my mind is filled with Sebastian and I realize I'm only now beginning to admit something to myself.

I like him. I really like him.

And the thought scares me half to death.

Chapter Seventeen

"Tell us about your horse ride with Sebastian," Cindy asks as I sit in a chair with bright lights shining on me, a camera catching my every look and word. My mic pack digs into my back, and I shift my position.

"It was great to get some one on one time with him, even though I wasn't exactly confident on my horse. First time riding for me."

"What did you talk about?"

"We talked about his job and Timothy. Timothy is my activewear label, not my boyfriend, in case you were wondering."

"Have you developed any feelings for Sebastian?"

A small smile creeps across my face before I can stop it. Even though I've begun to, I don't want to tell her about it. "He's a great guy."

"Can you expand on that? Start with 'The way I feel about Sebastian is.'"

This is so natural.

"Sure. The way I feel about Sebastian is ... I like him. I didn't think I would, but I do."

"Why didn't you think you'd like him?"

"Because he's—"

"Begin with 'I didn't think I would like Sebastian because,'" Cindy says, much the way a mom says to her child for the four hundredth time that day.

"Right. I forgot. I didn't think I would like Sebastian because he was so reserved when we first met, but now I'm getting to know him and I like him a lot more."

Cindy gestures for me to continue, so I add, "Of course he's super hot and charming, but he's got a playful side to him, as well."

"Like the time he read your note and told you he couldn't go to your room?"

"For the record, as I've said before, I did not invite him to my room in that note. He was kidding about that. It was hilarious, when you think about it."

Which it wasn't.

"He called you a firecracker today. How did you feel about that?"

I think of our horse ride, before Hayley rode up and stole him away, and something stirs in my chest. "I liked that he called me a firecracker," I begin, remembering what I'm meant to do, "because it was cute. I *am* a firecracker at times."

"In what way?"

"When I go after something, I really go after it. I'm like a dog with a bone."

"Like with Timothy, your label?"

"Exactly. I'm working really hard to get Timothy off the ground, which, now that I think about it, makes it sound like a blow-up character, floating in the air." I laugh lightly at my own joke, but Cindy just looks at me.

Tough crowd of one.

"Is your label the reason why you came on this show, Emma?"

I blink at her. "No," I reply in an entirely unconvincing way. "I came on the show to find love."

"Not to promote Timothy?"

I shake my head vehemently. "No way."

She tilts her head to the side, watching me, and I know I've got to convince her—and the American people.

"I've been a fan of reality TV dating shows since forever. Me and my friend Penny watch them, like all the time. I adore the romance, the suspense, the whole thing. I guess I'm in love with love, you know what I mean? I watched people fall in love on these shows. And I figured that if others can do it, why not me? And trust me, I am here for the right reasons. I'm here to fall in love with Mr. Darcy."

I hold my breath. I've pulled out every cliché known to dating show contestant-kind. One of them has got to do the trick.

"Camille must have got that wrong, I guess," Cindy says pleasantly.

I lock my jaw. I should have known it would be Camille. "She has."

"Good to know. Okay, Emma, we're done here. The card ceremony is coming up soon, so you've got an hour or so before then."

My mind swimming with thoughts of the traitorous Camille, I thank Cindy, remove my mic, and head back to my room.

Of course I get why Camille would tell the producers

about my label. I've made no secret of the fact my clothes are all by Timothy. I told a bunch of contestants on my first night here.

I reach the empty bedroom and flop down on my bed, thankful for the rare solitude.

Camille's playing the game, that's all. She wants to get me kicked off the show. In a way, I should see it as a compliment: I'm sufficient enough competition in her mind to make her want to get rid of me.

The problem for her is, if Sebastian follows through on getting Timothy some air time, she's got no clue the star of the show is in on the whole thing.

It's another card ceremony and the final two are standing on the other side of the room from us. Hayley and Shelby are clutching onto one another as though the Titanic has struck the iceberg and Leonardo DiCaprio is nowhere to be found.

Despite knowing how Shelby manipulated Sebastian with that whole fake fainting saga, I still feel sorry for her. She genuinely thinks they're destined to be together, and by the looks of the confusion and hurt on her face right now, she's having a hard time processing her current predicament.

Then there's Hayley. I'm not going to lie, Hayley being sent home would make my life here considerably less like a scene from *Mean Girls*, not to mention the absence of the Oompa Loompa in drag will mean Camille might not be quite so horrible to be around.

Who am I kidding? She'll continue to look down her aquiline nose at me and work behind the scenes to get me thrown off the show.

I guess all's fair in love, war, and reality TV.

"Who's it going to be?" Kennedy mutters under her breath at my side.

"I know who I *want* it to be."

Johnathan has his hands steepled as he looks at the two girls, waiting for the drama to build until he puts one of them out of her misery. "Shelby. You have been invited to stay. Please, join The Lizzies."

Shelby instantly bursts into loud sobs as she hugs a shocked Hayley.

Hayley pushes her away, throws her hands on her hips, and glares at Sebastian. "Are you freaking kidding me? We went on that horse ride together. I told you things about me. I opened up to you. I was real. And this is how you treat me?"

"Thank you for doing that, Hayley. I appreciate your honesty and ... enthusiasm," Sebastian replies.

I hold in a giggle. "Enthusiasm" is one word, but I can think of a bunch of other words for Hayley, some of which I would not repeat in polite company.

"There was one tiny detail you omitted from your conversation with Sebastian, though. Wasn't there, Hayley?" Johnathan says.

"I don't know what you're talking about," she sniffs.

"We have recently learnt something about you that we found unexpected."

Hayley shifts her weight, her plumped up lips pulled together. "I can get a divorce," she spits.

Wait, what?

Hayley's *married*?

I turn and gawp at the women around me. Everyone looks as stunned as me, riveted as the scene unfolds before us.

Johnathan's voice is calm but firm as he says, "All contestants are required to be single, Hayley. Had we known you were married before filming began we would not have been able to have you on the show."

"Yeah, whatever," she huffs as she crosses her arms. "It's a stupid rule."

I flick my eyes to Kennedy. "It's a stupid rule that the contestants on a dating show have got to be single?"

She chortles as she shakes her head. "So unreasonable."

Shelby has been watching along with the rest of us. She sniffs loudly and wipes the tears from her eyes before she collects her card and joins us on the other side of the room.

Meanwhile, Hayley is still fuming that she's been found out, and I'm not sure she's going to go quietly. "Sebastian, you should know that you've missed a major opportunity here. *Major.* No one else here comes close to me. I am the full package." She does a little shimmy to show us all just how full her package is. "And now," she adds with a waggle of her finger, "you can't touch this."

I half expect her to break into that old MC Hammer song. She doesn't, which is a shame as the mood in here could really use some "Hammertime" to lighten it up.

"I'm sorry, Hayley," Sebastian replies. "You're a wonderful woman and I'm certain things will work out for you."

"You got that straight, mister," she spits at him.

Johnathan jumps in. "Hayley, rules are rules, and as you have broken one of them, we have no choice but to send you home. I ask now that you say your goodbyes, pack your bags, and leave."

"All right. I'll go. This show sucks, anyway." She scowls at him before she holds her hand in the air and exclaims, "Later, bee-otches!" to us. She turns on her slipper-ed heel and waltzes out of the room, her hips swinging from side to side like a pendulum.

I'd like to say I'm sad to watch Hayley leave, but we all know that would be a bald-faced lie. She's been nothing but horrible to me the whole time we've been here. Seeing her sent home has me punching the air. Well, metaphorically anyway. The cameras are trained on The Lizzies so I don't want to look too happy.

A tall guy from the crew follows her out, probably to ensure she doesn't set the house on fire or something, and we're instructed to stay where we are for more filming.

Beside me, Shelby asks, "After what's just happened, I thought we would definitely be done for the night."

"There's a special announcement coming up," one of the crew replies. "Hold tight. We'll be right with you."

I glance over at Sebastian. He's now on the other side of the room with Johnathan, their heads down as they talk.

"That was brutal," Kennedy says. "Who knew she was married?"

"I know, right?" I reply.

"She's an idiot," Camille announces.

I shoot her a sideways look. "I thought you two were friends?"

"I'm not here to make friends," she replies scathingly. "This is *Dating Mr. Darcy*, not *Making New Friends*. Particularly not when they're stupid enough to think they can get away with something as big as being married and no one would be the wiser."

"You're so right, Camille," Lori, my sleep-talking room-mate says as others around me agree. "It's good she's gone now. At least all of us are here for the right reasons."

I work hard at not rolling my eyes.

"Why do you think they're going to film some more tonight?" Phoebe asks.

Reggie turns around to face us. "Maybe they're gonna announce a second guy."

"Darcy's best friend, Mr. Bingley, maybe," I offer, watching Johnathan and Sebastian on the other side of the room.

"Mr. Bingley would be nice," Phoebe replies.

"Or Mr. Wickham," Reggie says. "I could take a scoundrel like George Wickham for a twirl right about now. I bet a man like him would be real excitin'."

"Gosh, yes," one of the other contestants nearby agrees as others pile in with their ideas.

A few moments and a lot of eager chatter between the contestants later, they call for order and the camera lights flick back on.

Johnathan stands before us once more, flanked by Sebastian. "Ladies, with Hayley now gone we are down to you as our Lizzies. Congratulations to you all." He beams out at us. "Now, I'll hand over to Mr. Darcy to say a few words. Sebastian?"

Sebastian steps forward, looking serious. "Ladies, it's been wonderful to be here at the ranch, but I'm afraid our time must come to an end. Hayley won't be the only one leaving."

What?

"I need to ask each and every one of you to return to your rooms and pack your bags."

We dart stunned looks at one another. Are we all being sent home?

"I need you to pack your bags," Sebastian continues after the crew is satisfied the contestants have got sufficiently worked up, "because tomorrow we are all taking a flight to England to stay at Pemberley, my family's home." His smile stretches across his face and I can tell it's the real deal now.

My face on the other hand, probably more closely resembles a deer in headlights.

The women around me erupt in excitement, hugging, whooping, and thanking Sebastian. I do none of these things. Instead, I stand rooted to the spot, my brain on fire. I'm going to England? But that's a thousand miles away. No, more. A *lot* more. It's over an ocean. It's an entirely different country.

Sure, they said bring your passport, but I figured it'd only be for the contestants who got into the top few, and I had no plans whatsoever of being one of those women.

"Oh, one other thing, ladies," Sebastian says and the room falls quiet. "You'll be able to wear whatever you want on the flight. No need for Regency attire. Might I suggest some comfortable activewear, perhaps?" His eyes slide to mine, and I feel a shot of elation.

It cushions the blow.

As we're herded (cattle, remember?) back out of the room and directed to our bedrooms, I catch Sebastian's eye once more. He mouths "my room," and I manage to nod briefly before I move into the hallway, lost in thought.

I feel a hand on my arm and look up to see Kennedy, her face bright with excitement.

"Can you believe we're going to England tomorrow? England, baby!"

I knit my brows together. "I think I'm still processing."

"What is there to process? We're gonna have such an adventure. I've never been there before. Heck, I've never even left the country. Well, other than to go to Cabo, but everyone does that where I'm from."

"But it's *England*. It's, like, really freaking far away."

She looks at me sideways as we lift our petticoats so we don't trip on them as we climb the stairs to our rooms. "You okay, Emma?"

"Sure. I guess I should have worked out that we'd be going to England if we're on a show called *Dating Mr. Darcy*."

She laughs. "I know, right? This is going to be amazing!"

I chew on my lip. Why does it bother me so much? Is it because of the fact we're travelling far away from here, from my work, from my life? Or is it something else?

Whatever it is, I'm finding it hard to kick the unsettled feeling that's sunk in my belly.

Chapter Eighteen

L ater that night, once Reggie and Lori are lightly snoring and mumbling in their sleep respectively, I throw on some leggings and a tee and sneak on mouse-like feet down the hallway. As I round the corner a couple of doors down, I literally walk into somebody. I stagger back in surprise.

"Emma?"

"Phoebe?"

"Is everything okay?" she stage whispers.

"I, err, couldn't sleep," I reply, flustered. "I thought I'd go for a walk."

"A walk? Oh. I thought you might have been going to the bathroom."

That would have been a lot more believable.

"What are you doing here?" I ask.

"Same."

I take in her cute tank and PJ shorts. They've got teddy bears and love hearts all over them. They're *so* Phoebe. "But you're in PJs."

"Oh, they're very comfortable for walking."

"Right."

"I guess I'm nervous about the flight tomorrow."

I'm eager to get away from her so I can get on with my clandestine activity, so I say, "You'll be fine. We can sit together."

She smiles at me. "That would be nice."

"Well, enjoy your walk."

"You, too," she replies before she takes off down the hall as though her pants are on fire.

I watch her leave and am once again alone in the darkened hallway. What was she doing here? There was no way she was going for a walk. I chew on my lip as a fresh thought fills my brain. Had she been to see Sebastian? I didn't think any of the other contestants had a clue where he slept. But then, maybe I'm totally naïve and he's been seeing contestants in his room all this time.

Despite knowing that rationally it shouldn't matter to me even if he has, my belly sinks to the floor. I know this is a dating show. He's got his choice of eager women, and he's here to fall in love. At the end of this show he's got to name his "Mrs. Darcy" and propose.

I need to shake it off. Sure, I've started feeling things for him that I wish I didn't, but I'm not here for him. I'm here for my label.

But lately, I find I've got to keep reminding myself of that.

Things are beginning to get complicated.

I press on down the hallway, moving as swiftly and quietly as I can. I knock lightly on his door and wait. A moment later, I'm met with Sebastian in a white T-shirt and pair of jeans.

His face lights up as his eyes land on mine. "Brady Bunch," he says with his sexy accent.

"Hey." I feel like a goofy teenager meeting a boy she's got a crush on.

He pulls the door open and stands back for me to enter.

As I do, I round on him, those crush feelings replaced with something else. "Tell me something straight up, okay?" I raise my index finger in warning. "And you cannot lie to me."

He darts me a quizzical look. "When have I ever lied to you?"

"Umm, maybe by not dropping the hint we're going to England today when we went for a horse ride?"

"We had cameras on us. Plus, I didn't want you to appear like you knew about it already when they filmed everyone's reaction. As it turned out, you looked like a stunned mullet."

"It came as a bit of a shock, that's all."

"A good shock, I hope?"

"When is a shock ever good, Seb?"

His face falls. "Are you saying you don't want to go?"

"I didn't expect it, that's all."

"Well, I for one am glad you're coming. I would love to show you Martinston."

"What's Martinston?" I ask. I glance down at his jeans and my eyes bulge. No, he couldn't be that guy! He might be getting a bit flirty, but he's not the type. Is he?

"Martinston isn't the name for your—" I nod at the crotch of his jeans.

"What? No!"

"Oh, thank goodness," I say with a rush of relief.

I am not a fan of guys naming their appendages. I should have known a pompous British aristocrat wouldn't name *his*. Well, not something like "Martinston," anyway.

More like "Little Sebastian," or "Lord Wiener." Oh, please stop me now.

"So exactly what is Martinston?" I ask.

"It's my family's home. They're calling it 'Pemberley' on the show because of the book, of course, but that's not its real name. Martinston has been in our family for generations. It's really special to me."

That's why his smile flipped to genuine when he told the contestants about it. My heart squeezes at the thought he wants to show me his home—and the fact he's not the type to name his err, manhood, either.

"I'd like to see your home, Seb."

"I'm glad." His eyes lock with mine and I wonder what it was that I hated about him so much. He's a good guy. Sure, he's still a total douche to choose to go on a reality TV show to find love, but none of us are perfect. Right?

"I hope you'll like it."

"It's a castle, Seb. I'm sure I'll love it."

"Not a castle."

"Sorry. My bad." I raise my hands in surrender. "A manor house. *So* different from a castle."

He opens his mouth to reply but seems to think better of it. Instead, he says, "What was it you wanted me to answer honestly?"

"I saw Phoebe in the hallway on the way here. She seemed flustered. She told me she was going for a walk."

He cocks an eyebrow. "Much like you were?"

"Fair point," I concede. "But I was coming to see you. What was she up to?"

"I honestly don't know. But in case you're indirectly asking me what I think you are, I assure you, Phoebe was not here with me. Nor does she know where my room is, as far as I'm aware."

The heaviness in my belly lifts and I'm surprised at how relieved I feel to hear him say it. "I'm glad we cleared that up."

He takes a step closer to me, and I catch a hint of his scent, his physical presence making my heart thud like a beating drum. Why does he have to stand so dang close? Doesn't he know it's confusing for me?

More than confusing.

"What is interesting, Brady, is how the thought of another woman visiting me has clearly upset you so much."

"I'm not upset. I'm only—" I search for the correct word. "—concerned."

"You're concerned."

"Yes. I'm concerned about our deal." He holds my gaze and I fight the urge to wrap my arms around him and kiss him.

Wait, *what?!*

Me, kiss Sebastian? Have I completely lost my mind?

I clear my throat. "Speaking of which, I need to thank you for the chance to promote my label tomorrow when we travel. It's really great of you to set that up for me."

"I'm only pleased I could help."

"You're a total lifesaver. Truly."

"Well, there's only so many times I want an angry Texan turning up at my room in the middle of the night."

I bat him playfully on the arm. "Oh, you love it."

"Once you've got your label on camera, I imagine you'll want to leave."

Getting away from here is all I've been able to think about since the Regency clothes bomb was dropped. But that was before I began to feel things for Sebastian I never expected to feel. Confusing things.

Wonderful things.

I nod. "That's the plan."

"As impossible as I imagine you'll find this, I will be sorry to see you go."

My heart rate picks up again. "I thought I was a pain in your butt."

A smirk spreads across his face. "What makes you say that?"

"Are you serious right now? I haven't exactly been nice to you."

"Granted, you are pushy, and you came here to promote your label, which I might remind you is against the rules. And not only that, you get extremely bolshie when you don't get your way."

"Don't hold back there, cowboy."

"Despite it all, Emma Brady, I find you intriguing. Irritating beyond belief, but intriguing all the same."

A blink at him. Sebastian finds me intriguing? I swallow down a rising lump. "You do?"

"Is that so hard to believe?"

"Well, I am a thoroughly intriguing person," I deadpan.

His eyes crinkle as his smirk reaches across his face. "And extremely modest, as well."

"So, what's so intriguing about me exactly, huh?"

Please don't judge me. It's not every day a guy who looks like Sebastian compliments me like that.

"How about we start with the fact that you're the only contestant who's not trying to impress me in the least. In fact, you've made it abundantly clear you want nothing to do with me."

My heart sinks. I'm intriguing because I've shown no interest in him. "That sounds like a classic avoidance strategy to me."

"Perhaps it is, Brady, but I like having you around."

My breath catches in my throat. He likes having me around? Does that mean ... ?

I swallow, my mouth suddenly dry. "You do?"

"I do."

Although my tummy does a flip at the thought, I narrow my eyes at him and reply, "No, you don't."

"Who are you to tell me who I do and don't like? I think I'm the best judge of that."

I chew on my lip, watching him. "Sure, you're right," I concede. "But you're also wrong."

He arches an eyebrow. "Thank you for being so very clear."

"What I mean is, you think you like having me around, when really you don't."

"Might I refer you to my earlier statement about me being the best judge of how I feel?"

"Let me spell it out for you. This is a totally artificial environment. We've been thrown together, we're all dressed up, y'all are pretending to be Mr. Darcy, I'm one of The Lizzies." I roll my eyes on behalf of Jane Austen. "It's only natural that we would develop feelings for one another."

His face creases into a smile. "You have feelings for me, Brady?"

Dang it! Did I just say that?

"No, I don't!" I insist far too firmly.

"You just said you do."

"Well, tell me this then: why do I want to leave, Mr. Know-It-All?"

"You see, that's where you're wrong. You don't want to leave."

"I do."

"You did, but you don't anymore."

Ha! The cheek of the man! The fact that he's right is totally beside the point.

"For your information, I have put my own very important needs aside so you could dispense with the crazies." I land on an appropriately grand sounding word to describe my sacrifice and add, "I've been magnanimous."

"But you still want to stay."

"Seriously?" I throw my hands on my hips. "And you call *me* irritating."

His eyes smolder as his gaze holds mine. It does things to my insides as thoughts race through my mind.

Does he ... ?

Do I ... ?

Will we ... ?

My eyes drop to his mouth.

Are we...about to kiss?

"Well," he says.

I swallow. "Well."

"Whether or not you want to stay, we've got a long flight tomorrow. I expect you'll need your sleep."

"Right."

He's not going to kiss me. He doesn't feel it, too.

To my surprise, I feel like I might cry, which I know is insane. There are a million reasons why kissing Sebastian would be a completely terrible idea. Like the fact he's not my type. He's formal and uptight and I bet if you looked up the word "overprivileged" in a dictionary, you'd find a picture of Sebastian Huntington-Ross, smiling that sexy smile of his. Or what about the fact that he's from an entirely different world from me? A world that, frankly, scares the crap out of me. Or how about the doozy of all doozies: he's come on this show to find love? Surely that's *got* to be the biggest deterrent of all?

But none of them mean anything right now. Because as I look at him, all I want to do is feel his lips against mine, his body pressed up against me.

"I guess I'll go, then," I say, but of course I mean the opposite.

"Yes. Of course," he replies.

"Now. I'll go now."

He opens his mouth as though to say something, and then closes it again. He nods. "I'll see you tomorrow."

I let out a resigned puff of air. "Tomorrow. Sure."

His lips curve into a smile I can feel right down to my toes. "Good night, Brady."

As Sebastian closes the door behind me, I lean up against the wall and scrunch my eyes shut.

He told me he likes having me around, but he didn't kiss me. I wanted him to, and he didn't. I let out a heavy breath.

I'm a total fool.

Falling for Mr. Darcy was never in the plan.

Chapter Nineteen

I barely sleep, I'm so amped. Thoughts race around my head, competing for thinking space. Promoting Timothy, staying longer on the show, going to England. But there's one that keeps fighting the others off for pole position.

I think I'm falling for him.

It gets my head spinning so much, I fear it ricocheting off my neck and slamming up against the bedroom wall.

How could I have let this happen? The plan was to get enough exposure for the label to move from fledgling start-up to profitable business and then get the heck out of dodge. Not fall for the guy I'm morally opposed to for going on reality TV to fall in love, a guy who's from an entirely different world from mine. A guy with whom it could never, in a million years, work.

Eventually, the sun rises and Reggie's alarm sounds. I get a temporary reprieve from obsessing over him. Today is the day we go to England.

I spend the morning racing around the contestants, offering them Timothy activewear for the flight. I tell them it's super comfortable and perfect for a long flight, which it is, and since most of them brought a wardrobe full of sexy low-cut dresses and bikinis—neither of which exactly scream Regency or long haul travel—I get a few of them choosing to wear it. Of course, the fact that all the tops I hand out have "Timothy" emblazoned across the chest along with our cute monogram is just a happy coincidence.

We're filmed leaving the ranch, traveling to the airport, boarding the plane, and in the bus on the drive from Heathrow Airport to Sebastian's family home. I'm not sure it's going to be riveting TV for the audience, but at least the label gets some screen time.

We've been on the bus for half an hour when Kennedy yawns loudly in the seat beside me. "This is the longest trip I've ever been on. I don't care if I ever see a bus or a plane again."

"Tell me about it. I had Shelby snoring next to me half the flight, and the other half she kept talking about how she and Sebastian are made for one another. It got old super fast."

"Did she warn you away from him?" Kennedy asks.

"She told me that it didn't matter if he showed me any 'special attention,' as she called it, because she is his destiny." I use air quotes.

She raises her eyebrows. "Special attention, huh? Like kissing your face off?"

"What? No!" I protest, although I'm sure the color in my cheeks gives me away.

"Are you telling me that if you were presented with the opportunity to kiss our wonderful Mr. Darcy, you would turn him down?"

Heck no. I'd be on that in a flash. I don't say it. I'm still fighting these new feelings I've got for him—feelings that aren't reciprocated, no matter how much he might tell me he likes having me around. Instead, I reply, "I don't know. You?"

She bats me lightly on the arm. "Hey! Stop deflecting, girl. Would you kiss him if you were given the chance?"

Camille's face pops up over the back of the seat in front of us. "I bet she already has."

Great. That's all I need: Camille weighing in with her two cents' worth, only in her case it's a dollar's worth, thanks to her family's wealth.

"What makes you say that?" Kennedy asks as I glare at Camille.

"Haven't you noticed the way she's always making googly eyes at him, like he's her favorite flavor of ice cream?"

"I do not!"

"Yeah. You do. I bet you follow him around like a lovesick puppy."

"Camille, you're just jealous because Sebastian obviously likes my girl here, that's all," Kennedy says.

"You see, that's where you've got it wrong," Camille replies. "A man like Sebastian, with all his wealth, fine breeding, and sophistication would never go for someone like *her*." Camille shoots me a look that tells me the mere idea is beyond disgusting to her.

"I suppose he'd prefer someone like you. Right, Camille?" Kennedy replies.

"Naturally," she replies with a lift of her skinny shoulder. "We're from similar worlds, you know. We understand each other. Sebastian and I are *sympatico*."

Kennedy rolls her eyes. "*Sympatico*? More like psycho."

I try not to scoff, but I'm pretty sure I fail. "You're trying to tell us you're an English aristocrat now, Camille? Because I've got news for you. You're not."

"Sticks and stones, girls. Sticks and stones. We'll all see who comes out on top soon enough, and I can tell you one thing for sure: it won't be 'your girl,' Kennedy."

"I guess we will see, Camille," I reply with as sweet a smile as I can manage, which is to say it probably resembles more of a scowl.

Deciding her work is done, with a flick of her hair, Camille turns her back on us and disappears behind the seat.

"I've said it before and I'll say it again: She is just lovely," I mumble, and Kennedy and I both burst into snorting giggles as we try to keep our voices down. No one wants to poke the Camille beast twice in one day.

A few miles later, the bus slows and turns off the charming country road we've been traveling down, with its rolling green fields and quaint stone fences, into a long tree-lined driveway. We pass by two tall pillars flanking the entranceway and I read the word "Martinston" on a brass metal plate.

"Oh, my God," I say. "We're here."

Kennedy leans over me to get a better view. "Seriously? Is he the frigging king of England?"

The coach crunches along the gravel driveway, under a line of old trees that form an archway over our heads. Surrounding the driveway are fields of lush, green grass, speckled with cows and sheep. And then, after what feels like minutes, the house comes into view.

It takes my breath away.

It's magnificent. There's no other word for it. Three-stories tall, the huge building with its turrets and long windows towers over gardens leading to a gorgeous pond. I've got no clue about architectural styles, but I can tell it's old, maybe a few hundred years. Just the sight of it transports me back to a time of horse-drawn carriages and ladies and gentlemen playing croquet on the lawn. It's elegant and whimsical and looks like ... well, it looks like Mr. Darcy lives here. Which is quite appropriate, really, considering he does.

I stare out of the window at the house, utterly transfixed. A lump rises in my throat as an odd sensation spreads across my chest.

"Would you look at this place," Lori exclaims. "Pemberley is gorgeous!"

"Wow, this guy is seriously loaded! I had no idea," Reggie says as she stands up to get a better view.

"Welcome to *Downton Abbey*, girls," Kennedy says to nods of agreement.

"Only much, much better," Phoebe agrees, "because it's real."

We come to a stop and the doors to the bus open. Everyone rushes to get out. I sit, collecting my scrambled thoughts. Seeing Sebastian's house—if that's what you call a building the size of an office block—suddenly makes this all feel so much more real.

He may be playacting as Mr. Darcy, but he's the real thing. I always knew we were from different worlds. Seeing his home makes me realize we're from different planets. A girl like me would never fit into a place like this.

Lizzie Bennet joked with her sister Jane that she realized she was in love with Mr. Darcy the moment she laid eyes on Pemberley. For me, seeing Sebastian's home, as stunningly fairy-tale perfect as it is, only assures me beyond a whisper of a doubt that he and I could never be together.

Any misguided feelings I have for him need to be left to wither and die.

"You coming, Em?" Kennedy asks, interrupting my train of thought.

I pull myself back to reality. "Of course." I collect my things and make my way to the exit.

Outside the bus, the place is even more overwhelming. There's an ornate fountain that looks like it could have been transplanted from Florence, a bunch of topiary trees and shrubs running past the house, and sitting right on top of the highest level of the house, there's a flag pole, proudly flying the Union Jack.

As if we need a reminder that we're not in Kansas anymore, Toto.

We go through the process of collecting our luggage and are then grouped together in front of the house, mics attached and cameras at the ready. Although it's summer here, the temperature has dropped about a hundred degrees from the unrelenting Texas heat we were used to, and it takes determination not to throw on a sweatshirt over my Timothy apparel.

"Mr. Darcy will be stepping out of the front door onto these steps in about thirty seconds time," Carl, one of the crew informs us, and my belly does a flip at the prospect of seeing Sebastian again. "I want you looking super happy to see him, and excited to be here at 'Pemberley.' Okay?"

"We *are* super happy to see him and excited to be at 'Pemberley,'" Shelby says, and a bunch of the contestants agree.

"Awesome," he replies with more than a hint of sarcasm before he yells, "Quiet on the set!"

Right then the oversized wooden doors at the top of the stone steps swing open and Sebastian appears, looking quite the gentleman of the manor in his Mr. Darcy breeches, buttoned up jacket, and top hat.

The sight of him has my tummy doing flips, and I find myself wanting to slip behind the contestants so he doesn't see me.

There's a ripple of excitement that flows through the group, and every eye in the place watches as he strides through the door and out into the weak English sun.

"Ladies, welcome to Pemberley," he says with a smile.

We all murmur our thanks, then fall silent once more.

"I trust you travelled well and are happy to be here at 'Pemberley.'" He shifts his weight and I wonder whether he's uneasy giving his much-loved Martinston the fictitious name.

"I wonder where Johnathan is," I hear Phoebe whisper behind me.

"Oh, I'm sure he's lurking in the house somewhere," Camille replies.

"He probably got lost. The place is huge," Reggie comments.

"Once you are settled and changed into attire befitting a lady of Pemberley, we shall all meet for drinks on the terrace. Until then, adieu." He smiles at us all and then turns and walks back through the large doors and into the house.

Sometime later, we are allocated our rooms up the huge staircase on the second floor. I am beyond excited to find that not only am I no longer sharing with Reggie the snorer and Lori the sleep talker, but I've got Kennedy, my new bestie, in a room all to ourselves. And our room is off-the-charts gorgeous. It's massive with its own seating area and a huge four-poster bed, complete with a top canopy and curtains to make us feel like princesses. There's a second bed near the ornate fireplace that looks like it has been added so that we can both sleep comfortably. The view is of the formal gardens below, with their boxed hedging and sculptures, and the most gorgeous stone pergola atop a low-lying hill in the middle distance.

"Em, this place is incredible," Kennedy says, her eyes wide as she also takes in the room. "It's like stepping back in time to a really, really rich person's house. Which it is, when you think about it."

I drop my luggage on the chaise at the bottom of one of the beds and gaze out the window. "It sure is something."

"Are you kidding me? Did you see the portraits on the walls as we came up the stairs? All the art, the tapestries, the furniture? I didn't quite realize it back in Texas."

I turn back to face her. "Realize what?"

"Sebastian is an actual, bona fide English gentleman. As in a sir or something."

I bite my lip, my insides churning with too many emotions. "He lives a different life from us, that's for sure."

A life I know I could never be a part of.

Chapter Twenty

I t's the first soirée at 'Pemberley,' and we've been instructed to wear our Regency clothes and curl those ringlets around our faces once more. With a sigh of regret for my twenty-first century self, I pack my Timothy activewear in the room's chest of drawers. Sebastian followed through on his promise to allow me time to showcase my designs. Now it's my turn to play the part of one of The Lizzies.

The place is abuzz with chatter as Kennedy and I reach the terrace. It's a beautiful, mild evening, and as usual, the drinks are flowing. Again, as usual, once Sebastian arrives, he's surrounded by a gaggle of eager women vying for his attention, their voices high and loud, interspersed with frequent giggles.

I'm sitting with Kennedy, Reggie, and Phoebe, sipping a glass of wine, the ever-present cameras hovering nearby.

"Welcome back to 1813, ladies," Kennedy says as we settle back against the firm cushions of one of the wrought iron couches.

I take a sip of my wine. "I know, right? We had a small

taste of our fashion freedom, and now it's been ripped from us once more."

"I like it," Reggie declares. "It seems right to be wearin' these in a place like this. It's romantic."

"I agree," Phoebe says.

"Do y'all have huge rooms with four-poster beds like we do?" Reggie asks. Her Southern drawl oddly seems to fit in the English aristocratic surrounds.

"Yup. Our room is amazing," Kennedy replies.

Reggie whistles. "That's a lot of bedrooms, and that doesn't even include Mr. Hottie over there, or his family, who I expect to be lurkin' 'round here somewhere." She gestures at Sebastian and I look in his direction. Camille is now smiling broadly as she leans up against him as though he were a man-wall, placed there for her benefit. He looks happy enough, but then the cameras are perpetually trained on the guy, so who knows? It could be all for show.

The lines are definitely blurred between what's real and what's not on reality television.

I turn my attention back to my friends. "It was a workout just to walk down here tonight, this place is so huge."

Kennedy waves her glass in the air. "I am not looking forward to all those stairs tonight after a few of these."

"Right?" Reggie agrees. "I wish there was an elevator."

I scrunch up my nose. "I'm not sure they had those in 1813."

"You know what I wish?" Phoebe says. "I wish I could Google Sebastian. Find out about him and his family. I bet the history of this place would be fascinating."

"I'd like to Google him to find a photo of him with no shirt on," Reggie says as she eyes Sebastian across the terrace. "Am I right, ladies?"

"Heck, yes," Kennedy replies and I smile as I try not to think of Sebastian without his shirt on ... and fail.

Has the temperature suddenly risen about twenty degrees out here?

"Back in the States, I figured he was just some guy acting the part," Kennedy says. "Sure, you could tell he's English, and clearly came from a fancy family. Now, being here, you see he's the real deal. I saw his family crest in the house, and it looked old. Not like those ones you can buy off of the Internet."

"You can buy a family crest off of the Internet?" Phoebe asks and Kennedy nods her assent.

I roll my eyes. "Remind me to do that when I get back home to my tiny rented apartment on the wrong side of town."

"Oh, you won't be headin' there anytime soon," Reggie says.

"What makes you say that?"

"He's into you, darlin'. It's plain as day." She leans forward and adds, "Whatever your secret is, please let me in on it. That man *does* things to me I'm not tellin' my mama about, if you know what I mean."

My heartrate kicks up. "He's not into me."

"You sure about that?"

"Look out, girls," Phoebe says as she sits more upright in her chair. "He's coming our way."

A moment later, Sebastian arrives. "Good evening, ladies," he says in that sexy accent of his, and I have to work hard at resisting the urge to leap into his arms.

I have got to get a hold of myself. If he reciprocated my feelings, he would have kissed me when he had the chance.

And he didn't.

"How are you all this evening?" he asks.

"Good," I reply, feeling thoroughly awkward as the others chat with him about the house and the journey here. He smiles and answers everyone's questions, even Reggie's about whether he's ever gone for a swim in his pond in just a pair of pants and a see-through white shirt, like Colin Firth in the famous BBC adaptation I used to watch with my mom.

"I have not," he replies with a twinkle in his eyes. "But I'll certainly add it to my to-do list."

"As long as you tell us when you're doin' it. We would hate to miss the show," Reggie purrs.

"I'll be sure to do that, Reggie," he replies smoothly.

After talking with us for a while about his home and how we're finding the place, he says, "Emma, would you like to go for a walk with me? I would like to show you the garden shrubs we were discussing earlier."

We both know we didn't discuss plants of any kind. "Garden shrubs. Sure."

He stands up and I do the same.

"Until later in the evening, ladies," he says to the group.

"I'll be holdin' you to that," Reggie says as we turn to leave. "I've got a sudden fascination with your garden shrubs myself now, too. Maybe we can go for a walk later?"

"I would enjoy that," he replies.

Sebastian offers me his arm, and I hook mine over it all lady-like as we walk away.

"Shrubs, huh?" I ask.

"Actually, I wanted to show you the gardens. I think you'll like them."

"The fact you said 'gardens' with an 's' tells me they're going to be a whole lot more impressive than my little window box."

"You have a window box?"

"Don't pretend to be impressed."

"I imagine it's a lot less work than our gardens."

"Watering a few gerberas every day or two isn't exactly work, you know."

"Are you all settled in? Do you like your room?"

"Oh, it's totally gorgeous," I can't help but gush.

The skin around his eyes crinkle as he smiles at me. "I'm glad you think so."

"It would be hard not to. Your house is seriously amazing. You've got to know that."

"It's not my house, per se. It's my family's. We all live here. My mother, my grandmother, and my sister, too."

"A bit crowded, huh? I hope no one hogs the bathroom in the mornings."

He smiles and asks, "Which room are you in?"

"Why? Are you planning to pop in for tea and crumpets?"

He shrugs. "I'm interested, that's all."

"I'm staying with Kennedy in the most incredible room with a massive four-poster bed, which I gave to her."

"Because you're so magnanimous?"

I know he's using my word to describe myself, and his playful tone has me relaxing from a tightly bound knot. "You got it."

"You'll need to narrow the room down for me. All the guest accommodations have four-poster beds."

"How tricky for you to keep a track," I jest. "You've clearly got too many guest rooms. If you stayed with me, you'd be lucky if y'all got half the couch. Frank would claim the other half."

"Frank?"

"My tabby cat." I think of my fur kid and my heart gives a squeeze. "I miss him. He's so cute and fluffy. He can be quite prickly though, even with me, but we've come to an understanding: I feed him and let him do whatever he wants and he doesn't maul me with his sharp cat claws."

"He sounds charming."

"Oh, he's the best. He was a rescue. The shelter said he was mistreated before I got him. I figured he'd gone through some crap, so he could keep his foibles."

"As well as his fur balls?"

I look at him in surprise. "Is that a joke, Mr. Darcy?"

"I do believe it is, Miss Emma."

"Next time, how about you put your hand up so I know when you're joking? That way I can make sure to laugh."

"It's reassuring to know you care so much for my ego," he says with a laugh. "Now, what color is your wallpaper and bedding?"

"Blue."

"Light or dark?"

"How many bedrooms have you got?"

"A few. Light blue or dark?"

"Light."

"In that case, you're in the Peacock Room."

"The Peacock Room. I'm so glad we cleared that up."

He smiles and warmth spreads across my chest, and it's then that I know I'm sunk. Everything about him draws me in and holds me there. I want to spend time with him, even in front of the cameras. I want to get to know him, to learn all about him. I want to be with him. Period.

Only, despite signs to the contrary, it's clear he doesn't want to be with me.

He comes to a stop and turns to face me. "Tell me, Emma, what do you think of my home?" he asks softly.

"It's breathtakingly beautiful."

"I'm glad you think so."

"Who wouldn't? It's got these beautiful grounds and all those bedrooms you seem to find so hard to keep track of. And the staircase? That thing is insane!"

"It's quite something, isn't it? It was designed in the eighteenth century during extensive renovations to the original Elizabethan design."

A fresh smile spreads across my face.

Sebastian notices and says, "What?"

"You're very knowledgeable."

"Isn't everyone about the place they live in?"

I let out a laugh. "All I know about my place is that it was built in the '90s with the thinnest walls known to humanity, the AC can be temperamental, and my rent is a pain in the butt. But then you wouldn't have any clue about rent, would you? You get to live in this spectacular place, where your parents lived and their parents before them, forever and ever back to when Adam was a cowboy."

"You're right," he replies after a beat and resumes walking through the pretty garden. "But we all have our crosses to bear, Emma. Just because I live here doesn't mean I don't have mine."

"You mean like having to remember how many bathrooms you've got?"

"Something like that."

We've reached the edge of the terrace now, and I notice several of the contestants approaching us with eager looks on their faces.

"There you are, Sebastian," Camille says as she hooks her arm through his and literally tries to pull him away from me. I let go of his arm and his eyes find mine briefly before he turns to Camille.

She pouts. "I've missed you. I hope Emma hasn't been boring you talking about her label."

God, she's horrible.

"On the contrary, Camille. Emma is quite delightful," he replies, and I can't help but shoot her a smug smirk. I'm delightful. Take that, Camille.

Clearly nonplussed, she ignores me and tugs on Sebastian's arm. "Can we go for a little chat? I want to learn all about life at Pemberley." She glares at me and adds, "Alone."

"Of course. Shall we go for a walk?"

"Actually, I've got us a place to sit and chat, just over there." She points at the picturesque swing seat flanked by topiary bushes in the garden. "Doesn't it look adorable?"

"Adorable is exactly the word I'd use," he replies.

I look down and allow myself a small smile. The Sebastian I've come to know would never use the word "adorable."

As he and Camille leave, and the cameras with them, I spy a spot on a couch next to my reality bestie, Kennedy, and plunk myself down against the comfortable cushions.

Kennedy hands me a glass of wine. "Nice chat with Mr. Darcy?"

"It was fine," I reply noncommittally.

She props herself up and eyes me. "You like him, don't you? Like, genuinely like him."

If I were smart, I'd deny it. What use would it serve to admit to my feelings when I never planned on a) falling for the guy, and b) being here for this long? Not to mention our mics are on and we're being filmed.

Only, I've realized I want to stay, and it's not for my label. I want to be here for Sebastian.

And it's probably the least sane thing I've wanted in my whole life.

Instead of replying, I deflect. "What about you? Do you like him?" I ask.

"Off topic."

"It's totally *on* topic. We're all here to date Mr. Darcy, remember?"

"I admit, I had wondered about him. I mean, the guy's hot, he was very sweet on our date, and I'm only flesh and blood." She gives me a sardonic smile. "But then I saw the way he's been looking at this friend of mine lately, you know, when he thinks no one is watching him? He's all gooey-eyed and smiley."

Does he do that? My tummy does an involuntary flip.

"No, he doesn't look at me all gooey eyed."

"Oh, honey, he does. I worked out pretty fast there's no point in even trying, not when he's got it bad for my friend Emma."

I do my best to ignore the hope rising inside me. "No, he doesn't," I reply weakly. "He's being nice, that's all."

She takes a sip of her drink. "Sure he is."

Kennedy's words catapult around my head. Sure, he pulls me aside to talk with me at the soirées, and he can be very flirty with me when we're alone, away from the cameras. But nothing has ever actually happened between us. And even if he did feel something for me, how do I know he doesn't have feelings for the other girls, too?

It's all too hard and far, far too confusing.

"Emma?" Kennedy questions when I don't reply.

I change my position to get closer to her, even though I know every word we utter is being recorded. "If I do feel something for him, and that's a big if, I know it'll never work out. We're from different worlds."

She shrugs. "So were Romeo and Juliet, and they are the greatest love story of all time."

"They both died. Plus they were from the same worlds. Their families hated each other."

She waves my protest away with a flick of her hand. "Whatever. Forget about your different worlds. Surely you know opposites attract?"

I look down at my hands. "I don't know if I can see it working once the show's over. We're too different. I'm from literally the wrong side of the tracks. Home was a tiny two-bedroom house with a small yard. Now it's a rented studio apartment with a crappy window box. I'm not polo and luncheons and Chanel jackets. I'm baseball and hotdogs and a Budweiser with my bestie watching reality TV."

Kennedy maneuvers herself so she's facing me full on. "Em? Do you like him?"

I chew on my lip and then nod, wishing we were having this conversation anywhere but here.

"Then tell me something. How often do you get to meet a guy who sets your soul on fire?" she asks.

I know what the answer is. I know how I feel about Sebastian. It's crept up on me, so quietly I didn't even notice it. And now he's virtually all I can think about.

I swallow, my heart fluttering like a hummingbird. "He's not what I expected at all." A small smile busts out across my face. "He's kind and funny and smart. All the things I thought he wouldn't be. He told me he likes me, but I don't know if that's romantically, or as friends, or what."

"Of course it's romantic. He's hot, you're hot. You'll have gorgeous babies together."

I let out a surprised laugh. "Babies? Let's not get ahead of ourselves here."

"You truly like him, so you've got to go for it. You know that, right?"

I glance over at Sebastian and Camille, sitting in the

love seat together, their backs to us. Could Sebastian and I have something real? Something that could overcome our differences? Something that could survive outside of this reality show bubble?

My insides twist. "He lives *here*. My entire apartment could fit into his dining room."

"What does that matter?"

It matters for a whole host of reasons. What it all boils down to is that I'm scared. I'm scared to fall for someone whose life is so different from mine. I'm scared to put my heart out there, fearful he could choose another girl. I'm scared that if I let myself fall for him, he won't love me back.

Fairy tale endings are all very well in books and movies, but in real life? Not so much.

So instead, I reply in a light, breezy tone, "I don't know."

Kennedy pushes herself upright, her gaze on something behind me. "Oh, my God."

"What is it?"

"She's going in."

"What?" I turn to look at the swing seat.

Camille has got her hand hooked around the back of Sebastian's head as she gazes up at him, her face only inches from his. Sure enough, a moment later, Camille pulls his face down to hers and plants her lips on his.

My insides twist painfully.

It's no big deal, I tell myself. It's her kissing him, not the other way around. And I know Camille. She wants to win and she's not the kind of girl to take a backseat.

But then, he lifts his hand and pulls her in closer, and it becomes clear he's kissing her back.

I look away quickly and push down the unpleasant feelings rising inside of me.

Kennedy nudges me. "You okay, Em?"

"Fine," I mumble.

I'm convincing no one.

She places her hand on mine. "You're not fine."

I stick on a smile. "He's allowed to kiss anyone he wants. This is a dating show."

She narrows her eyes at me. "It's fine not to be okay with this. We're in an insane environment. You'd never watch a guy you liked kiss another girl in the real world. Not without throwing your drink in his face, anyway"

"You're right. It's all a bubble. It's a heat-of-the-moment thing, that's all."

"Atta girl."

Why did it have to happen about five seconds after I admitted to my feelings for him on camera?

"I think it's in bad taste, really. If she wanted to kiss him, why couldn't she go do it somewhere else without us all seeing?"

"You know Camille. Little Miss Competitive." I take a quick glance in their direction and a wave of relief washes over me as I see the kiss is now done. Camille's hanging onto his arm, beaming out at everyone.

I take a deep breath, close my eyes, and pretend to relax. Inside, I'm back to being that tightly-wound ball of string.

I know it shouldn't bother me. Heck, it's not like we've even had a romantic moment that's led to a kiss. But dang it if I don't feel like packing my bags right now and running away from here. And doing my best to forget Sebastian, the show, Martinston, and this whole dang thing.

Chapter Twenty One

I t *doesn't bother me. It doesn't bother me. It doesn't bother me.*

If you say it enough, does it come true?

The image of Sebastian and Camille engaged in a game of tonsil hockey keeps flashing in front of my eyes. No matter how many times I picture it, it doesn't get any less horrendous.

The kiss wasn't like the time Shelby kissed him after she pretended to faint. That was so obviously one-sided, and lasted all of a second or two.

And back then, I didn't feel the way I do about him now. Back then, all I wanted to do was get out of this place and get back to my real life.

This kiss was different. He participated.

I ease under the covers and take a deep, kiss-cleansing breath. Well, that's the plan, anyway. It doesn't work, and before you can say "Emma is being the most pathetic version of herself *ever*," I'm back on that terrace in my mind, watching them kiss once more.

Dang it! Why does it have to bother me so much? I've

199

got no right to Sebastian. None of us have. Sure, he and I have spent time together, and I've got to know him in a way I never thought I would. But he's also spending time getting to know *all* of us.

I'm not special.

No one in their right mind would be a contestant on a reality TV dating show and expect an uncomplicated journey to fall in love. Well, maybe Shelby would with her ideas of destiny, but no rational person would. The entire premise of the show is for Sebastian to choose one of us, and for that to happen, he's got to spend time with each of us—and indulge in some tonsil hockey with my archnemesis, it would seem.

I flip over onto my back and stare at the bedroom ceiling. I need Rational Emma back. The Emma who was only ever going to come on this show to promote Timothy. The Emma who thought Sebastian was a pompous, overprivileged douchebag.

The Emma whose heart was safe.

The fact that there was a card ceremony after the infamous kiss and poor Lori was sent home after spending less than a day here in England barely gets any screen time in my mind. Instead, while Kennedy sleeps the sleep of the unbothered in the other bed, I'm tossing and turning, twisted up in jealousy over one lousy kiss.

And I hate myself for it.

There's a knock at the door and I sit bolt upright in bed. I freeze, wondering if I'm hearing things, the silence in the room enveloping me once more. Then, I hear the knock again. I whip the covers off, and pad in my bare feet over to the door. I crack it open and peer out into the dimly lit hallway. My heart skips a beat when I see who it is.

Sebastian.

He's wearing a T-shirt and jeans and he's holding a bottle with a couple of wine glasses upside down by the stems. "Do you feel like a chat over a glass of red, Brady Bunch?" he asks in a hushed voice.

For a drama queen-infused moment worthy of *The Real Housewives*, I contemplate slamming the door in his face, maybe even grabbing the bottle of wine from him first.

But then I remember I'm a sane, rational person and not some Botoxed diva caricature. So instead I lock my jaw and ask, "Why?"

"I want to talk to you."

I glance at the bottle of wine and glasses in his hands. "Or seduce the next one in line?"

"Emma, please."

I study him for a moment before I let out a sigh. Despite the fact that part of me would like to slam the door in his face—the part of me that forgets this is a reality TV show and he's "dating" a bunch of girls at the same time—another part of me is curious to know what he's got to say.

I glance back at Kennedy. She's still blissfully unaware of our visitor as she breathes evenly in her bed. "Give me one sec."

"Thank you," he replies, and I'm sure I catch a note of relief in his voice, but I might be imagining it. This show is messing with my mind.

I pad across the floor and locate a pair of sneakers at the bottom of the closet. I slip them on, grab a sweatshirt—because this is England—and step out into the hallway.

"Come with me."

"Where are we going?" I ask as he leads me down the darkened hall.

He puts his finger to his lips, and I clamp my mouth shut as he leads me down the stairs and down a long hallway to a room I've not been to before. He opens the door for me and I walk inside. Moonlight floods through large window panes, lending the place an eerie atmosphere.

He closes the door and flicks a light switch, instantly flooding it with a warm glow. I look around at the walls, lined with old, leather-bound books nestled in book cases reaching high up toward the ceiling. There's a large white stone fireplace with a portrait of a beautiful, but somehow sad looking woman hanging above it, and a group of comfortable chairs scattered around the room on top of an oversized Turkish rug. Book lovers everywhere would fall head over heels in love with this room.

"This is the library," Sebastian announces unnecessarily.

"I kinda got that already, what with the gazillion books in here and all."

He places the bottle of wine and glasses on a low table in front of the fireplace and squares me with his gaze. "I thought you could tell me why you ignored me all evening."

I nod at the bottle of wine. "Are you planning on taking that to someone's room after we're done here?" I know I'm completely ignoring his question.

He steps closer to me. "Please, Emma. Tell me how I've offended you."

I cross my arms. "I'm not offended." My words are at total odds with my body language.

"If it's what I think it is, you need to know that *she* kissed *me*."

"Sure. And I dug Jimmy Hoffa up in my mom's back-yard while I was planting petunias last week."

"I thought you lived in a flat."

I roll my eyes. "It's called an apartment, Seb, and I was being snarky."

"So it *is* Camille."

I give a short, sharp nod. There's no point in pretending otherwise, despite the fact I know I'm coming off like a jealous girlfriend. Which I'm not. Well, not the girlfriend part, anyway.

"Emma, Camille kissed me."

"You kissed her back."

"I had the cameras on me."

"So?"

"So, if I'd rebuffed her, it would look bad."

I scoff. "That's ridiculous."

His eyes are soft. "It's not ridiculous. This is a dating show, in case that fact skipped you by. I'm meant to be trying to find the woman I want to marry, and that means kissing some frogs."

I picture Camille as a frog. I like the image.

"Look, Seb. Who you kiss is your business. You're the star of the show, and I'm here to promote my label. We are two people going about our business." I can't resist to add, "Only, my business doesn't involve sticking my tongue down anyone's throat."

He raises his eyebrows at me.

"End of story," I add with authority.

He moves so close to me we're almost touching. "Is it?" he asks gently, and I swallow, electricity sparking through my body.

"Yes," I reply, although it comes out a little more breathless than I expect.

Why does he have to stand so close, smelling the way he does, with that impossibly sexy voice of his? It's making it hard ... to ... concentrate ...

"I made you jealous. I'm sorry, Emma. I never intended to do that."

"I'm not jealous," I protest feebly, because it's obvious to anyone with half a brain that I am.

He places his hand on my arm and it sends a shock of electricity straight up it. "I was in an impossible situation. Camille is very persistent. It seemed letting it happen could diffuse her somewhat. I didn't want to kiss her. I wanted to kiss someone else entirely. In fact, I've been thinking about it for some time now."

I nod, because with him this close to me, telling me what I think he's telling me, it's all I can trust myself to do.

He pushes a strand of hair away from my face, his fingers brushing against my skin. "I like your hair down like this."

With my heart thrashing around in my chest, I try to make light. "Not a fan of the ringlets?"

"I think you look beautiful in anything."

I gaze back at him and the little voice in the back of my head telling me it will never work between us grows quiet. All that's left is him, here, right now, his eyes on mine, his hand gently cupping my head.

And then it happens. I don't try to stop it. I want it to happen, despite our differences, despite Camille, despite how I know this will end.

Despite all of it.

His eyes intense, he lifts my chin, and brushes his lips tantalizingly against mine. It's gentle and incredible and makes me feel like the air has been sucked from my lungs.

He pulls back enough to look me in the eyes. "You're the one I want to kiss, in case you were wondering," he murmurs, his deep voice doing things to my insides.

"I kinda got that," I reply.

"Good." He kisses me once more.

"Mmm," is the sum total of my response. Well, my

verbal response, anyway, because before you can say "Camille who?" we're kissing some more. Only this time, there's no gentle lip brushing. No siree. It's a full on, no holds barred, we want to devour one another kind of kiss. The kind of kiss you feel from the top of your head to the tips of your toes.

My head spins, my knees go weak, and everything, *everything* melts into nothingness around us.

After we come up for air from frankly the most heart-stopping kiss of my life, his smile spreads from ear to ear, the skin around his eyes crinkling. "You have no idea how long I've wanted to do that."

"Really?" I ask as I catch my breath. "Since when?"

He slips his hand into mine. "I could say it was from the moment I laid eyes on you, but you were on the ground, swearing like a fishwife, with a dress attached to your hair in that particular moment."

"Not my best moment."

"No, but I could tell you were feisty, and it was hard not to be attracted to that. Then, you asked me to send you home during that first conversation in my room. It was that moment when I wondered what it would be like to kiss this woman who didn't seem to care what I thought of her."

"So I was a challenge?" I tease.

He laughs as he toys with my hair, sending shivers down my spine. "You weren't some sycophant who would do anything to be with Mr. Darcy, no matter who he was."

"You got that right. But I was convinced you hated me."

"I was convinced you hated *me*," he counters.

"I did. But I also secretly thought you were totally hot."

He grins at me. "That makes the hate so much better."

I reach up and kiss him again. Mainly because I can, but

also because kissing Sebastian is my new favorite thing to do.

"Is that wine for us," I ask without a drop of subtlety, "or were you actually on your way to Camille's room when you decided to bring me here?"

His laugh is low as he shakes his head and reaches for the wine and glasses. "Shall we sit?" He gestures at the couch by the fireplace, and we sit down next to one another, our thighs touching.

"I thought we could get to know each other better over a glass of Châteauneuf-du-Pape."

I giggle and it ends in a snort. "All I got out of that was fancy French wine from some château."

He removes the cork with a corkscrew he produces from his pocket, and pours us a couple of glasses. "It's from a beautiful region in the Rhône, near Avignon. But that's not why I like it. It's a superb red." He hands me a glass. "My father was very fond of it, as was his father. I imagine you could say it's in the Huntington-Ross blood."

"I think Budweiser's in the Brady blood," I reply with a self-deprecating chortle. "Or maybe moonshine, back in the day."

"That sounds like a story."

"Believe me, it's not. We Bradys are regular folk. Nothing special."

"I would have to beg to differ." He lifts his glass. "To the intriguing Miss Brady."

"Dude, I might not be all classy like you, but I do know I can't drink to myself."

"In that case, here's to Mrs. Watson. Long may she wear that deeply attractive handkerchief on her head."

I let out a laugh as warmth spreads through me. "I'm sure it's a shower cap."

"To Mrs. Watson's shower cap, then."

I clink my glass against his. "I would never have guessed you'd have a good sense of humor, Mr. Darcy."

"I have hidden talents, don't you know," he replies.

"I've just been finding out about some of those."

He pulls me in for another head-spinning kiss.

I take a sip of my wine. "Holy crap, that's good," I say before I remember that I'm sitting on a couch that's probably older than my great grandmother, in a room that was "extensively renovated by the late Victorians," with an aristocrat at my side. A hot one, but an aristocrat all the same.

He grins at me. "I'm glad you like it."

I take another sip. "It's even better than Bud," I declare with a laugh.

"High praise indeed."

Our gazes lock and we grin at one another. Can anything beat this moment? The moment when you've both admitted to having feelings for one another after not knowing if the other felt the same? The moment when you realize the object of your desire wants you back?

"I didn't expect you, Sebastian Huntington-Ross," I say. "I thought you were pompous and self-interested, and only came on this show to stroke your already massive ego. Either that or you were a total nut job, expecting to find love on reality TV. But you're not like that at all."

"I'm not pompous, self-interested, or deluded? Emma, you are so good at flirting. You should write a book."

"I do try to make y'all feel special."

He laughs. "You've made me feel a lot of things since you came on the show, Brady."

"Angry, annoyed, unvalued?" I offer.

"Don't forget frustrated and irritated."

I spread my hands out to my sides. "My work here is done."

He takes one of my hands in his. His tone is more serious when he says, "I hope not. In fact, I hope you might agree to stay. And not just for your label's sake."

My breath catches in my throat. "You want me to stay? Here, at Martinston?"

He bites his lip, his eyes glowing warm gold. "I can ask that you be allowed to wear your label on camera again, of course, but, Emma, I want you to stay for more than that. I want you to stay for me."

"I—" I break off. I look down at my hand in his. "Seb, I didn't come here to look for someone."

"I know," he replies softly.

I lift my eyes to his. I open my mouth to speak, but I can't find the words. I cannot deny I've got feelings for him, but I also know that this could never work. Different worlds, different lives, not to mention the fact we're in this weird land of reality TV that distorts everything.

"Before you answer, I need you to know I feel something for you. Something I don't feel for anyone else. Something I didn't expect in a million years to feel on this show. You came along and changed all that." As he looks at me, there's a vulnerability in his eyes I've not seen before.

"But you came on this show to find love. You told me that on the first night."

He takes another sip of his wine and stares at the empty fireplace. After what begins to grow into an uncomfortable silence between us, he tilts his head to face me once more. "I agreed to do the show because Martinston is under threat. The Huntington-Rosses may have a long line of notable aristocrats, but what we don't have so much of these days is money." There's a note of anger in his voice.

"You can't tell me you're broke. Your house is freaking huge."

"We're not broke. But a place like this takes a lot of upkeep, which takes money. My family and I live here together. Although Zara and I both work, it's not enough for us to support Mother and Granny as well as pay all the household bills."

"Oh."

"When Johnathan learnt about the fact the production company was looking for a Mr. Darcy, he suggested I apply as a way to make some fast cash."

"I guess it beats a bank robbery," I say to lighten the mood. "What would have happened if you hadn't done the show?"

His jaw locks, his features hardening. "I would have gone down in history as the son to lose the family estate."

I squeeze his hand. "Seb, I had no idea."

"Of course you didn't. I'm meant to be here to find love, not save my family home." He looks up at me and I can see the pain behind his eyes.

"Why now? What's happened?"

"It turns out I didn't know my father very well at all. When he died, we discovered he'd racked up debts through gambling. I always knew he enjoyed going to the races. He loved horses. But I what none of us realized was quite how much he 'invested' in them. He'd emptied the family coffers, if you will."

I can't imagine even *having* family "coffers," let alone emptying them through gambling.

"I'm really sorry to hear that, Seb. It's a lot for you to have to deal with."

He gives a tight nod. "I'm trusting you to keep this information to yourself."

"Of course. I won't tell a soul."

He takes my glass and places both his and mine on the table. "Thank you."

"That must be so hard," I say. "I can't relate to it, because I grew up in a total dump I was happy to see the back of. But this place is so special. I can see why you love it so much."

He leans in and kisses me gently on the lips. "Perhaps now you can see why you were such a revelation to me. We both came here for reasons other than love. We're not so very different, you and I."

"I guess we're not." Happiness bubbles up inside me as I lean in to kiss him once more. My fears about us being different melt away at his touch, and I finally allow myself to fully admit to my feelings for him.

Neither of us went into this thing looking for the other. But somehow we found each other, and suddenly the prospect of being here to the end, knowing Sebastian and I can be together, has me grinning from ear to ear.

Chapter Twenty Two

"**B**owls!" Mrs. Watson's beaming smile makes her look like she's just told us we've all won the lottery, rather than we've got to play a game where we roll heavy black balls across a lawn to try to get them as close to a smaller ball as we can.

I mean, really. What is the point?

"The ladies and gentlemen of the Regency period had time on their hands and, consequently, they were fond of many games. Lawn bowls is one such game, and you will be competing with one another to win time with Mr. Darcy. The runner-up will have high tea with him in the parlor, and the winner will be treated to a romantic dinner for two this evening."

Two dates in one day? I almost feel sorry for the guy.

"Awesome. Another game to dent our dignity," I murmur to Kennedy.

"What's left of it," she replies. "And anyway, isn't this usually a game played by old guys on artificial turf?"

I snort and quickly clear my throat when Mrs. Watson glares at me.

"Whatever you do, don't look at the shower cap," Kennedy murmurs.

I look at the shower cap and instantly burst into giggles, which I try to stifle with my hand over my mouth.

Mrs. Watson turns her scary school teacher glare on me. "Are you quite well, Miss Emma?"

I think of terrible things to stop from giggling. "Yup. All good, Mrs. Watson," I reply as all eyes turn to stare at me.

Mrs. Watson tightens her features and raises her eyebrows, telling me exactly what she thinks of my little outburst, and I feel like a naughty tween, messing around when I should have been doing algebra back in Mrs. Tosca's math class.

"Look around you. You're already standing in your teams," Mrs. Watson continues and I glance at Camille to my left.

I roll my eyes at Kennedy. Lucky us. We've got the darling Camille on our team.

"Miss Camille, you're the captain of your team. Miss Shelby, you're the captain of yours, and Miss Reggie, you're the captain of yours. You will decide the bowling order."

Camille turns to us and declares I will go first, followed by her and Kennedy. We agree, because we couldn't care less about bowls, and Camille is kind of scary.

"First team to bowl is Miss Shelby's team," Mrs. Watson announces and Shelby and her teammates collect their black balls from the wooden cases on the table.

"We are going to win," Camille instructs us as we peel away to the nearby chairs to watch.

"Are you especially fond of high tea, Camille?" Kennedy asks facetiously.

She scrunches her brows together. "Of course not. I

don't eat carbs and I definitely don't drink tea." She gives us a look that questions our sanity. "I want that dinner date, not the consolation prize. Now, watch the others and imitate the ones who know what they're doing."

"Camille, I don't think any of us know what we're doing on account of the fact we're not men in our eighties," I reply.

"Actually, I heard that lawn bowls has the highest mortality rate of any sport," Kennedy says. "Although I think that's more to do with the average age of the participants than any real danger."

"Good to know."

"It's all about ball skills," Camille states.

"Riiight?"

"I'm sure you've both got them. That's all this is." She turns to watch as Shelby takes her first roll of the bowl. It misses the jack by about fifty yards and Camille sniggers. "Don't copy that dingbat Shelby."

"I couldn't care less about winning, but I do like the idea of high tea," I say to Kennedy.

"I thought you'd want the dinner with Mr. Darcy. So romantic." She waggles her eyebrows at me and I'm mortified to feel heat creep up my cheeks.

Camille doesn't miss a beat. "As I told you before, Sebastian and I are a perfect fit. Even if you do win, Emma, you having dinner with him won't make any difference to that fact. You and your stretchy pants business and air of desperation."

I think of the time I spent with Sebastian in the library last night, and my cheeks flame. The only desperation I felt then was when he ran his fingers through my hair and I ... never mind. It was hot, and that's all you need to know.

"You just keep telling yourself that, Camille," Kennedy says in my defense.

She ignores the jibe. Instead, she twirls one of her ringlets around her finger, and says, "We vacation in some of the same places, we know some of the same people, we both come from serious money. Can either of you say that?"

"Oh, my gosh, Camille. Have you ever wondered if you're related?" Kennedy asks, wide eyed.

I do my best not to laugh.

"Don't be ludicrous. The only way Sebastian and I are going to be related is through marriage when I win," she replies, looking especially pleased with herself.

"I walked into that one, didn't I?" Kennedy says under her breath to me.

"Kinda did, babe." I nod at the cameras. "And it was all recorded."

"Oh, Shelby!" Camille exclaims in delight as Shelby mis-bowls a ball, this time rolling it into a bush on the other side of the garden. It misses the jack by about the length of Sebastian's house, give or take. "You're meant to try to get the ball as close *to* the jack as you can, not as far away from it." She giggles at her own joke and receives a scowl from Shelby.

The atmosphere changes around us and I look up to see Sebastian walking across the lawn toward us. He's dressed as Mr. Darcy, of course, and when his gaze lands on me, my heart contracts.

"Hello, ladies," he says as he comes to a stop. "Did someone mislay this?" He holds up a ball.

"Oh, that'll be mine," Shelby says bashfully. "I'm not very good at this game."

He holds it out for her and she takes it in her hands as

though it's a rare and wonderful baby bird. "That's a shame. I was hoping to spend some time with you, Shelby."

I know he's playing the game. He's got to at least show willingness with the other contestants. But it stings all the same.

The other members of Shelby's team bowl their balls and then it's Reggie's team's turn. Reggie is terrible but good humored about it as always, and then Mrs. Watson announces, "The next team is Miss Camille's team, Mr. Darcy. We have Miss Camille, Miss Kennedy, and Miss Emma." She points at each of us.

He smiles at us and says, "I'm glad I didn't miss this."

Mrs. Watson claps her hands. "Positions please, ladies."

Kennedy, Camille, and I collect a ball each and move over to the mark.

"If this were ten-pin bowling, I'd smash the lot," Kennedy says to me.

I narrow my eyes at her. "You don't look like the bowling type."

"What's the type?"

"You know, protruding belly, terrible shoes. Plus you're not a balding, middle-aged man."

"I grew up with a dad obsessed with it. I couldn't *not* be the type."

"You go first, Emma," Camille instructs.

"But Kennedy's got the 'ball skills,'" I complain.

"Just do it," she snaps. She turns to smile sweetly at Sebastian.

I could argue, but what's the point? I'd may as well get this thing over with. I step onto the little green mat and line up my shot. Without any strategy whatsoever, I aim for the jack and roll the ball in its direction. I watch as it slows and comes to a stop about five feet from it, knocking one of the other team's balls out of place.

"Hey! Not fair," Shelby complains.

"Sorry," I say to her with a conciliatory shrug.

"Don't be sorry, Emma," Camille says. "You're doing great." She hands me another bowl and I almost fall over at the compliment.

"I've got to go again?" I ask.

"Haven't you been watching? Each player gets four balls to bowl."

I let out a puff of air. "Okay."

I bowl the next ball and it ends up crashing into a garden seat way off course, and the next ball barely makes it half way down the green.

"Would you like some help, Emma?" Sebastian asks.

"Sure," I reply breathlessly as he collects a ball and moves over to me.

"I think it might be your technique."

"Do you know much about bowls?" I ask him under my breath.

"Next to nothing," he replies, and I snort with laughter. He passes me the ball and moves to stand behind me. "Line up the jack."

I hold the ball up in front of me as though I'm going to bowl a ball down an alley at ten pins.

He puts his hand on my arm and I can feel his firm body pressed up against mine. It feels amazing, and I find myself wishing we were alone in the library away from the glare of the cameras and the other contestants. "Now, pull it back like this, and then direct it at the jack."

I release the ball and, with his body still pressed against mine, we both watch its progress. It knocks my other ball out of contention, sitting pretty only a couple of feet from its target.

"You're a professional, Miss Emma," he says and I turn and smile up at him, my heart going all kinds of crazy.

"My turn next," Camille announces.

With regret, I pull back from Sebastian and return to Kennedy on the edge of the green.

"Will you show me how to do it, too, Mr. Darcy?" Camille asks, looking up through her lashes at him.

"Of course, Camille."

"You'll need to do exactly what you did with Emma. I'm afraid I'm not very good at bowls."

I roll my eyes at Kennedy. Camille sure knows how to play the damsel in distress card.

As Sebastian takes Camille's ball and positions himself behind her as he had with me, a burning sensation takes hold of my chest. Although my rational brain tells me he's playing the game for the cameras, it's hard to watch.

And Camille milks it for all it's worth. She asks for his help with every ball, and I'm forced to watch the whole thing unfold, pretending I'm fine with it all.

"Oh, Mr. Darcy. With your help, I think I might win today," she simpers when her last ball has been bowled. Praise the Lord.

Kennedy has her go next, and she makes a point of not asking for Sebastian's help, even though she could quite obviously use it. She manages to knock one of my balls out of contention, but the rest of them go awry.

And then it's time for Mrs. Watson to assess who has won.

She calls for quiet. "Congratulations, Camille. You have won the romantic dinner for two with Mr. Darcy tonight."

Camille smirks and thanks everyone as though she's just won an Oscar and not some game played by the elderly.

"The runner up is Phoebe, who will enjoy some high tea with Mr. Darcy this afternoon."

Phoebe smiles her beautiful smile at everyone.

"Well done, you two," Sebastian says. "I look forward to seeing you later." His eyes flick to mine briefly, and I hope he means me.

"Everyone else has a free afternoon," Mrs. Watson says.

"Poor Sebastian, having to have dinner with *her*," Kennedy says once we're back in our room and our mics are firmly off. "She'll probably be all over him again, telling him how well they're matched."

"I say bring it on," I reply.

"Oooh, someone's feeling confident."

"If I tell you something, will you promise not to say anything to anyone? And I mean anyone."

"This sounds juicy."

"Promise?"

"I promise." She leans closer to me and asks, "What is it?"

"I met up with Sebastian last night."

"You what?" she shrieks and I shush her straight away. We might be alone in our room away from the cameras, but you can't be too careful on a reality TV show. I know. I've watched them.

"He came to our room and I snuck out with him," I say.

"Oh, my gosh. Are you serious? I slept through the whole thing?"

"You did."

"So? How was it?"

"It was wonderful. He's wonderful."

She beams at me. "Tell me everything."

"I may leave some things out," I lead.

She laughs. "Move over Camille. Emma has already won the prize. And what a prize he is."

I grin at her, happiness spreading across my chest. Camille may have won today, but I've won what really matters here. I've won Sebastian's heart. And I could not be happier.

Chapter Twenty-Three

I t's one thing to be questioned on camera about a guy you're pretending to like. It's quite another to actually like him, have spent a pretty amazing clandestine visit with the guy, and now have to behave as though none of it has happened. Not to mention the fact that he's also dating a bunch of other women while everything is being filmed.

"Complicated" doesn't even begin to describe my life right now.

"Tell me how things are going with Sebastian," Cindy says, the bright lights trained on me.

"Oh, things with Sebastian are great."

"You opened up to Kennedy."

Of course she's seen the footage. I knew the cameras were on us, but I pushed them from my mind as we spoke. Now, I wish I hadn't.

"I did. I told Kennedy I like Sebastian and that he's not what I'd first thought. He's kind and fun and cares about things." I can't stop the smile from creeping across my face. "Whoever ends up with him will be one lucky gal."

"Do you want that to be you?"

I pause. Of course I want it to be me, but I don't want to be *that* girl, the one who admits to falling for the guy on camera only to get publicly rejected. But, I guess that ship has already sailed, thanks to my chat with Kennedy.

"I do really like him, but it's still early in the game. Who knows what will happen in the coming weeks? We're only just getting to know each other right now, plus he's dating a bunch of other girls, I hear."

"Speaking of which, tell me what you think of Camille," Cindy asks.

"Camille's great," I reply with a wide smile.

"What do you like about her? And remember to start with 'What I like about Camille is.'"

"What I like about Camille is—" I rack my brain for some positive things about her. I don't come up with much, but I know I need to at least appear to be authentic. Well, as authentic as anyone is in these confessional style producer interviews. The last thing I want to be cast as is the show's bitch. "—her hair. She's got really pretty hair. Nice highlights. And the cut's good, too. Yup, that's what I like about Camille: her hair."

Cindy raises her eyebrows and I know she wants more than "hair."

"I also like the way Camille's shared her story with us all."

"Her story?"

"You know, how she lives on Manhattan's Upper East Side, how she went to a prestigious school, and how her family has a bunch of places named after them. Basically how she's from *Gossip Girl*."

"Would you say she's impressive?"

She's a pain in the butt, that's what she is.

"Oh, yes. Camille is very impressive."

I know I sound like a robot reading from a script, but I'm working so hard at not pulling a face or laughing or scoffing that something's got to give. In my case, it's a complete lack of natural expression in my voice.

"What do you think she and Sebastian are doing on their date right now?"

"Having a great time, I bet."

"Camille and Sebastian shared a passionate kiss on the terrace. Do you think they might be kissing? Or, maybe, something more?"

I shift in my seat as a weird feeling rises. Why the heck is she asking me that?

"I dunno," I reply inarticulately.

"They've got use of a hot tub tonight."

"That's not very Regency," I scoff before I can stop myself. "I mean, Mr. Darcy in a jacuzzi? That's all kinds of wrong."

"Does the idea upset you, Emma?"

"No," I reply sounding thoroughly upset. Because come on! I want to think about Sebastian in a hot tub with another girl about as much as I want Linda the Torturer to pluck every last hair from my eyebrows.

"I don't know about you, but I would be really upset if a guy I had feelings for was sitting in a hot tub with a gorgeous girl right now, and I had no idea what they were up to. What with them in nothing but their swimwear."

My heart begins to thud and I've got to work super hard at not showing any jealousy. It is one tall order. "It's fine. Totally fine," I lie.

"That's good to hear, Emma, because we believe they have something special. I know you told Kennedy you have feelings for him, but Camille is definitely the front runner right now."

"Good for her." My smile probably makes me look like The Joker, it's so painted on.

"Here. You look a little shaky. You might want to have some of this." She passes me a shot glass of clear liquid.

I offer her a wry smile. "Tequila, huh? Are you trying to get me drunk?"

"I thought you could do with it. You seem a little upset, that's all. We want you to be as comfortable as possible during these interviews."

I eye the tequila. There's no way I'm drinking that. I need to be in control of what I say right now. "Thanks, Cindy, but I'm good."

Cindy doesn't appear to want to give up. "Camille is so great, isn't she?"

I know what I want to say. I want to say that Camille is *not* great, that she is in fact a terrible human being who thinks she's better than the rest of us just because she carries purses that cost more than my monthly rent. I want to say that she'll stop at nothing to win this show, even if she doesn't have any genuine feelings for Sebastian.

I don't say any of these things, despite being sorely tempted to do so.

"You're right. She's great. If Sebastian chooses her I'll be happy for both of them."

Cindy arches an eyebrow. "Are you sure about that?"

She's not going to draw me on this. I've seen what happens when contestants do that, and it ain't pretty. I nod, resolute. "I am sure."

After more questions about Camille, Phoebe, and whether I thought Sebastian may have feelings for half the contestants, I leave the interview on unsteady feet. I feel as though I just dodged a missile, intended to make me break down in a sobbing, hysterical mess.

So, really, just your average day on a reality TV show.

But I don't want to let Cindy and her cameras in. What Sebastian and I have together is too precious for that. I need to keep my wits about me, and definitely not go for the tequila.

* * *

Although I'm expecting the knock on our bedroom door later that night, when it comes, it still makes me jump. This time, though, I'm prepared. I'm wearing my favorite Timothy ensemble of three quarter length leggings and a cute take on a baseball tee that I think makes me look the right level of sporty—not too much, not too litte. My hair is brushed and hangs loose around my shoulders, without a librarian's bun or ringlet in sight, and I've sprayed myself with a cloud of my favorite perfume.

I'm Mr. Darcy ready.

Kennedy is still awake. "Sneaking off with Mr. Darcy? Whatever will Mrs. Watson say?"

"I bet her shower cap would shoot off her head in outrage if she knew."

She giggles. "Maybe her ringlets would curl up and drop off."

I pause at the end of her bed. "You're okay about this, right? I mean, you're 'dating' him, too."

"Honey, he's hot and all, but I know when a ship's sailed. You go get yours."

I beam at her. "If you say so."

"Oh, I say so."

I reach the door and look back at her, propped up in her bed. "See y'all soon."

"Don't do anything I wouldn't do," she replies with a coy grin.

I pull the door open and see Sebastian standing there. Although I know he's been out on a date with Camille, allegedly sitting in a hot tub in not much at all, I hadn't thought about what he would be wearing. He's back in that James Bond tux from the very first time we met, looking every inch the man of any woman's dreams.

"I have a rather good bottle of red awaiting us in the library, if you would care to join me?" he asks in his adorably formal way.

My limbs feel light as a smile spreads across my face. "I *would* care to join you. Thank you." I glance quickly back at Kennedy, who gives me the thumbs up before I close the door behind me.

We scoot down the stairs and long hallway on silent feet, reaching the sanctuary of the library, where Sebastian closes the door behind us and instantly pulls me into him for a kiss.

"I have so missed you," he breathes into my hair. "I've missed this."

"Even though you were in a hot tub with Camille?"

"I beg your pardon? We had dinner and talked. There was no hot tub. They're not very Regency, you know."

Cindy, you sly devil, trying to trick me into saying things I'll regret.

"That's what I thought." I kiss him hard on the lips. It's such a firm, passionate kiss that it leaves me dizzy when we finally pull back.

"All you need to know is that the whole time I was with Camille, I wanted to be here with you."

"That makes two of us." I take him by the hand and lead him over to the couch where we sat last night.

He pours us a glass of wine each, and we clink glasses. "Châteauneuf-du-Pape?" I ask.

"She's learning."

"I read the label."

"Never give away your secrets, Brady."

"Well, right now *you're* my secret."

His smile is flirty and oh-so cute. "I think I like being your secret."

I gaze back at him with what I know is a totally goofy grin. Because why not? This thing between us has come out of nowhere and it feels amazing. *He's* amazing. "I like being your secret, too," I murmur.

He pulls me in for another kiss, and it's so perfectly wonderful it makes my head spin. He wraps his arm around my shoulder and I nestle into him.

"I picked the bottle from our cellar before I went out this evening."

"You have a cellar? What am I saying, you live in a house the size of a stadium. Of course you have a cellar."

"I'll take you there, if you like."

"How big is it?"

"In square feet or in the number of bottles?"

"You know both?"

He gives a self-deprecating smile. "Actually, I don't know either, but I thought it sounded good to say that."

"You're funny, did you know that? I never would have thought it." I take his hand in mine and toy with his fingers.

"Why not?"

"Well, when I first met you—"

"When you fell onto your bottom," he interrupts.

I snort with laughter. "Bottom? You're hilarious."

"Should I say arse?"

"You do you. 'Bottom' is fine. It's cute, that's all."

226

"My goal is to be cute, of course, as is that of any thirty-one-year-old man."

"Huh, you're four years older than me."

"And so much wiser."

I nudge him on the arm. "Y'all tell yourself that."

"What did you think of me when we first met?"

"I didn't think we'd have anything in common whatsoever. You were stiff and formal and kind of mean."

"Mean?"

"I had to talk you into letting me get the do-over, remember?"

"To be fair, I was told to greet each contestant as they presented themselves. I thought perhaps you were on the quirky side and wanted to make an entrance."

"By falling out of a limo?"

His shoulders shake as he laughs quietly to himself. "It was rather funny."

"It wouldn't have done anything to help Timothy."

"Tell me about your label."

"We're partners, Penny and me. She does all the creative stuff, and I do the business side of things."

"Why is it called Timothy?"

"Both of our dads are called Timothy. My dad is ... *was* a good man. I want to make a success of Timothy to honor him."

Sebastian gives me a squeeze. "Emma, I didn't know. I'm so sorry. When did he pass away?"

I feel a stab of sorrow and cast my eyes down. "It will be four years in September. He had cancer. Mom had been trying to get him to go to the doctor for a year for his cough before he finally agreed to go. By the time he was diagnosed, it had already taken hold."

"Lung cancer?"

I nod. "Asbestosis. He was a builder and got exposed years before. He was fifty-six when he died."

"Young."

"Yup."

"You were close."

I point my thumb at myself. "The original Daddy's Girl, right here."

"Tell me all about him."

I lean back against his chest, feeling his warmth emanating through me. "He was a great dad. He told me he loved me every single day of my life. Which of course I found incredibly embarrassing as a teenager, but I never doubted his love for me. He was firm but fair when I was growing up. Smart as a tack, too. I could never get anything past him, which was incredibly frustrating. Everyone said I was just like him, right down to the way neither of us would let something go until it was either dead or done."

"Not literally, I hope? I have an image of some poor creature meeting its grizzly end."

"More if we made our minds up on something, we wouldn't let anything get in our way."

"Not even a Jane Austen dress."

I tilt my head back to look at him. "You got it. Things got hard when he lost his job. He worked for this big shot who developed commercial buildings around Texas. Daddy worked for him for years, then one day, out of the blue, he was told not to come in. He was fired. Just like that." Heat rises in my cheeks as the memory smarts.

"Did he find another job easily?"

I shake my head. "With more time on his hands, Mom made him go to the doctor. He was diagnosed and couldn't work. We thought things had been tough before then, but they got a whole lot worse."

"Financially?"

"Yup. I was rooming with Penny but decided to move back home to help out. I contributed some of my salary, of course, as well as helped Mom with the house and looking after Dad. She was so grateful. She had someone else to help carry the load, you know?"

"I do," he says quietly.

I push myself up to look at him. "Did your dad have cancer, too?"

"No. Heart attack. It's the Huntington-Ross way. My father died from one, his father, and his father before him. You should watch out if I turn red and begin to clutch my chest."

I bat him gently on the arm. "Don't joke about things like that."

"We've all got to go from something, don't we?"

"I guess, but I'm only just getting to know you. I can't have your heart giving way out of the blue."

He plants a kiss on my forehead. "I've got a good forty years before then."

"What was your dad like?"

He casts his eyes down. "He wasn't like your father in the least. He was strict and had his ideas of what his only son should be. He was older and more old fashioned, I suppose. Not one to say 'I love you.'"

"Ever?"

He shakes his head, his mouth tight. "I never heard him say it, not once."

My heart hurts for him. "How awful."

"It was just the way he was. I knew he loved me. He was my father. He shook my hand from the age of seven rather than hug me, sent me away to boarding school at eight, and told me what line of work to get into. But he did one thing for me that no one else could: he left me all this."

"What do you think he would say if he knew you were playing Mr. Darcy on a reality TV show?"

He lets out a sudden laugh. "There's no doubt that he would be utterly appalled."

"But what if he knew you had to do it to save Martinston? He'd understand that, right?"

Sebastian's jaw tightens and his features harden. "Perhaps," is all he says.

I decide it's best to change the subject. "What about your mom? I bet she's great. You had to have gotten it from somewhere."

"My mother is an exceptional woman. She's involved in many charities, and started a foundation in my father's name to help young artists develop their talent."

"And?" I lead.

He shakes his head, his smile firmly in place. "And she's a lot more loving and understanding than my father ever was. We're close."

"Good." A thought occurs to me. "Why isn't she the one trying to save Martinston? I mean, this is the twenty-first century, not the Dark Ages. Women can be responsible for their property, you know."

"I suppose you could say I'm helping her to carry the load," her replies, using my own words. "I feel an obligation to my family, Emma. Being Mr. Darcy seemed like a relatively easy way to do it."

"I like that you're trying to look after your family by saving their home."

"You'd do the same in my position, I'm sure."

I think of my little apartment, with its tiny kitchen and

cheap kit-set furniture. It's not much, but it's mine, and I would hate to lose it. "You're right. I would do the same."

"How's the wine?"

I collect my glass from the table and take a fresh sip. "It's bold and sassy and I'm getting undertones of spice and," I rack my brain for something wine snobs would say, but all I come up with is, "grapes. Lots of grapes."

"Wine with undertones of grapes?" he asks as he tempts me with more kisses to make me swoon. "Who'd have thought."

As I kiss him back, I forget all about undertones of grapes or anything else. This. This is what I want. To be alone here with Sebastian, sharing our stories, learning about one another.

I know I'm falling for him, and this is exactly where I want to be.

Chapter Twenty-Four

I close the door to my bedroom as quietly as a mouse. Not that mice are all that quiet, in my opinion. Who makes these sayings up, anyway?

With my sneakers in my hand, I tiptoe across the hardwood floor, aiming for the bed, where I pull off my clothes and slip under the covers.

"Fun night?" Kennedy says, making me almost leap out of my skin.

I put my hand over my chest and feel my heart pounding. "Don't do that to me."

"Sorry."

"Did I wake you?"

"I've been lying here thinking about things half the night." She sits up and flicks on her bedside lamp and, instantly, the room fills with a warm, golden glow.

I sit at the bottom of her bed. "Something on your mind, babe?"

"Oh, you know: life, the universe, and everything. Oh, and the fact my bestie on this show is sneaking off to have a torrid affair with the guy I'm meant to be competing against her for. So clearly, I'm not going to be the one walking down the aisle at the end of the show."

My tummy does a flip and I begin to feel all giddy. Giddy and more than a little freaked out. I mean, walking down the aisle? It all feels so ... final.

Final, but also, kind of incredible.

"So, pretty general things?" I ask with a smirk. "And it's not a torrid affair. It's—" I pause as I try to land on the word to sum up what Sebastian and I have together. Whatever it is, wherever it's going to go, I know one thing for sure: it feels wonderful.

She pushes herself up on her elbows and scrutinizes my face. "Oh, Miss Emma, I do believe you are blushing."

"No, I'm not," I protest, doing precisely that.

"Girl, you've been out with the guy half the night. I think you're fully entitled to blush." She sits more upright in bed. "So? How was he?"

"It's not like that," I reply defensively.

The look on her face tells me she's not buying it in the least. "Mmm-hmm?"

"Sure, there was some of that, but mainly we talked."

"You spent all this time off camera with the totally hot guy everyone is falling over themselves to be with, and you 'mainly talked?'" She uses air quotes. "Tell me at least you kissed the guy."

I try to suppress the smile busting out across my face. "I did."

"And? What's he like? I bet he's good at it. He looks like he'd be good at it."

"Heart-stopping, knee-melting, star-seeing good."

She returns my smile. "That's more like it. Oh, Em. You so have got this show in the bag. Camille is going to want to scratch your eyes out with her French manicured nails."

I let out a light laugh. "That doesn't matter. I don't care about the show or Camille. I only care about him."

She shakes her head at me. "You've got it bad, girl."

"It's kind of scary," I admit, "but also kind of amazing. We've got a lot more in common than I ever thought. I remember when we met, I thought he was the biggest douchebag to walk the face of the Earth." I smile at the memory. "Now? Well, let's just say I don't."

"You're Lizzie Bennet."

I crinkle my brow. "So are you in this weird, messed up reality TV world. The Lizzies. Ugh."

"No, I mean you're *really* Lizzie Bennet. Think about it. She hated Mr. Darcy when she met him. Then, once she got to know him, she hated him some more. Same as you."

"Ah, but I had feelings for him while I hated him."

"I bet Lizzie did, too. Jane Austen just didn't put it out there in black and white, like, 'Lizzie told Jane she had the hots for Darcy, even though she thought he was a total dick.'"

I giggle. "I can totally imagine Jane Austen writing that exact line."

"And now, just like Lizzie, you've realized the error of your ways and have fallen in love with Mr. Darcy. Only, there was no Mr. Wickham running off with Lydia to mess it all up."

Things flutter around inside me. Have I fallen in love with Sebastian?

If I haven't, I'm at serious risk of doing so.

"How does he feel about you?"

"You'll have to ask him that," I reply evasively.

"Yeah, like I'd get a straight answer out of him. Unlike you, I don't sneak off to see him off-camera. Any time I'm near him there are a bunch of cameras nearby, poking their nose into everything." She rolls her eyes and grins at me. "When you win this thing and live happily ever after in this place, can I come visit you and your army of impossibly beautiful children?"

My laugh is shot with nerves and excitement. "Let's take it day by day, okay?"

"Babe, you don't have the luxury of that. Even if he's fallen madly in love with you, he can't spend every waking hour with you. He's got to play the game for the cameras, make it at least look like we've got a fighting chance."

My smile threatens to take over my entire face.

She reaches over and pulls me in for a hug. "I am so happy for you, Em. Finding love on reality TV is as rare as a unicorn. But you've gone and done it."

I beam at her, happiness spreading from the top of my head to the tips of my toes. "I have, haven't I?"

* * *

The following morning, due to lack of sleep, the news that the day's activity is learning how to dance Regency style is not exactly music to our exhausted ears.

It turns out Regency dances are ridiculously complicated and surprisingly physical for something that looks so sedate. It's not helped by the fact Kennedy and I spend half the time giggling in the corner rather than paying close attention. How the ladies and gentlemen of the Regency era managed to look poised and elegant and not like they'd run ten miles uphill is a mystery to me.

After at least two hours of practice we get to take a much-needed break in the afternoon. No costumes, no dancing, no cameras. Bliss. After lazing around, talking to

Phoebe and Kennedy, I decide it's time I stretched my legs before they turn completely to Jell-O.

I stand up and stretch, my back clicking as I reach for the ceiling. "I'm going for a walk. Anyone want to come with me?"

"No, thanks," Phoebe replies. "I'm going to have a lie down before the dancing tonight. That session really took it out of me."

"Not me," Kennedy says. "My poor feet are aching from having to wear those stupid ballet slippers the whole time. No arch support."

"Suit yourselves." I turn to leave, only to bump into a smug, smirking Camille.

Yippee.

"Emma." She casts her eyes over me. "How nice to see you in your sweats again. Tell me, do you ever wear anything else? Or is this your ... 'look?'" She scrunches up her nose in distaste so I'm in no fear of missing how little she thinks of my choice of attire.

I take in her outfit of a floral print dress, cinched in at the waist, and a pair of heels. Her hair is held back with an Alice band, and her makeup is absolutely perfect. It's a look anyone from *Gossip Girl* would be happy to sport, and it's the way she dresses, even when it's just us girls, chilling out away from the cameras. Mom might think she's got standards, I think she's got a serious case of the "I'm better than everyone else-es."

Instead of rising to her bait, I reply, "I guess it is my look, Camille. My label is very comfortable."

"Elasticated waistbands *are* very comfortable, I'm told. I wouldn't know. I wouldn't be found dead in any clothes with one."

That could be arranged...

"It's not elasticated. It's Lycra."

She waves her hand in the air. "Potato, po-*tah*-to." She flashes me a condescending look worthy of Lady Catherine de Bourgh herself, Lizzie Bennet's arch rival. "Did you enjoy the dance practice this morning?" she asks, and I go to reply when she cuts me off with, "Because I wondered whether dancing is really your thing." She cocks her head to the side as though she's genuinely wondering, rather than just messing with me in her usual, evil way.

God, she's annoying.

"I'm sure Sebastian will take pity on you and ask you to dance tonight, anyway. I mean, he's very kind and thoughtful to all of the contestants. Even the ones he's not interested in."

"You mean even me?" I say, my tone dripping with enough sarcasm to fill a bucket. Not that I was bad at the dancing portion or anything. Well, no more so than anyone else. It was complicated and hard to keep track of all the steps. And there were a lot of steps.

"That's the attitude, Emma," she replies with a fake smile.

I've had enough. "See y'all later." I turn and walk toward the door leading out onto the terrace.

"You're not going to win, Emma," she says with a harsh edge to her voice.

I stop and turn. "Maybe. Maybe not," I reply with a shrug. I'm working hard not to get my hackles up right now.

"I would say *not*." Her pretty features are hard. She steps closer to me. "You see, Sebastian and I are right for one another. We're a fit. We're the same. He understands me and I understand him." She trails her eyes over me once more. "You would never fit into a life like his. You'd have no clue how to handle it, you and your comfy pants and ponytails."

What's wrong with ponytails?

Her steel blue eyes are trained on me, and I half expect to turn to dust with their evil force. "He's mine, Emma. Get used to it."

"Don't tell me you've gone all Shelby on me now, Camille. I'm not sure her destiny approach worked out quite how she imagined it would."

"Don't be ridiculous," she scoffs. "I'm trying to warn you, as a friend, that you may as well give up. You can't win."

As a friend? Sure she is.

I glare back at her for a moment because two can play this game, and screw her. So what if Sebastian and I lead different lives? Opposites attract. Doesn't she know that?

I ignore the tiny voice at the back of my head telling me she's right. Because, dammit, she's not.

"Whatever, Camille."

She smiles sweetly at me. "I'm glad you agree, Emma. Enjoy your flight home."

Chapter Twenty Five

I
t takes all my strength not to pull the spangly, expensive-looking Alice band from Camille's hair and hurl it across the room. Although I bet if I did that, it would only go to prove her point that I'm too low class for Sebastian and she's not.

I turn my back on her and march across the terrace and out onto the wide expanse of grass, bypassing the formal gardens with their fountain and rows of topiary. Instead, I head for the untamed woodlands up a small rise to the west.

What I wouldn't give to tell Camille the truth! To rub her perfect face in my happiness, to let her know in no uncertain terms that she is so, so wrong.

But what good will that do?

Nothing, that's what, and it would probably get me kicked off the show to boot.

I just need to bide my time and bite my lip.

I reach the woodlands and purposefully slow my pace. I take a few deep breaths and look around. It's beautiful here. The trees stretch tall above me, the light filters through from above, and the ground is covered in dried leaves with patches of green. It's English country perfection, what I imagine the country was before it gave way to cities and roads like the rest of the world.

After rambling through for a while, I find a fallen tree. Checking for spiders and other creepy crawlies, I climb up onto it and take in the view of the forest around me. The wild beauty helps me push Camille and her patronizing attitude from my mind, and I let out a deep breath.

"Be careful you don't fall. You don't have a good track record with that."

I look around in surprise to see Sebastian gazing up at me, a smile on his face. He's wearing his off-duty clothes of a T-shirt and pair of shorts, and he looks like he's been working out.

"I've been practicing my balance skills since then, and anyway, no dress headpiece this time. See?" I hold my pony-tail in my hand as proof.

"You are improving," he replies with a glint in his eye.

I climb down from my spot on the tree and land a couple of feet from him.

"You're also a gymnast." He loops his arms around my waist and kisses me, full on the mouth. "So many hidden talents, Brady."

"Oh, you have no idea, Mr. Darcy."

"Sorry, I'm all sweaty."

"Don't be. I like it," I murmur against his mouth.

"That bodes well for me," he says between kisses as he holds me close against him.

"Ahem." Someone clears their throat behind us and we immediately stop what we're doing.

Fear twists inside me. "Uh-oh. We've been busted." With trepidation, I stand on my tippy-toes to peer over Sebastian's shoulder to see a woman I've never laid eyes on before. She's dressed in a pair of shorts and a singlet top, her hands on her hips, and she's staring at us with a look of delight on her pretty face.

"Aren't you meant to be saving that for the cameras?" she asks. Her accent is just like Sebastian's. She's so cute, I bet she has guys falling over themselves to be with her.

Sebastian hooks his arm around my shoulders and turns to face her. "Zara, that's the last thing I would want to do, and you know it."

She grins at us. "You must be Emma, and if you're not, I'm going to have some serious words with Sebastian."

I look in confusion from the woman to Sebastian and back again. "I am Emma," I reply. "Have I missed something?"

Sebastian chuckles. "You weren't meant to meet like this, but as it's happened, Emma, this is my sister, Zara."

"Your *sister?*" I exclaim in surprise.

"Hello there," she says. "It's lovely to finally meet you, despite all the kissing. As a side note, Seb, no sister should ever have to witness that."

I tilt my head and eyeball him. "Seb, huh?"

He has the good grace to look bashful. "I was messing with you. All my friends and family call me Seb."

"Is that so?"

"To be fair, you were very prickly at the time."

"Fair call." I unhook myself from him and go to shake Zara's hand. Instead, she pulls me in for a quick hug and says, "Seb's told me all about you."

He has?

I glance back at him. He's still looking bashful, but in a very manly and sexy way, of course.

"He's told me about you, too," I reply. "Although he

didn't tell me you look like that gorgeous British actress. You know, the one in that Bond movie?"

"Gemma Arterton," Sebastian says.

"That's right. It makes sense Mr. Darcy would have a Bond-girl for a sister. You know, in some parallel universe somewhere."

Zara rolls her eyes as she laughs. "I get that all the time," she says in her posh rounded English vowels, looking and sounding exactly like Gemma Arterton.

"And that's a bad thing?" I ask.

"It's fine," she replies as though I haven't told her she looks like a totally beautiful actress. "We've been out for a run. Seb makes me do it whenever I'm home."

I raise my eyebrows at him. "Does he now?"

"Oh, yes. He says my life in London is far too unhealthy and I need to get some fresh Martinston air in my lungs. Since I've been summoned home for a family get together this afternoon, he's roped me into this."

Sebastian places his hand on Zara's shoulder. "My sister is a single girl about town in London."

"That sounds fun to me."

He raises his brows at me. "You want to be single?"

As I look up into his eyes, my chest expands. "No."

He gazes back at me and replies, "Good."

We share a smile.

"Oh, you two!" Zara exclaims. "First the kissing and now longing gazes? Could you get any cuter? And when I say cuter, I mean vomit-inducing, of course."

Sebastian nudges her on the arm. "Sisters," he says to me.

I shrug. "I wouldn't know about those. I'm an only child."

"Lucky you, not having to put up with a bossy, overbearing older brother who makes you run through forests when all you want to do is catch up on Netflix, drink wine, and eat cake."

"Which is precisely why you need to go for a run, little sister," he responds.

I watch them as they verbally spar with one another like they're pre-pubescent teens in the back of their parents' car. Which, now that I think about it, is probably a Rolls Royce or a Bentley or something. They've got that whole sibling closeness thing going on where they can say anything and they'll still love one another as brother and sister. It's something I never had, and watching them now, I feel like I missed out.

"Oh, Seb, will you give it a rest please? I promise not to party as much with Tabitha."

"She is a very bad influence on you, Zara."

Zara rolls her eyes at me. "Tabitha's been my best friend since we were babies. Seb here can't seem to accept that means something and going to the occasional party or night-club with her in London is perfectly fine."

I put my hands up in the air in the surrender sign. I've got no clue who this Tabitha person is or whether she's a good influence or not. "Don't involve me, you two. Innocent bystander here."

"Speaking of Tabitha, I promised to call her after our run," Zara says. "Emma, it's so nice to meet you. My brother has amazing taste." She pulls me in for another quick hug. "And you?" she says to Sebastian. "I'll see you back home once you've finished kissing Emma's face off."

I let out a giggle that ends in a snort.

"Bye," she says as she runs away.

"You're only winning today's race because I got distract-ed," Sebastian calls after her.

"You keep telling yourself that, brother," she calls back as she disappears behind a clump of bushes.

With Zara now gone, Sebastian and I are left in the woods alone.

"You're going to kiss my face off, are you?" I ask and he laughs.

"It would be rude not to."

I stand on my toes, hook my hands behind his head, and we do just that.

"I hope that was okay, meeting Zara that way? I had wanted to introduce you when we were less, well, sweaty."

"Are you kidding? She's terrific."

He beams at me. "She liked you."

"She did?" Of course I could tell she did, but I adore hearing it from him.

"Definitely."

I can't help but feel like Lizzie Bennet when she met Georgiana Darcy in *Pride and Prejudice*. Lizzie knew that by introducing them, Darcy was showing he was totally into her. If Darcy wanted Lizzie to meet his sister because he had fallen for her, did that mean Sebastian has fallen for me? Of course, things took a turn for the worse after the meeting, but I know they won't for Sebastian and me.

And yes, I know I'm taking this whole *Pride and Prejudice* thing a little far. I blame Kennedy for putting the idea in my head.

But as Sebastian cups my face in his hands and plants a tantalizing kiss on my lips once more, I know nothing can stand in our way. Any doubts I may have had have well and truly disappeared.

Chapter Twenty Six

I t's the evening of the dance and the contestants are buzzing, and not just because we've all been given new clothes to wear. Of course they are still Regency, but they're a step up from the ones we've been wearing since the whole "dress like it's 1813" thing was sprung on us. The new clothes are only half the excitement. We've been told that Sebastian is sending someone home tonight, and Reggie has been taking bets ever since. Apparently, Shelby and Camille are the horses to back, although I know who *I* would prefer to see go home. No prizes for guessing it's not Shelby.

I stand in front of the mirror in Kennedy's and my room. My top is low-cut to show off what cleavage I actually have, with short, girly puff sleeves finished with pale green ribbons. I'm wearing what Mrs. Watson told us is a redingote, which is a long, pale green dress that splays open mid-thigh to reveal—no, not an Angelia Jolie-inspired leg, more's the pity—my ivory dress and petticoats beneath. The mandatory slippers on my feet and long, white gloves above my elbows complete the look.

I feel pretty and weirdly sexy, even if my petticoats do reach the floor. Despite the fact the design means I've still got to wear the world's most uncomfortable bra, I've ditched the baggy bloomers in favor of my regular underwear.

"Breaking the rules feels so naughty, doesn't it?" Kennedy says as she pulls our door open to head downstairs.

"Who knew plain white cotton underpants could be quite so risqué?" I reply with a laugh. "If only Marni were here to enjoy the revolution. She missed her Spanx."

"How can anyone miss Spanx?"

"Bloomers versus Spanx? It's all relative, babe."

She laughs as we make our way down the stairs. We reach the ballroom—yup, Sebastian's house has a ballroom, naturally—as Phoebe and Camille also arrive. I greet Phoebe with warmth, and nod a cool hello at Camille.

Together, we walk inside. They've lit it so it feels like candlelight, because of course it would be too much of a fire risk to have real candles. You can't trust a bunch of contestants on a reality show not to start a fire, apparently. Thanks to Penny and her obsession with all things reality, I've watched a bunch of episodes of *The Real Housewives*, so I've got to agree.

I look up to see the most stunning row of chandeliers hanging from the ceiling, glinting in the soft light. The walls are lined with old oil paintings of people and landscapes in between Roman-looking columns. There's a group of musicians in the corner, dressed up in their Regency clothes, looking just the part.

The overall effect is breathtaking, and I can't help but feel swept up in the occasion, like Lizzie Bennet herself at the ball at Netherfield.

Camille walks one way as we enter so Kennedy and I walk the other.

Reggie sails over to us. She takes a hold of Kennedy's and my hands and tells us we look like princesses, ready for the ball.

"You look beautiful yourself," I gush as I take in her red redingote and turban. Yup, you heard it right: Reggie is wearing a turban. And what's more, it's got a big brooch on it and pink feathers sticking out the top. It's really quite something.

The weird thing is, she looks amazing in it.

"Nice hat, Regg," I say as I reach out to stroke one of the feathers. "Ooh, soft and silky."

She does a little shimmy for us. "I figured if I'm leavin' tonight, I'd may as well go out with a bang, darlin'. Where else could I wear one of these in my regular life?"

"The laundromat?" I offer. "Or maybe Costco?"

"Oh, definitely Costco," she coos.

"Who said you're going home?" Kennedy says. "It could be me. I've had a grand total of one date with him, and I tell you, it was nothing to get excited about."

"That's one more than me, darlin'. I'm here as the eye candy, don't you know?"

"Well, you're doing that just fine," I reply with a grin.

She winks at us. "And getting my Insta followin' up too, with any luck."

I hook my arms around both of their waists. "I don't want either of you to go home. You're the only thing keeping me sane on this show."

"The *only* thing?" Kennedy asks, and heat burns through me at the thought of Sebastian.

"Well, I know one thing for sure, Emma, darlin'. You've

got nothing to be nervous about tonight," Reggie says. "Mr. Darcy wants to keep you."

"Oh, I don't know," I reply. It's weak and completely unconvincing. I know it just as much as they do.

Sebastian isn't sending me home tonight.

"Yeah, you do," Reggie replies with a wink. "But whatever happens, we need to have a good time tonight."

Kennedy grins. "Amen to that."

"Come on girls. Let's get a drink," I say. "No one should have to do those dances we had to learn today without alcohol in their bloodstream. It would be criminal!"

We amble across the ballroom and collect some drinks from the bartender. As usual, there's no beer, only wine. Mine's a glass of white, and Reggie and Kennedy both get glasses of red.

"To the dance," Kennedy says as she raises her glass, and we all clink.

"Who do y'all reckon Sebastian will dance with first?" Reggie asks, and I feel quite silly at how much the mere mention of his name makes my heart rate rise.

Seeing him this afternoon in the woods was so unexpected, and meeting Zara was wonderful. Well, to be perfectly clear, Zara mentioning that Sebastian had talked to her about me was the wonderful part, although she did seem pretty great, too. Like someone I could be friends with. Not that Sebastian would approve of that, by the sounds of things. I smile to myself at the thought. Protective older brother Seb. I kind of like that.

"Oh, I think I know who he'll choose first," Kennedy says as she smiles at me.

Phoebe smiles as she arrives at our group, accompanied by Camille. "Hi, girls," Phoebe says. "Isn't this exciting?"

"It'll be much more exciting when Sebastian gets here," Camille says gruffly. "Where is he, anyway?"

"I'm sure he's on his way," Phoebe replies. "Do you think they'll provide other men for us to dance with?"

"No!" I reply as Kennedy says, "Are you kidding right now?" and Reggie says, "That would be so nice."

"Maybe Johnathan will come with him?" Phoebe offers.

"I don't care if Prince William himself turns up, as long as Sebastian gets here soon. And I've got the first dance. Got it?" Camille takes a sip of her drink and scowls at us.

"I see Camille's being her usual friendly self," Kennedy says to me out of the corner of her mouth and I stifle a giggle.

"Can you imagine if Prince William actually did turn up?" Phoebe says wistfully, like she always does. I tell you, I have never met anyone so sweet and nice as her.

"I think if Prince William turned up here, Mrs. Watson would have a heart attack," I say.

"Or faint in his arms, like Shelby did with Sebastian." This from Phoebe.

"Oh, that was entirely staged. I lost all respect for her when she did that. Imagine, throwing yourself at a man like that. Literally," Camille sniffs. "Sebastian deserves so much more."

Finally something we can agree on.

"You mean he deserves *you*, Camille?" Kennedy asks.

She moves her drink from one hand to the other and toys with the string of pearls around her neck. "All I'm saying is that he deserves more than people playing games." She shoots me a pointed look.

What games does she think I'm playing?

"Good evening, ladies," a low voice says behind us and we all turn to see both Sebastian and Johnathan standing in the ballroom. They're dressed the same as each other in what must be Regency evening wear for men: long black pants, cream waistcoats with white shirts, and those black jackets with the tails.

Although both of them look like total swoon-worthy romantic heroes, Sebastian is the one who has captured my heart.

"At least we've got two male dance partners," Reggie says to me as the other contestants greet the men. "Although I bet one of them only has eyes for you."

I look through my lashes at Sebastian. He's standing stiffly as Camille flirts her Regency bloomers off, twirling her ringlets, batting her eyelids, and pawing his chest. He's clearly not enjoying it, and I cannot say that makes me feel bad.

You pull out all the tricks you can, Camille. I know something you don't, and when you find out, you're not going to like it one little bit.

I wander over to the bar and ask for a glass of Sebastian's favorite wine, Châteauneuf-du-Pape. The bartender looks at me as though I've asked for a ticket to the moon.

He picks the bottle up and reads the label. "The red is a Californian merlot. It's this or the white."

"Right." Of course. I forgot: minimum-cost alcohol for maximum effect, even for Mr. Darcy. "I'll have a glass of that, thanks."

With my offering in hand, I join Sebastian's group of Camille, Kennedy, and Reggie. Reggie is telling them about something to do with crocodiles, and all I catch are the words "ate the poor creature," and I'm glad I missed the rest.

"Why do you choose to live in such a horrible place?" Camille asks in that special, nonjudgmental way of hers.

Reggie shrugs, looking totally unaffected by her. "It's

home, darlin'. Just like New York is for you. Staten Island, right?"

Kennedy and I share a look of amusement at Reggie's deliberate mistake. My eyes lift to Sebastian's, but he's looking at Reggie.

"I live in Manhattan," Camille corrects tersely. "Upper East Side, to be precise."

"Oh, silly me. It's all tall buildings, traffic, and pollution, as far as I'm concerned." Reggie waves her hand in the air and smiles the smile of the seasoned tormentor.

"Maybe if you made it out of Hicksville, Tennessee every once and a while you'd know more about the world?" Camille offers.

Reggie's hand flies to her chest. "Are you invitin' me to stay? Oh, Camille, you are so kind. Can I bring Puddin'?" Her accent has become thick and strong now as she lays it on.

Camille blinks at her. "Pudding?"

"My pet possum. He's house trained. Mostly. Oh, and Gigi. She's the baby alligator I keep in the tub sometimes. You'd love her. I think I'll leave the coyotes at home, though. They can get awful rambunctious."

Unable to hold it in any longer, I snort with laughter. I look at Sebastian once more. His eyes are still trained on Reggie, and he doesn't seem to get the joke. Maybe he thinks Reggie is serious about all her pet creatures?

I place my hand lightly on his arm. "Sebastian, I got this for you. It's a crappy cheap wine by the sounds of it, but it is a red."

He seems to study the glass in my outstretched hand before he lifts his eyes to mine. He looks rigid and uncomfortable, like he's Mr. Darcy at the Meryton assembly where he thought everyone was beneath him.

He pauses for a moment before he takes the wine from me and says, "Thank you for thinking of me, Emma."

I smile back at him. "You're welcome."

He immediately averts his eyes from mine, and says, "I believe the musicians are about to begin. Camille? You mentioned you would like the first dance. Shall we?"

I feel a sting of rejection. Which is crazy, I know. This is the guy who I spent a considerable amount of time kissing in the woods only a few short hours ago, the guy who had told his sister about me. I know it's for the cameras, nothing more, so I try not to let it bother me.

"Of course, Sebastian. I would love to have the first dance with you," Camille replies, beaming at him as she takes his outstretched arm.

As the musicians begin to play, Kennedy puts her hand on my elbow and says, "Poor guy having to dance with *that*."

I roll my eyes at her, feeling instantly better. "I know, right? Would you like to try out your dance moves with me?"

"Can I twerk?"

I laugh. "I'm absolutely positive twerking was a big part of the Regency dance scene."

"Along with pole dancing, right?"

We line up and face one another to begin the dance we learned this afternoon. I've got Phoebe on my right, facing Johnathan, and Sebastian on my left, facing Camille. As the music begins, we start out like professionals, moving in sequence, no one stepping on anyone's toes, no one bumping into anyone. It lasts for all of thirty seconds before I take a wrong step and slap against Phoebe.

"Sorry!" I call out.

"Totally fine," she replies.

I concentrate hard. Two steps forward, slap hands in a

ladylike fashion with Kennedy, then three steps to the right, walk elegantly around Johnathan like I've got a carrot up my butt. Now, step backwards on my toes into formation, and there, I've got it. Sort of. I look to my left where Sebastian is meant to be, only to see he's at the other end of the line, his hands held against Camille's. Oops! I totally messed up.

Man, this is hard.

"Emma. Over here," Kennedy calls and I dash past Phoebe to her, where we twirl around each other. "Oh, we are so messing this up, babe."

I glance at one of the cameras nearby. We've already made a total hash of the dance steps, so the way I see it, we'd may as well enjoy ourselves. "Just go with it." I hook my arm through hers and we do a silly jig.

The steps are entirely forgotten now, and even Sebastian has lost some of his formality and smiles as Camille and everyone else fudge their moves.

When we get to the part where we switch partners for a few steps, I find myself facing him. I waggle my brows at him and say flirtatiously, "We really must stop meeting like this, Mr. Darcy."

Instead of replying with an equally flirty quip as I've come to expect, he merely nods at me, his jaw locked, his eyes flicking away from mine.

"Is everything okay?" I ask him as we move around the other couples.

"Yes, fine," he replies brusquely.

I knit my brows together in concern as we return to our original partners, and I can't help but notice Sebastian's smile returns as he takes Camille's hand.

What is with him tonight?

When the musicians thankfully come to the end of their

253

tune, we pretend like we've danced like a group of accomplished Regency dancers, and bow and curtsey the way Mrs. Watson showed us.

"We could make a career out of that," Kennedy says as we collect our drinks.

I eye Sebastian across the room. He's now talking with Phoebe and Johnathan, as Camille hangs off his arm. The cameras are trained on him, as usual, but this time they're also on Kennedy and me. I paste on a smile. "I think I'll stick with my day job," I reply absently.

"Well, I need more wine. Waiting around to be asked to dance by one of two guys isn't exactly rock 'n roll. Want another?"

I hold up my almost full drink. "I'm good."

"Suit yourself."

As Kennedy makes her way to the bar, I watch Sebastian. Something has changed, and I don't know what it is. But there's one thing I do know for sure, I need to find out.

Chapter Twenty Seven

I don't have to wait long.

During the next dance, when I find myself facing him once again, he says to me under his breath, "Meet me in our place in ten minutes."

I nod my eager assent and instantly feel the weight of worry lift from my shoulders.

As he moves away to his partner, Reggie, I chew on my lip. This weirdness has all got to be for the cameras, nothing more. He's playing the game, making sure it looks like an even playfield, as though he hasn't already given me his heart.

A few minutes later and I've told anyone who will listen that I need to visit the little Lizzies' room (read: bathroom), I've switched off my mic, and am now staring out at the evening sky from one of the long library windows.

Sebastian quietly enters the room.

I turn and smile at him, relieved to see him away from the glare of the cameras, the contestants, and Camille.

Especially Camille.

I move across the floor and wrap my arms around his waist. I close my eyes and tilt my head up to kiss him, but when I don't feel his lips on mine, I ping them open. "There are no cameras here, Seb."

His body rigid, he says, "Emma," in a way that immediately makes my tummy twist with apprehension.

This hasn't got anything to do with cameras. This is something else instead.

I drop my arms to my side and gaze up at him, fear rising inside. "What's going on?"

He pinches the skin between his eyes and steps away from me. He reaches the fireplace, where he places his hand on the mantle and looks back at me. "It's not going to work."

"What's not going to work?" I ask in a measured tone as I take a couple of tentative steps toward him. "The show? Saving Martinston? What?"

His eyes bore into me. "I'm going to cut to the chase, Emma. You deserve that in the very least."

"Cut to the chase about what?"

He clenches his jaw. "I-I need to send you home."

I let out a surprised laugh, certain this has got to be a joke. "Sure you do."

He doesn't look like he's joking.

My heart begins to thud. "Seb?"

"I'm so sorry, Emma."

He's sorry? Sebastian's sorry he's sending me home?

"What? Why?" I ask, totally flummoxed.

Of all the things I thought this was, being sent home wasn't one of them.

"It's the way it's got to be."

I blink at him in shocked disbelief. "You're actually sending me home? As in back to the States?"

He gives a short, stiff nod. "Yes."

Is this really happening?

"But-but why? I don't get it."

"Because I have to. I've got no choice in the matter."

"Of course you've got a choice. You're Mr. Darcy."

His features tighten. "It's not that simple, Emma. I wish it was but it's-it's out of my control."

"It's out of your control? I don't understand." I reach his side and place my hands on his arm. The thudding of my heart drums in my ears. "Tell the production company to leave you alone, Seb. You can make up your own mind who you choose."

He casts his eyes down. "It's not them."

It's not the production company?

If it's not them, that means ... that means it's him. It's *his* decision. *He's* sending me home.

I swallow down my rising desperation. "Why?" I ask once more, my voice growing harsh.

He lets out a heavy breath. "Emma, what we have has been so very special, and I'll never forget you. I wish it didn't have to be this way. I wish—" He stops abruptly. His eyes tell me he's finding this hard, that he doesn't want to do it.

But dang him, he's doing it anyway.

I pull my hands away as I fight back the urge to cry. "What about all time we spent together, Seb? All the things we talked about? You opened up to me. You don't do that when all you're doing is having a bit of fun with some-one." Tentatively, I place one of my hands back on his arm. "This afternoon, when I met Zara, she said—"

He interrupts me with, "Zara says a lot of things." He turns away from me, and my heart sinks to my belly.

He means it. I got it wrong. I made something out of nothing, and now it's come crashing down around me.

This reality show has messed with my head.

He's messed with my head.

And I'm the total fool who believed it all.

I let out a defeated puff of air, my head spinning at a hundred miles per hour. Even if I've got to go, even if I'm not The One for him, I deserve the truth.

I lift my chin. "You need to tell me why." My voice is edged with steel.

His jaw tightens. "There are things out of my control here. Please understand."

"How can I understand when you won't explain it to me?"

His eyes find mine once more, and I see naked pain where once there was resolve. "I'm so sorry. For all of it. I never meant for this to happen."

"What the heck, Seb?" I blurt out. I don't care who hears me, I don't care if we get found out. He's ending this with me, and I deserve an explanation. "You have feelings for me, just like I do for you. You told your sister all about me. Who does that if they're only in it for a quick fling? You asked me to stay for you, remember? The night we first kissed. You asked me to stay here for *you*. And I did."

His eyes glide away from mine. "Emma, you deserve someone who can give you their heart completely. Someone who's less complicated. Someone who doesn't have to... someone better than me."

I throw my hands onto my hips and glare at him. I might be dressed like a pre-feminist lady, but I'm not taking this lying down. No siree. "That's bull crap, Seb, and you know it."

"If I could turn back the clock, I would."

His words cut deep.

His face is drawn when his gaze locks with mine. "I only hope you can find it in your heart to forgive me."

I blink at him in utter shock. I cannot believe he's doing this to me. To *us*.

With my stomach in knots, I reach out to touch him. "Seb, please."

He whips his arm away, and I know that he means what he's said. It's over, and I've got no choice but to accept it. Because even though it takes two to make a relationship, it only takes one to pull it apart.

"We need to get back to the ballroom." He strides away from me toward the door, and I watch him as though in a daze.

I open my mouth to reply and then clamp it shut. What am I going to say? We've fallen for each other? He feels the same way as I do?

My worst fears bubble to the surface.

He doesn't feel the same way. All of it—his sister, the woods, the time together here in the library—has been a fantasy. *My* fantasy.

None of it has been real.

I've been nothing more than a brief diversion for him to fill the time while he makes his money to save his precious house. I'm the easy girl from the wrong side of the tracks. The girl he knew would never fit into his real world.

I'm not going to chase after him. I might not have much, but I have my pride.

He reaches the door. With his hand on the handle, he pauses before he looks back across the room at me. "I'll be sending you home at the card ceremony tonight."

I nod dumbly at him.

His mouth twists, his features drawn. "I'm ... I'm sorry, Emma." He pulls the door open and slips out of the room.

I'm left standing alone, trying to make sense of what's just happened, my heart in pieces on Martinston's grand library floor.

Chapter Twenty Eight

"I cannot believe these numbers. Will you look at them?" Penny thrusts her tablet in front of me for about the seventeenth time this morning. And it's only ten o'clock.

"I know, they're totally great, Penn," I reply.

She spreads her arms out wide. "Come on, bring it in."

I push myself up from my desk and allow her to collect me in a hug. "Do we have to do this every time we get a new order? 'Cause it's totally creasing my shirt," I ask, half smothered by her mass of auburn curls.

"Since when have y'all cared about shirt creases?" She hugs me tighter. "You deserve every hug and every ounce of my gratitude for what you put yourself through for our label. I hate what he did to you." She pulls back and fixes me with her gaze. "You doing okay, Em?"

"I'm fine," I reply with a shrug that's convincing absolutely no one.

"I don't believe you."

"How about if I say I will be fine given a little more time?"

"And a few thousand more amazing orders like this one?" She holds her tablet up again and my eyes land on the dollar total at the bottom of the screen.

I read the company name. "D. A. B. is stocking more of our stuff?"

"Yeah, baby! D. A. B., the largest sports chain store in the Pacific Northwest. Boom!"

"Huh."

Penny knits her brows together. "We get an order with that many zeros, and all you can say is 'huh'?" She narrows her eyes at me. "You need coffee and chocolate chip cookies from Cardinelli's, and you need them now."

I smile weakly at her. "That sounds perfect, but I've got some prep to do before this interview in an hour."

"Em, you are more organized than anyone I know. We will kill the interview and probably get a stack more orders from it, too. Let's go."

"Okay, you win. I will eat unnecessary sugar and drink caffeine with you."

"Atta girl."

As Penny returns to her desk, I collect my phone and notice a new message. It's from a number I don't recognize.

How are you?

I check the number. It starts with a "+44." Who could that be? I Google the area code. My heart leaps into my mouth.

England.

How many people do I know who have English cell-phone numbers? Answer: one.

Regardless, I tap out a reply.

Who is this?

I stare at the screen as my heart thuds, knowing it's him.

It's Sebastian.

My belly does a weird flip and I'm not sure if I'm going to pass out, vomit, or hurtle my phone across the room.

I do none of them. Instead, I simply stare at the words on my screen.

Another message arrives.

Not a day goes by when I don't think about you. I am so very sorry for what I did. I've wanted to talk to you for so long. I've wanted to explain. Really explain. My hands have been tied, but not anymore.

"You ready?" Penny asks, her voice cutting through my consciousness.

My jaw slack, I lift my eyes to hers.

"What is it? You've gone all pale."

"It's ... Sebastian."

Her eyes get wide. "Sebastian? As in Mr. Darcy dumping your butt, Sebastian?"

I bite on my lip and give a slow nod.

She rushes around to read my screen. "Oh, Em. *Now* he wants to explain? You tell him even though he's some English aristocrat, he's pond scum and you never want to hear from him again. Period."

I don't reply—to Penny or to Sebastian. Instead I sit, paralyzed.

I don't need to know how he got my number. He's the star of the show. He can have anything he wants. The question that's burning in my mind is why. Why now, seven weeks after I was dumped and sent back to Houston, my tail firmly between my legs?

"Em? What are you thinking?"

"I don't know what to think."

My phone pings again and we both read the message.

I want to see you.

Penny nudges me in the ribs. "He wants to see you."

"I can see that."

"Well?"

I lock my jaw. There are a million things I could say to him, things I've wanted to say for weeks. Biting things. Clever things. But what's the point?

He made his choice, and it wasn't me.

I tap out my reply.

It's all ancient history ☺ Good luck with your wedding.

My finger hovers over the "send" button.

"Good luck with your wedding?" Penny guffaws. "You're seriously going to say that to him?"

"He's only reaching out to me now because the show has begun to air and he feels guilty for what he did."

"How do you know?"

"Let me think. Because he booted me off the show after leading me on, I haven't heard from him since then, and now he's sent me a message telling me he's sorry."

"He wants to see you."

"Penny, I need to see this for what it is. He's just trying to feel better about the lousy way he treated me. Nothing more."

She shakes her head. "You're a bigger person than me, Emma Brady. I'd be sending him messages telling him exactly what I think of him."

"Oh, believe me, I want to do that. But it's not going to make a blind bit of difference." I press send before I change my mind, and slip my phone into my purse. "Done. Now it's time for that sugar fix."

Ten minutes later, we're sitting at our local coffee house, our coffee and chocolate chip cookies on the table in front of us.

Penny leans back in her seat, her arms crossed. "I'm gonna give it another week, tops."

"You're gonna give what another week?" I ask as I take a sip of the coffee I once fantasized about while on the show.

"This moping over Sebastian thing you're doing. You've been back for nearly two months, and now with that message you've sent him you've effectively told him you've moved on."

"I was wishing him the best."

She raises her eyebrows at me. "You sent him a smile emoji, Em."

"Well, it's a good thing if he thinks I've moved on. And it's not two months yet. It's seven weeks and two days," I correct, and instantly feel bad that I know precisely how long it is since Sebastian told me and the rest of America that I was no longer in the running to become the lady of his manor.

Not my favorite moment.

"Okay. Seven weeks and two days. You took about two months to get over Chad Macdonald dumping you a couple of years back, so I figure you've got about five days left before you'll be all 'Sebastian who?' and feel great again."

Right now, I can't imagine ever being "Sebastian who?" But the thought is nice.

For such a short relationship—we were really only involved with each other for a matter of weeks—this one hit me hard when it ended. I guess it was partly to do with the fact he dumped me seemingly out of the blue, and partly because it was all so weird being on a reality TV show together and having to hide our relationship from the world.

Not to mention that by sending me home, he'd broken my heart in two.

"I am still so angry with him, Em. I mean, you weren't there to fall for the guy, and you did anyway, and then he played you. If only I could get my hands on him ... "

I raise my eyebrows at her. "You'd do what? Penn, you're shorter than me, and he's, like, over six feet."

"I don't know. I'd call him some names, maybe draw a mustache on him with a permanent marker while he was asleep."

I surprise myself with a chuckle.

She taps her chin. "Let me think. What else could I do to him?"

"You could put his hand in a bucket of warm water as well, so he'd pee himself."

"Oh, yeah. Now we're talking."

I giggle. It's short lived and manages to lift my spirits for about two seconds.

"Any more messages?" she asks.

"I'm not going to check."

"I will." Before I can stop her, she reaches into my purse and pulls out my phone.

My belly begins to flutter as hope rises inside. Man, what am I? Some kind of masochist?

Her face falls. "Nothing." She slots my phone away. "I guess you're right."

The disappointment is so strong it winds me.

"You've gone pale again, Em. Eat."

I sink my teeth gratefully into my chocolate chip cookie. "OMG, that is so good," I say, my voice muffled by the chocolate yumminess. "I think I need to move onto a cookie-only diet. That'll fix me for sure."

"Mm-hm," Penny agrees. "By the way, I watched the latest episode of the show last night."

I don't need to ask which show she's referring to. "Good for you." I take another bite, willing the cookie to push my feelings away.

She leans forward and places her elbows on her knees.

"I know you're choosing not to watch it, and I totally get it, but I thought you'd like to know that you come across so well, and you look super cute in the label."

"So it's still the first day or two, before we're forced into the Regency clothes?"

"No. You've been in the clothes for a while now. They're showing two episodes a week, so we're racing through it."

"Cool," I reply noncommittally. "You'll get to watch him dump me on national television soon. That'll be super fun."

She reaches across and rubs my arm. "I'm sorry, Em. I promise, I won't mention it again. I just wanted you to know that what you did to promote Timothy on the show is totally helping our company, and I am so grateful."

I drink some of my coffee. "You said that already."

"Yeah, well, I kinda think you're pretty awesome, so you'd better get used to being told that. And that Sebastian guy? Total douche for passing you up."

I give a nod. "Total douche."

"Idiot."

"Dick."

"A-hole."

"Oh, so many things." I finish off my cookie and lick my fingers. "We'd better get back for the interview."

Penny presses her phone to check the time. "You're right."

Thirty minutes later, we're sitting with a journalist from *Lone Star Woman Monthly* in what Penny and I jokingly call the boardroom, which is in fact the only space in her garage not filled to the ceiling with boxes of activewear.

"Tell me about the inspiration for the name. Timothy is

not the type of activewear label we're used to seeing," the journalist, Sammy-Jo asks.

"It's in honor of our dads," Penny replies. "Both are called Timothy, and both are big influences in our lives."

"That is so sweet. I bet they're both super proud of your recent success."

Penny glances at me before she replies, "Oh, they are. So proud."

"You're a couple of Daddy's Girls, huh?" she asks with a grin.

"Definitely," I reply. "They've been positive influences in our lives, and we both owe them so much." I know Dad would be immensely proud of me if he were alive to see this. And it's all happened so fast. The first episode of *Dating Mr. Darcy* aired only weeks ago, and since then our sales have shot right up. It's made us think we can make a real go of this business.

"It says here you design the clothes, Penny. Tell me about that."

Penny talks Sammy-Jo through her creative process, and I interject every now and then with points about fabric sourcing and all the business aspects I take care of.

"Now," Sammy-Jo says once we've satisfied her questions, "I'm certain our readers want to know what it's like to date Mr. Darcy. Is he just as gorgeous in person as he looks on TV, Emma?" She looks at me with bright, expectant eyes.

I knew I would get questions about the show from people. Journalists, friends, family. Mom has barely been able to contain herself, telling me every five minutes how she always thought I would achieve great things—by which she means marrying a rich guy and living in a fancy house. Contractually, I'm not allowed to tell anyone anything, of course. And I've stuck to it religiously, except for with Penny. I had to tell someone, and being my best friend and business partner, she needed to know what a disaster it was for me.

And I needed a shoulder to cry on for the last seven weeks and two days.

I plaster on a smile and reply, "He is a very good looking guy."

"Good looking?" she says. "Girl, he's a dreamboat." She fans herself and looks like she might swoon. "I know y'all can't tell me anything, but did you get to go on a date with him? Maybe even kiss the guy? Please tell me you did."

"I'm sorry, Sammy-Jo. I can't tell you anything about the show right now. But I do hope you enjoy watching it."

"Oh, I do. Can I tell you what I think?"

Can I stop her?

"Sure. Go ahead."

"I think he's going to end up with that beautiful girl Phoebe. The one with the long blond hair. They're both tall and gorgeous. Those two would make beautiful babies together."

I think of how Camille would feel about Sammy-Jo's wish and this time my smile is genuine. "You'll just have to wait and see."

Penny shoots me a concerned look. "I think that wraps it up. Sammy-Jo, thank you so much."

"One more question," Sammy-Jo says, her eyes bright. "Did he do the pond scene? You know, diving in and getting all wet with that white shirt clinging to all his muscles?"

Penny stands up to signal the interview is now over. "Is that the time? Sammy-Jo, I am so sorry but we are going to have to go to our next appointment. It has been such a treat to spend time with you, though."

Her face falls. "Oh, of course."

I shoot Penny a grateful look. She's my bestie and she's totally got my back.

As she bundles Sammy-Jo outside, I slump back in my chair. Not only did I have to say goodbye to the man I thought was the love of my life, but now with the show airing, I won't be allowed to get on with forgetting about him.

I rub my forehead and let out a heavy sigh. I tell myself I will move on. I will get over him.

Although right now, it feels a million miles away.

Chapter Twenty Nine

Penny slips the straps of her handbag over her shoulder. "Promise me you won't bail. This will be good for you, Em. It'll give you closure."

"I still fail to see how watching a guy who dumped me propose to someone else is going to give me closure, particularly if it's odious Camille."

"Trust me, okay? My therapist friend told me it would help you."

"Why were you talking to your therapist friend about me?"

She gives me a sympathetic look.

"Yeah, okay. Don't say it."

She pulls me in for a hug. "I love you and I want what's best for you. Y'all know that, right?"

"I know,' I say as I breathe in a cloud of her perfume.

"Good. Then I'll see you at my place at seven. I'm sending Trey out, so it'll be just us girls. Don't forget to bring the dip."

I salute her. "No, ma'am."

"Less of the ma'am. I'm only three months older than you, remember?"

"I sure do, ma'am," I reply with a grin.

The episode in which I was unceremoniously sent home aired last week. I did not watch it. Penny agreed it was a good idea. Apparently, I looked like a stunned mullet as I stood waiting with Kennedy and Reggie to be told I was leaving. In an unusual twist, Reggie got sent home, too, which apparently she did with a smile. She was there for the follows, after all.

Mom, on the other hand, called me in floods of tears, telling me how upset she was I hadn't landed my prince. Or duke. Or baron. Or whatever archaic title Lord Huntington-Ross holds. I reminded her it was ages ago now, and assured her I had already moved on. Which I had.

Kind of.

Well, at least I wasn't thinking about him every waking hour of every waking day anymore. Not when we had so much more work to do now that Timothy's business had continued to grow.

And yes, Sebastian had messaged me a few more times, always telling me how sorry he was, asking if we could talk. After much consultation with Penny over yet more cookies and coffee in the past few weeks, I decided not to reply. I'd said my piece about being happy for him and his future bride. The last thing I was going to say was that I was still in love with the guy.

So, at seven sharp, despite serious reservations about watching Sebastian choose one of my fellow contestants to walk down the aisle, I ring Penny's bell. She swings the door open almost before my finger has left the button.

"That was quick," I say in surprise.

"Was it?" She pulls me into the hallway and closes the

door behind me. "I just happened to be by the door, that's all." She looks at my hands. "Is that the dip?" She grabs it and reads the label. "You went to Central Market!"

I shoot her a quizzical look. "That's where we always get the dip. They've got the best selection. Remember?"

"Right." She nods so fast she looks like she's attached to one of those fat wobbling machines that are meant to make you lose the pounds. "Now, let's get you into the living room. We've got some watching to do." She manhandles me —or womanhandles me, really—down the hallway.

"You okay, Penn?" I ask as we enter the living room.

"Me? Sure. Why?" Her cheeks are shiny and she's got a slightly manic look in her eyes.

"You seem weird."

"I'm all good." She gives me a smile that's meant to reassure me but makes me wonder if she's secretly on Ritalin. "Sit. The show's about to start."

I do as instructed, leaning back on her comfy leather couch. The large screen TV is already on, paused on an ad for tires. Penny places a bowl of chips on the coffee table along with the dip I brought, then settles down next to me and pours us out a glass of chardonnay each.

"No beer?" I ask.

"I thought wine was more appropriate. Cheers," she says and we clink glasses.

"Cheers. Here's to moving on dot com."

She collects the remote from the coffee table. "You ready?"

"No."

"It'll be okay, Em. You need this."

I blink at her. "I *need* to watch the guy I fell for propose to someone else?"

"Not when you put it that way."

273

"What other way is there?"

"I guess seeing him and knowing you're over him. Because you are over him, right?" She looks at me with expectation.

I give a firm nod. "Right," I say, more to convince myself than anyone else. Because I will get over him. Someday.

"Plus, everyone is going to see this and want to talk to you about it. You need to be prepared."

At least that point makes sense. "Okay."

"Ready?"

I chew on my lip, my tummy clasping in apprehension. "Hold up." I take a couple of large sips of wine and hold the glass to my chest. To get through the next sixty-or-so minutes, I'm going to need more of it, I'm sure. "Ready."

Penny presses play, and instantly orchestral music fills the room as the title of the show pops up on the screen over a backdrop of Martinston.

So far so ... okay. I mean, sure, the house looks spectacular, but it's just a house.

A moment in, Sebastian is on the screen. I feel like my heart could burst out of my chest at the sight of him. He's dressed up as Mr. Darcy, as I expected him to be in the finale of a show called *Dating Mr. Darcy*. Johnathan asks him about the final two contestants, and he answers with what sounds like expected platitudes to me.

They're beautiful and amazing women, and I'm very lucky to have had the opportunity to get to know them both.

As he smiles, to the world he looks happy and serene, waiting for his two potential brides to come down the "aisle," but I can tell his smile isn't genuine. It doesn't reach his eyes, not the way it did when he would smile at me.

But then again, maybe I got that all backwards? I'm not the one up there on the screen with him, am I? I'm the sad sack on my bestie's couch, clasping a glass of wine to my chest as a lifeline, about to watch him ask someone else to marry him.

"Who are the final two?" I ask Penny.

"Just watch and see."

Sebastian is now standing in a particularly picturesque part of the garden I recognize from my daily wanderings. I guess at least I should be glad he's not in the woods. That would be a step too far for me right now.

I gulp down more wine. As I take in his square jaw and brown eyes with the glints of gold, I know I'm not over him. Very far from it, in fact.

I let out a heavy sigh. Getting over Mr. Darcy is proving to be difficult indeed.

Penny eyes me next to her on the couch. "More wine." She takes my now warm glass and tops it up.

The screen pans across the garden to a beautiful woman in a long, navy, slim-fitting dress.

My heart sinks to my toes. "Oh, no. Not her."

Camille.

I watch as she walks toward Sebastian. She looks gorgeous in her dress, with her hair falling around her shoulders, and the broadest smile on her face. She reaches him and he takes her hands in hers.

"I think I'm going to be sick."

Penny pauses the show. "Don't worry, Em. They always reject the first one, remember? Camille is toast."

"I hope you're right. She is a truly horrendous human being, and I'm not just saying that because she's the one up there and not me."

"I know. I've been watching the show, remember? She's horrible." She presses play and I hold my breath, waiting to hear what Sebastian has got to say to her, hoping it'll be along the lines of "I'm feeding you to the lions. Enjoy."

The camera zooms in on Camille's face.

"Sebastian, my very own Mr. Darcy."

"Yup, vomiting now."

"Shh."

"You are everything I want in a partner. You're like me. You're focused, smart, and determined. You're also very handsome, which I think is a total plus."

She grins at him.

"We might be from different countries, but we are cut from the same cloth, you and I. Together, I know we can take on the world, and get everything we were both born to receive."

I roll my eyes. "She's still crapping on about them being supposed equals. Where are the actual, tangible feelings for him, Camille? Where, huh? Huh?"

"You know she can't hear you," Penny says.

I sit back in my seat and cross my arms. "I know."

The camera is now focused on Sebastian.

"Camille, it has been an adventure getting to know you these past weeks. You have so many qualities that any man would be insane not to appreciate in a woman. Other than your obvious beauty, you're strong, you're determined, and you will stop at nothing to get what you want."

The camera focuses on Camille's smiling face before it returns to Sebastian.

"I'm sorry to tell you, however, I must be insane, because as lovely as you are, I feel your qualities are better suited to another. I can't make you the lady of my manor. I do hope you understand."

My jaw slack, I look at Penny, wide eyed.

"Take that, Miss Camille I'm Too Good For Everyone!" she exclaims in obvious glee.

"Go Sebastian," I mutter under my breath.

Back on the screen, Camille's face is a study in utter shock. She must be feeling so humiliated not to have won. I feel sorry for her. Well, almost.

"But-but you need *me, Sebastian. Without me, you're absolutely lost."*

He's lost? What the heck does that mean?

"I know this is hard, Camille, and I am truly sorry. I wish you all the best for your future, and hope that in time, you will find the right man for you."

Camille's face is like thunder.

"You will regret this, Sebastian. You need me. You'll see. You're never going to do better than me."

Sebastian releases her hands and looks down. With nothing more to say, Camille turns on her heels and stomps away from him.

As the show cuts to an ad break, I'm suddenly nervous. "I am so glad it's not Camille, but who's it going to be?"

"Who do you want it to be?" She must see something in my face, because she adds, "I mean, if it can't be you."

"It could be Kennedy. If it is, I'll be happy for her."

"Really?"

"She's a great girl, and now that this whole thing is over I can't wait to get together with her over a drink or two. Plus, her last name is Bennet, like Lizzie's in *Pride and Prejudice.* I always thought that might mean something."

"It's back on," Penny says as the ads come to an end.

The camera shows Sebastian standing, waiting once more. We see the back of a woman walking toward him. She's in a pretty pale blue dress, her long blonde hair tied up in a ponytail.

"Phoebe?" I guffaw.

"She is so beautiful," Penny gushes. She tilts her head toward me. "I mean, nice dress. That would make anyone look amazing."

"It's okay, Penn. Phoebe is beautiful, inside and out. It's just I didn't think—"

"You didn't think he'd choose her?"

I chew on my lip. "Sebastian and Phoebe? As sweet as she is, I can't see them together. But then, I proved I knew absolutely nothing when he kicked me off the show out of the blue."

We watch Phoebe walk down a long red carpet toward Sebastian, between the topiary, lined with white ribbons and flowers. It's verging on cheesy, but somehow the majesty of Martinston keeps it classy.

As she reaches his side, she beams at him and he takes her hands in his, returning the smile. A genuine smile.

Something twists painfully inside. They are two impossibly gorgeous people, in an impossibly gorgeous setting, smiling at one another as though they've just won the lottery.

"I'm not sure I want to watch this," I mutter to myself.

"Phoebe," Sebastian begins, and I sink a little further into the back cushions. *"You are one of the most genuinely kind, sweet, and good people I have had the honor to know in my life. It's clear to anyone that you're stunningly beautiful, but you've also brought a sense of dignity to this process that was perhaps lacking in some.*

They share a smile. Phoebe is all those things and more.

And then a thought occurs to me. "Penn? I caught Phoebe in the hallway one night after lights out."

She pauses the show. "What?"

My mind twirls like a spinning top. "She said she was

out for a walk, and Seb assured me she hadn't been visiting him."

"Shall we keep watching?"

My heart sinks. He lied to me. "I don't know."

She takes my hand in hers and gives it a squeeze. "It'll be okay."

I chew on my lip for a moment before I nod. My stomach clenches in apprehension once more. She flicks on the show and we watch as they hug one another.

"Thank you, Sebastian," Phoebe replies. *"Coming on this show and meeting you has changed my life forever, and I am so grateful for it. Here I have met the love of my life.*

"He's choosing her," I say in resignation as my heart drops to the floor.

"Shh. Keep watching," Penny says.

"I know you have, Phoebe," Sebastian replies with a broad grin, *"And I am so very happy for you both."*

Huh?

I turn to Penny. She's got that glow-y, bright-eyed expression she gets on her face when she's watching the happily ever afters on these reality shows.

"Penn? What's going on?"

Sebastian takes Phoebe's hand in his and turns to the camera.

"As you will know, Dating Mr. Darcy *is meant to end with a proposal of marriage. Well, I hope you're all as happy as I am to know there will be a proposal. It just won't be coming from me."*

I pull my brows together. "What the—?" I look at my friend. She doesn't look quite as surprised as I would expect for such an out-of-the-blue pronouncement.

On the screen, Phoebe smiles at Sebastian and he steps out of shot. Then, the camera pans to Johnathan. He's dressed in his Regency finery, walking toward Phoebe with the biggest smile on his face.

"What the heck is happening?" I ask.

"Shh."

Johnathan and Phoebe are holding hands and gazing at one another.

Johnathan and Phoebe. *Johnathan and Phoebe!*

"Johnny, coming onto this show and getting to know you has been the most incredible experience of my life. You are my soulmate, and I am totally in love with you ... "

As Phoebe continues to tell Johnathan how amazing he is, I shake Penny's arm. "Did you know about this? Has it been in the show or what?"

She presses her lips together and replies, "Not at all. Isn't it shocking?"

There's something in her tone that has me narrowing my eyes at her. I return my attention to the screen. They're still holding hands, and Phoebe has tears streaming down her cheeks as she gazes at Johnathan.

"Johnathan Penfold, will you marry me?" she asks nervously, and it's impossible not to melt as he says he will and she leaps into his arms. He twirls her around, and the music plays, and I feel a few tears of my own slide down my cheek.

"That is so romantic," I say. "Phoebe's the sweetest person you'll ever meet." I wipe my tears away with the back of my hands. "And she was falling for Johnathan all this time? Who knew?"

That's who she was going to see that time I ran into her in the hallway after lights out. Johnathan! And there I was feeling angry with Sebastian for lying to me. He hadn't.

"It's *so* romantic," Penny agrees, her eyes glistening, her hand over her chest. "Ooh, look. It's Sebastian again. I wonder what's happening now?"

"But ... but what does that mean? He's not marrying anyone?"

"Let's watch."

I grab the remote from her and press "stop." "You don't seem overly surprised by any of this," I say.

"I am surprised," she insists. "Let's watch it, okay?"

I narrow my eyes at her. There's something going on with her tonight, I just don't know what it is.

She takes the remote out of my hand and presses "play" before I can protest further.

Sebastian's face fills the screen once more, and my belly does a flip at the sight of him again.

"Phoebe and Johnathan falling in love has been a wonderful surprise for me. I could not be happier for two people so well suited and perfect for one another. I also know this television show is called Dating Mr. Darcy, *and not* Marrying Mr. Darcy's Best Friend. *Please believe me when I tell you I had every intention of marrying the woman I chose. But you see, the thing is—"*

The thing? *I* say that. Not him. He *never* says that.

"—I sent the woman I fell in love with home from the show, and it was the hardest thing I've ever had to do. Because she stole my heart from the moment I laid eyes on her on that red carpet back in Texas. She had something stuck in her hair, you see, and I helped her out with it."

I try to swallow, but my mouth is dry.

Could he mean ... ?

Am I ... ?

I look at Penny for answers. Her eyes are brimming with tears, her hand over her mouth as she stares back at me.

And I know. I just know.

"It's me," I breathe, my voice choked with tears. "He means me."

Penny nods, her face bright as tears roll down her cheeks. "It's you, Em."

Sebastian is still talking into the camera.

"If you are watching—and I have done what I can to make sure you are watching this—you will know exactly who you are. I know I hurt you. I know sending you home the way I did was callous. I was a coward, and you deserve so much better. I put the needs of others in front of my own, and I hurt you in the process. I should never have done it. I sincerely hope you will give me the chance to make it up to you. Perhaps even one day, you may agree to let me make it up to you for the rest of my life."

Penny reaches across and squeezes my hand. "He's in love with you, Em. He's in *love* with you."

The doorbell rings, making my heart leap into my mouth.

"Penny?" I question.

"Could you get that?" she asks, acting all nonchalant, like the man I'm head over heels in love with hasn't just professed his love to me on national television.

I don't need to be asked twice.

I know exactly who it is.

I leap off the couch, slopping what's left of my wine over my Timothy leggings. "Dang it!"

"Forget about it," Penny instructs in a rush. "Go! Quick! Answer the door!"

I have so many questions, but now is not the time. I bolt out of the living room and into the hallway where I pause, my heart beating hard.

He's come for me.

Sebastian has come for me.

I grasp the handle and pull the door open to see him standing on the doorstep. He's holding a couple of bottles of beer in his hands. He smiles at me, and my whole body goes into overdrive: my heart races, my breath shortens, my tummy flips, and my legs go weak.

It's a small miracle I can still stand, really.

"Brady Bunch," he says in his deep, velvety voice.

"You're here," is all I manage to say.

"Were you watching the show?"

I nod, working hard to get myself under control.

His face lights up in a smile. "I brought a peace offering." He holds up the beer bottles. "I thought we could try your favorite."

"You brought Bud."

"I've heard it runs in the Brady family veins."

In a daze, I take the bottles from him and place them on Penny's hallway table. "Thanks."

Sebastian takes a step closer to me. "Emma, I am so sorry for doing what I did to you. I hope more than anything you can find it in your heart to forgive me."

I open my mouth to speak. I've got so many questions, so many things I need to say to him. But watching his heartfelt TV speech only moments ago, and now seeing the hope in his soft brown eyes, all I can say is, "I *want* to forgive you, Seb."

He lets out a relieved breath and reaches for my hands. "You do not know how happy I am to hear that."

But I have a few things I need to say to this Mr. Darcy.

"Why did you do it? Why did you send me away like that?"

"I'm not proud of my actions. I did what I thought I had to do. You see, the afternoon before the ball, Mother, Granny, Zara, and I met with our lawyer. She told us that the money I had made from the show wasn't enough and we needed to find more if we wanted to save Martinston."

"I don't get it. What has that got to do with sending me home?"

"Unbeknownst to us, Camille had smuggled in a mobile phone, and she put it to good use. Somehow, she found out that my family was in financial trouble. She came to me with a financial deal. She's from a wealthy New York family."

"You don't say," I quip.

"Indeed." He shoots me a sardonic smile. "She told me we would make a great team. My family name and home, and her money."

"That's very *Downton Abbey* of her," I scoff.

"I've never seen it."

"The Earl of Grantham marries a rich American heiress."

"How very *not* relevant to us." He shakes his head and smiles at me. "That afternoon, the day I saw you in the woods, I came under pressure from our lawyer to pursue the idea. She convinced me that it would work, even though she knew I didn't have feelings for Camille. It made sense: her money could save Martinston. All I had to do was name her as my bride. Immediately after that meeting was the ball, and then I sent you home. I knew I needed to do it then, or I wouldn't ever" He squeezes my hands. "I regretted it the moment I sent you home, my darling Emma."

I begin to tear up. "You put the needs of your family before your own. It's very noble of you. I mean, saving your home was the reason you did the show in the first place."

He nods. "It was. But in the end, it wasn't enough."

"Why did it take you so long to come find me?" I keep

my voice light, but my heart is thrashing around in my chest like a wild animal.

"I was going to go through with it right up until the last moment, until Zara told me what an idiot I was being to walk away from you."

I allow myself a small smile. "Go Zara."

"I've spent the last weeks waiting for that final episode to air. I felt after what I'd done to you, I needed a grand gesture to win you back."

I don't want to tell him that it worked, but it *so* did.

He moves so close to me we're almost touching. "You see, there was something I didn't share with our lawyer that day, something that has changed my life."

My breath catches in my throat. "What?"

"I've fallen in love with you."

I beam at him, my heart bursting. "You have?"

"Head over heels, completely and utterly, madly, deeply in love." He cups my face in his hands and I breathe in his intoxicating Sebastian aroma. The next thing I know, we're clasped together in an embrace, his lips on mine, my fingers tangled up in his hair, his hands pulling me close.

And in case you're wondering, it's an amazing kiss. Unforgettable. The kind of kiss that makes you see an entire universe of stars.

My grin threatens to crack my face in two. "I'm in love with you, too."

"Oh, Brady. You don't know how good it is to hear you say that."

"Oh, I think I do." I pull him down to me and kiss him with all my might.

"I should never have listened to our lawyer and I should never have sent you home. I am so very sorry."

"But Martinston?"

"I will find a way to keep it. I don't know what it will be yet, but I'm absolutely determined not to lose it. What matters to me is that I love you, and I want to be with you. I'm not going to let anything come between us ever again."

My heart soars high above the clouds as tears sting my eyes. "I promise to do whatever I can to help you save your home."

"I've missed you so much, Brady Bunch." He pulls me into him and smothers me in kisses once more.

He's here.

He came back for me.

He loves me.

My heart is so full of love, it could burst.

"Ahem." We turn to see Penny standing in the hallway, grinning her head off at us both. "I take it you've made up?"

"You must be Penny," Sebastian says, reaching past me to shake her hand. "Thank you so much for all your help."

I look, open mouthed from Penny to Sebastian and back again. "You've been in contact with Seb?"

"He called me after you stopped messaging him. At first, I told him to go take a flying leap at himself. But then, he told me all about trying to save the house and how much he loved you, and I knew you weren't over him. Even though you said you were."

"You know me too well, Penn."

"I hope you're okay about it. It felt weird going behind your back like that."

I let go of Seb long enough to pull her into a hug. "It's going to take chocolate. A lot of chocolate."

"Oh, chocolate I can manage."

We share a smile, my heart completely full.

"What does a man have to do to get invited into some-one's home here in Texas?" Sebastian asks.

"Oh, where are my manners," Penny says. "Come in. I'll pour you a glass of wine and get out of your hair."

"I brought some beer." He gestures at the bottles in the side table.

"Let me go open those for y'all," Penny says before she leaves us for the kitchen.

Sebastian slips his hand into mine and I look up at him. "Thank you," he says in his low, sexy voice.

"For what?"

"For not giving up on me, despite wanting to."

I loop my hand around his neck. "If you ever do anything like that to me again, I will personally hunt you down and kill you."

His laugh is low and reverberates through me, reaching right down to my toes. "I love you, Emma Brady."

I beam at him. My heart contracts, filled to the brim with the most wonderful feeling in the world. "I love you, too, Mr. Darcy."

THE END

Acknowledgments

I wrote this book while it seemed the world was on fire. New Zealand had been in total, country-wide lockdown to combat COVID-19 for several weeks, news from overseas was increasingly grim, and it felt like the last thing I could ever do was sit down to write something heartwarming, uplifting, and funny. But in between home schooling, endless dog walks (sorry, dogs), and trying not to read the news, I wrote a story that had been percolating away in my head for well over a year. As the words began to flow, I felt I'd found a way to escape the insanity and instead concentrate on finding some happiness. I absolutely loved writing this book, and Emma and Sebastian have a special place in my heart.

I've always been a huge fan of Jane Austen's work, *Pride and Prejudice* in particular, and the idea of having a Mr. Darcy figure in a modern, 21st century world was so appealing I had to write this book! In the process, I realized it could be more than one title, and so the *Love Manor Romantic Comedy* series was born and I get to live with these characters for a while longer.

Now, onto my acknowledgments . . . I am lucky to have the most amazing support people around me. My family is so understanding and supportive, even when they lose me to books for a while. They know how important writing is to me, and they give me the space and time to follow my passion.

I was lucky to have a couple of critique partners for this book. With her in-depth knowledge of reality TV dating shows and chick lit stories, Kirsty McManus helped make the dating show feel authentic and possible. Jackie Rutherford, as always, put me through my writerly paces, not allowing me to get away with any of my bad habits, and helping me create a book to be proud of.

I'm part of a few writers' groups that are wonderfully supportive. I was lucky enough to be invited to be a part of a small group of like-minded authors who share the same goal: to write the best books we can and to have them experience the success they deserve. Thank you to all of you in the Chick Lit Think Tank and Chick Lit Chat Head Quarters. You are all amazing and I'm so grateful to have your support.

Thanks also to my new editor, Melissa at Grapevine Editing for doing a great job ensuring my language is American and my t's were crossed and i's were dotted. I always learn something knew through the editing process, and this time was no exception.

And Sue Traynor, you took my vision and made it into the most gorgeous cover, as you always do. Thank you!

And finally, as always, thank you to you, my readers. I love having the opportunity to write for a living, and your readership is what makes that possible.

About the Author

Kate O'Keeffe is a *USA TODAY* bestselling and award-winning author who writes exactly what she loves to read: laugh-out-loud romantic comedies with swoon-worthy heroes and gorgeous feel-good happily ever afters. She lives and loves in beautiful Hawke's Bay, New Zealand with her family and two scruffy but loveable dogs.

When she's not penning her latest story, Kate can be found hiking up hills (slowly), traveling to different countries around the globe, and eating chocolate. A lot of it.

Made in the USA
Middletown, DE
08 May 2023